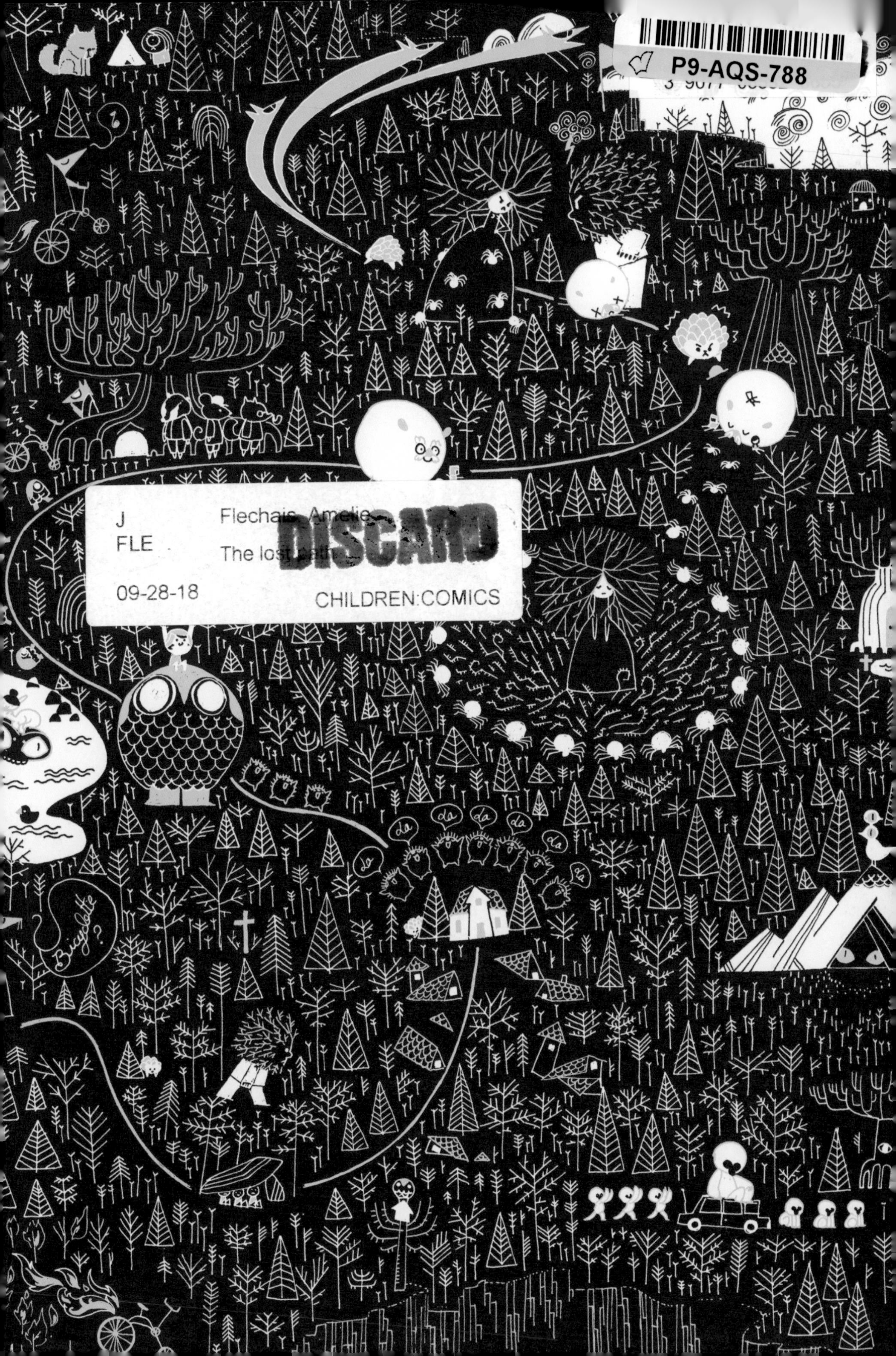

da
da
da
da
da
da
da
Bicyclette?

THE LOST PATH

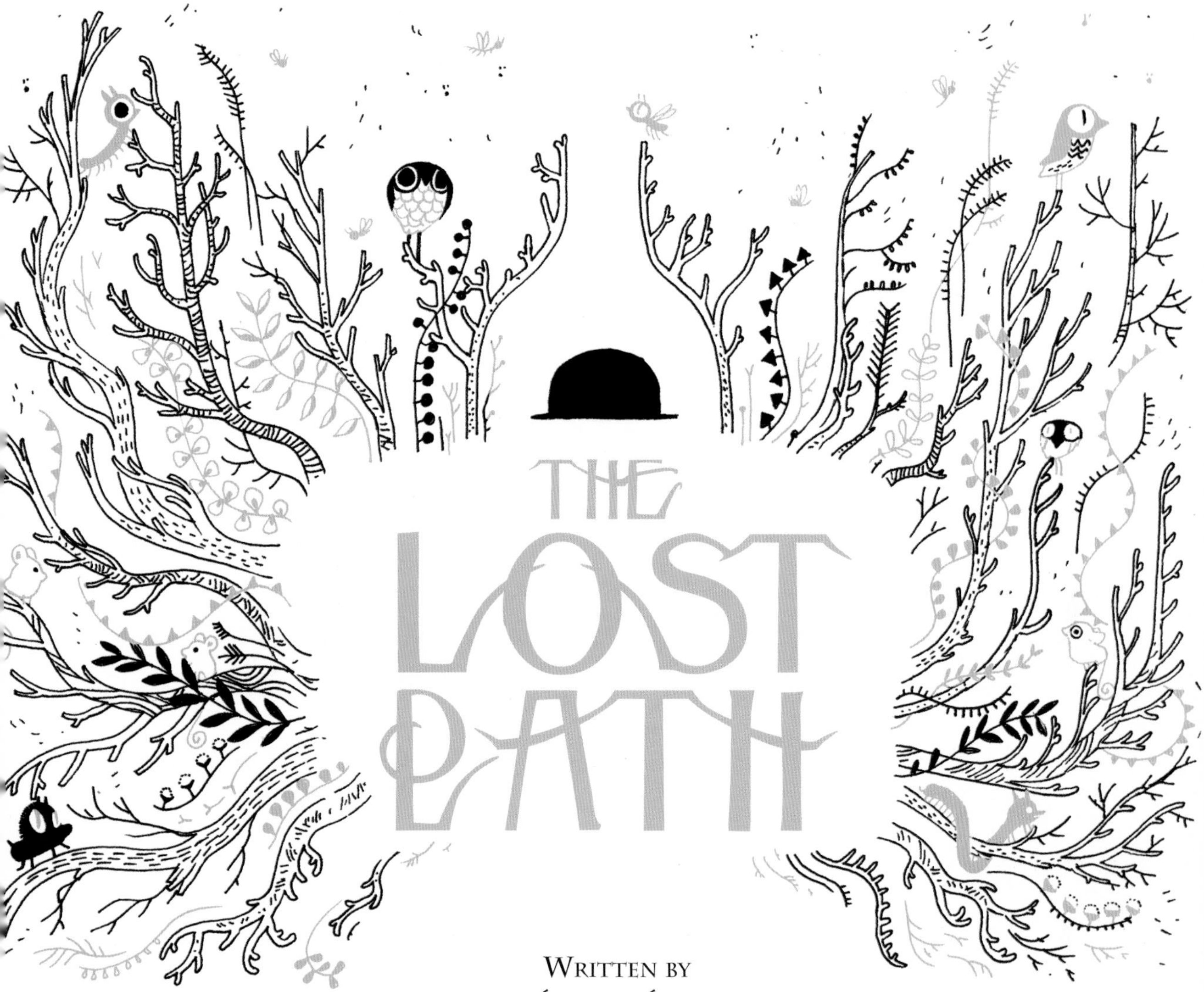

WRITTEN BY
AMÉLIE FLÉCHAIS
&
JONATHAN GARNIER

ILLUSTRATED BY
AMÉLIE FLÉCHAIS

CUB HOUSE

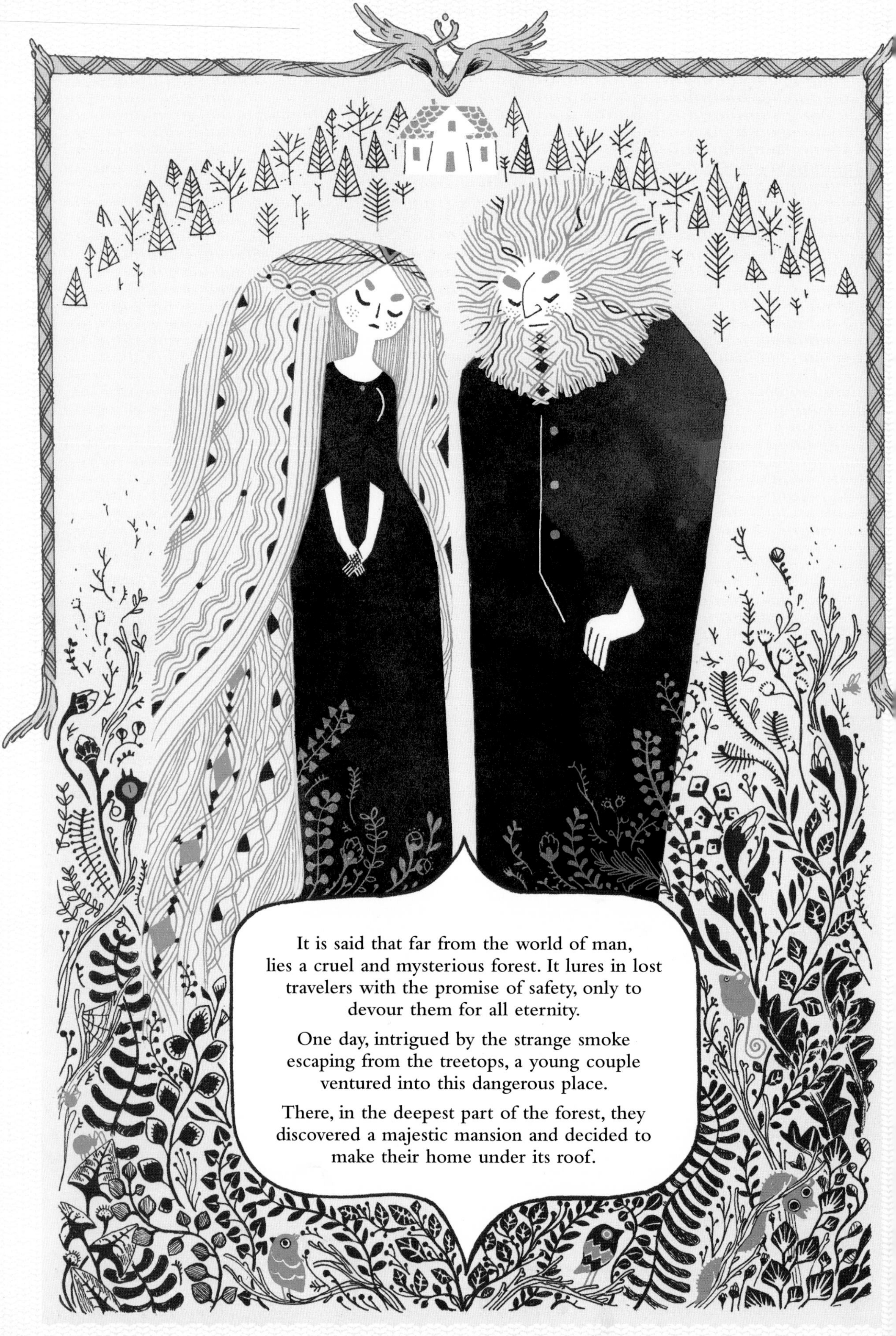

It is said that far from the world of man, lies a cruel and mysterious forest. It lures in lost travelers with the promise of safety, only to devour them for all eternity.

One day, intrigued by the strange smoke escaping from the treetops, a young couple ventured into this dangerous place.

There, in the deepest part of the forest, they discovered a majestic mansion and decided to make their home under its roof.

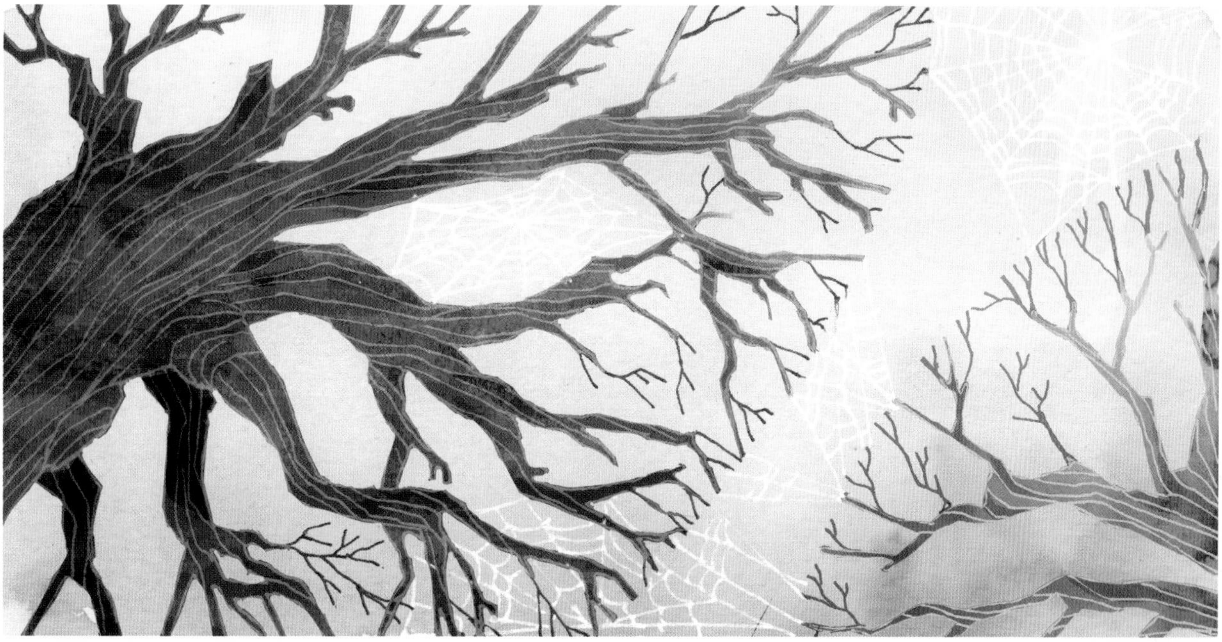

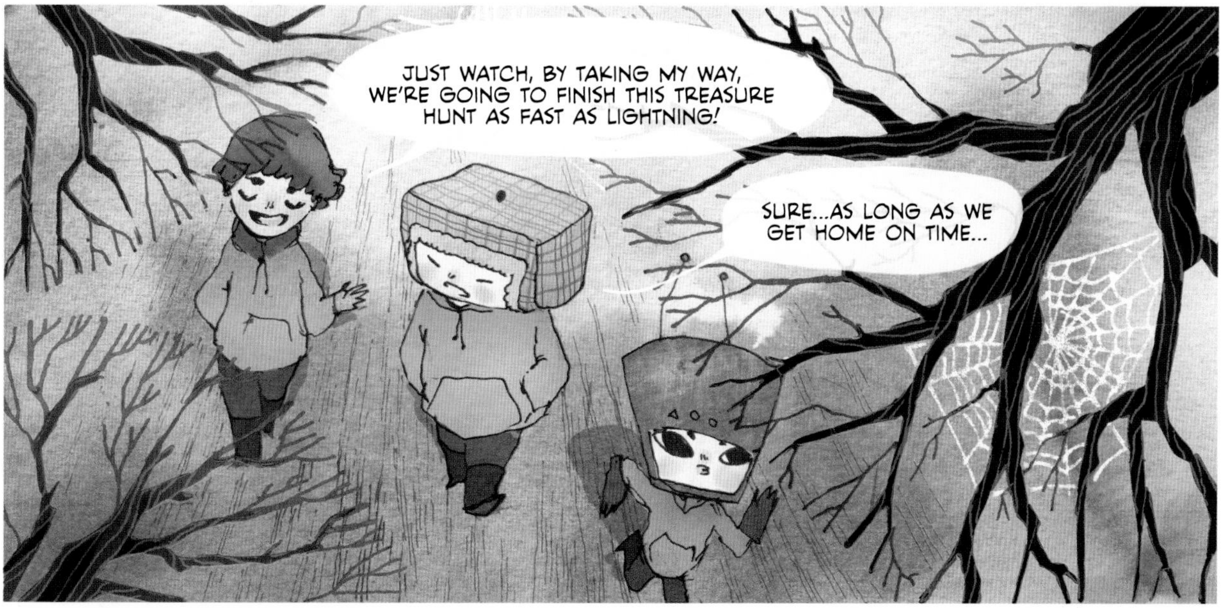
JUST WATCH, BY TAKING MY WAY, WE'RE GOING TO FINISH THIS TREASURE HUNT AS FAST AS LIGHTNING!
SURE...AS LONG AS WE GET HOME ON TIME...

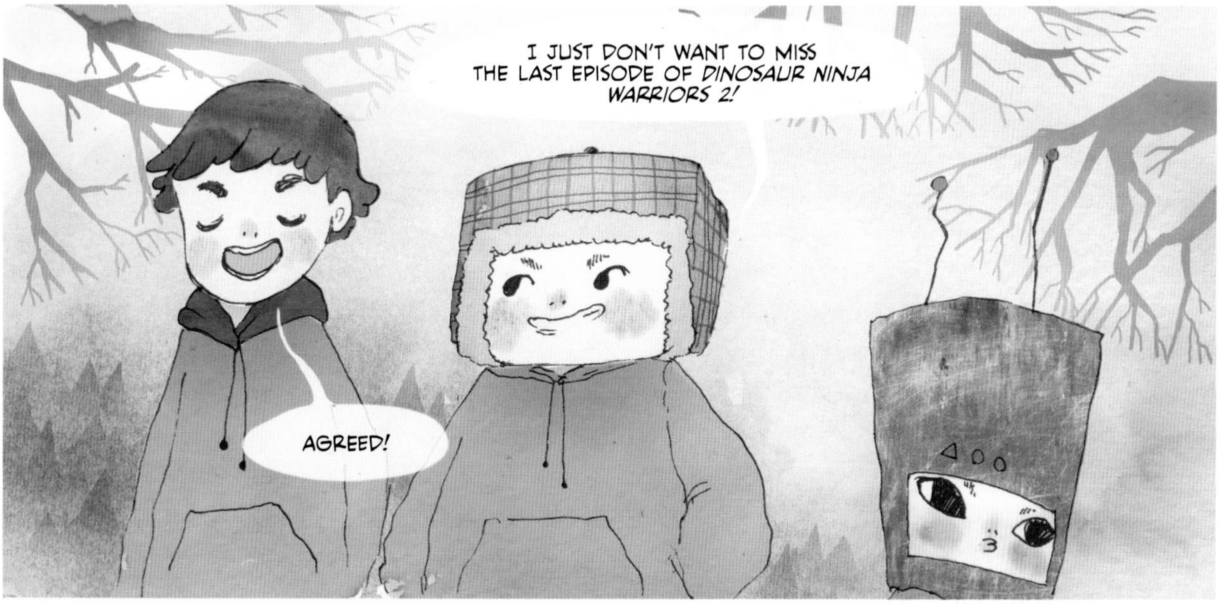
I JUST DON'T WANT TO MISS THE LAST EPISODE OF *DINOSAUR NINJA WARRIORS 2!*
AGREED!

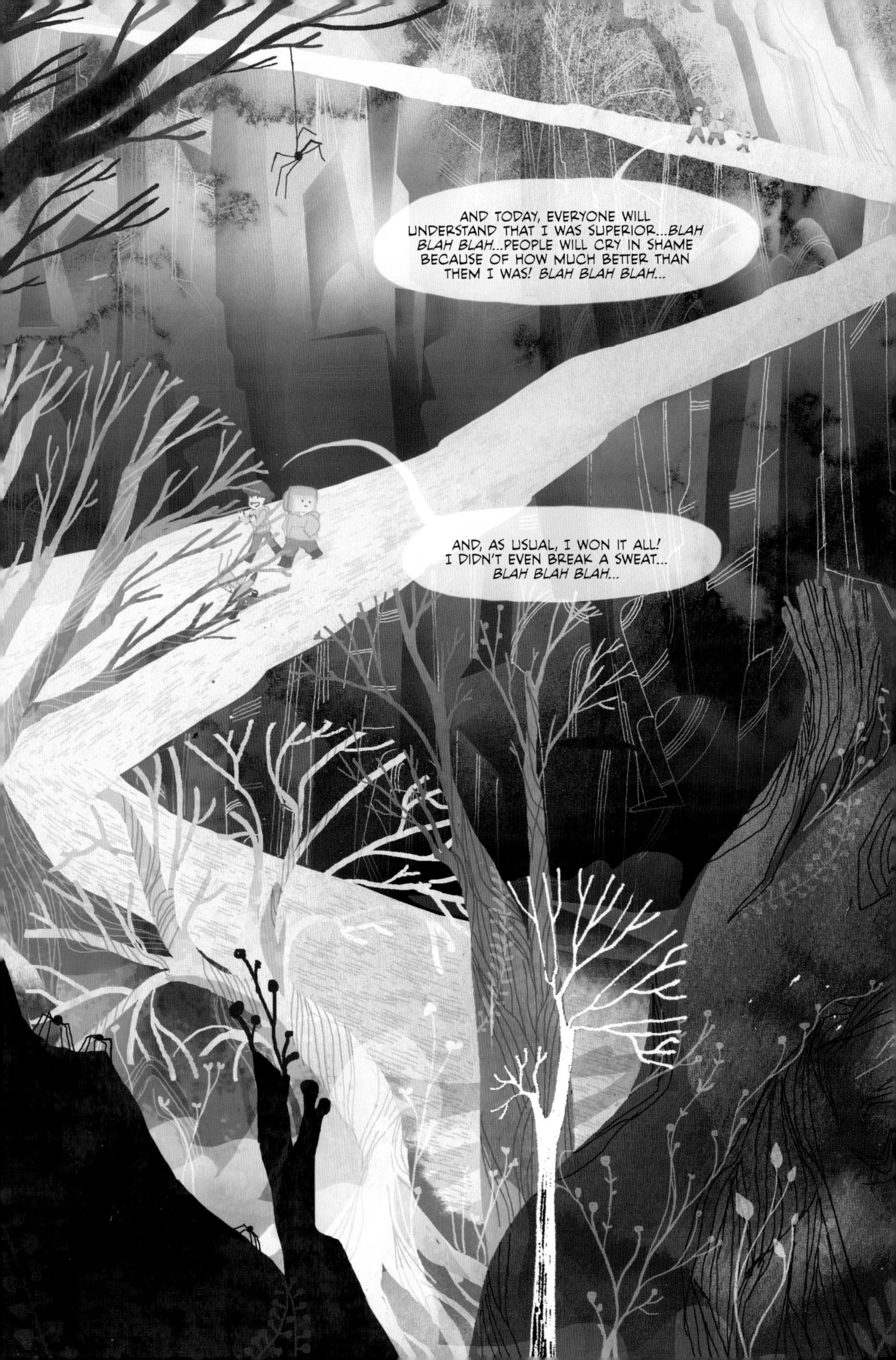
AND TODAY, EVERYONE WILL UNDERSTAND THAT I WAS SUPERIOR...*BLAH BLAH BLAH*...PEOPLE WILL CRY IN SHAME BECAUSE OF HOW MUCH BETTER THAN THEM I WAS! *BLAH BLAH BLAH*...
AND, AS USUAL, I WON IT ALL! I DIDN'T EVEN BREAK A SWEAT... *BLAH BLAH BLAH*...

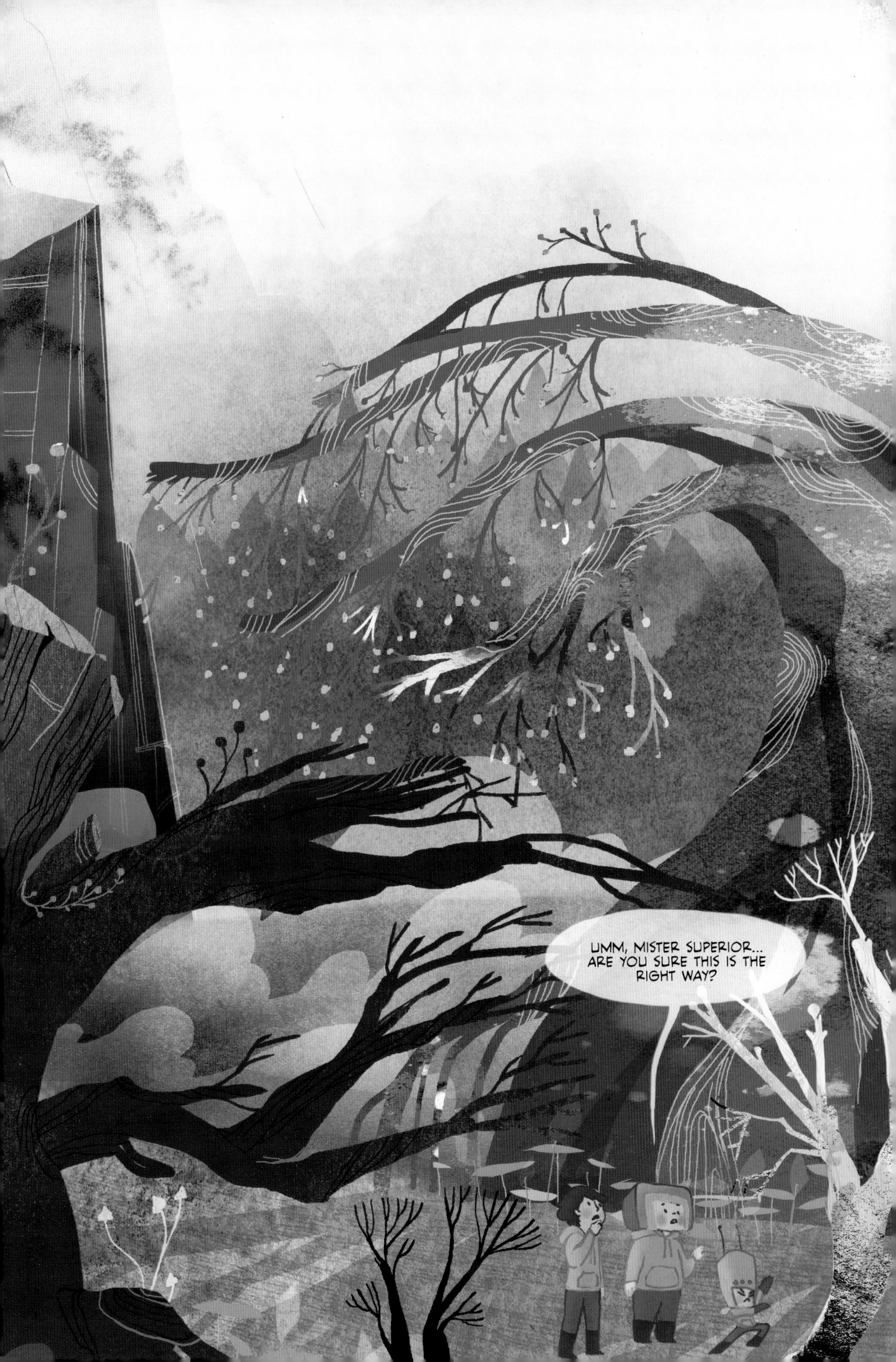
UMM, MISTER SUPERIOR... ARE YOU SURE THIS IS THE RIGHT WAY?

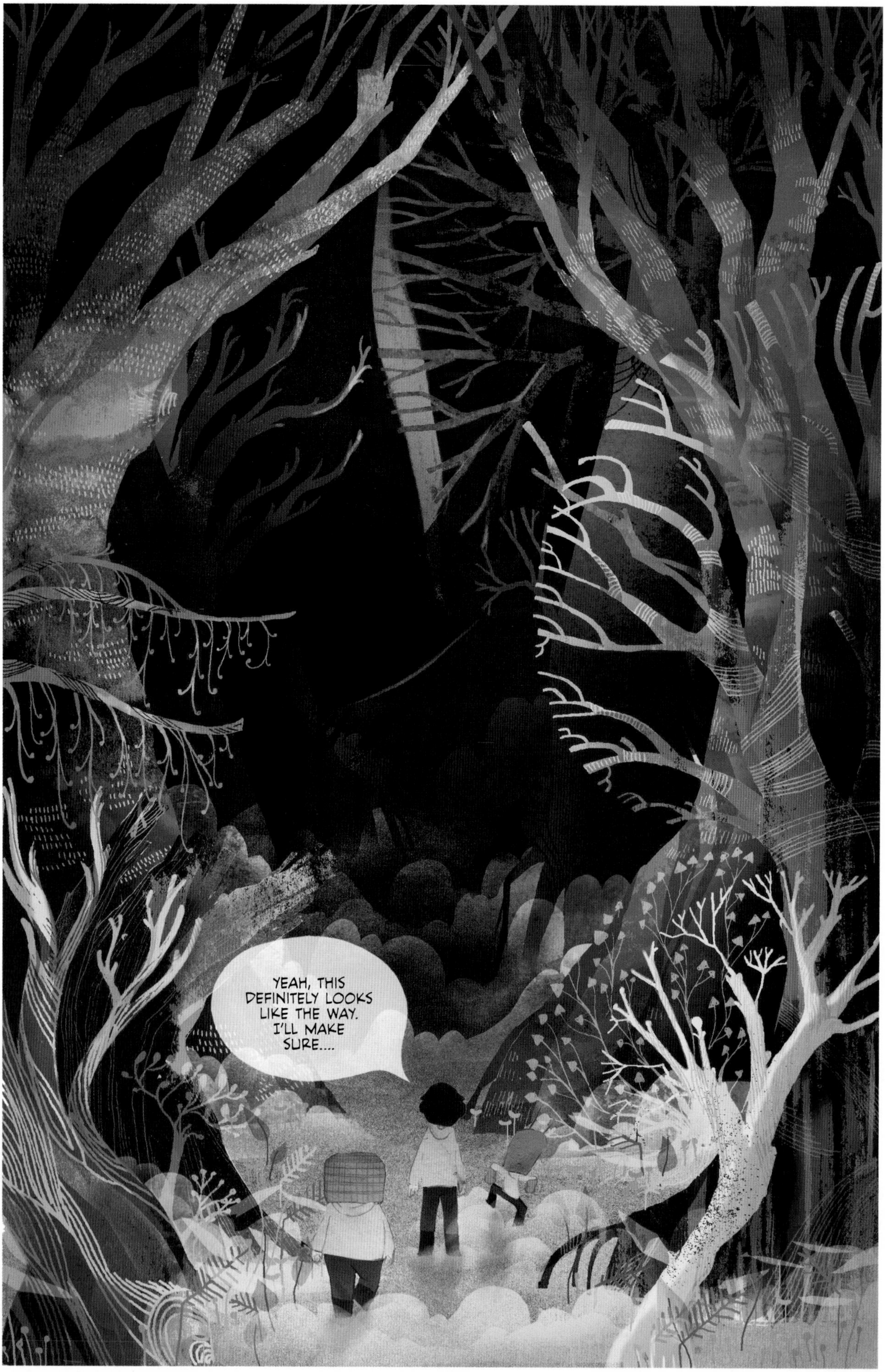
YEAH, THIS DEFINITELY LOOKS LIKE THE WAY. I'LL MAKE SURE....

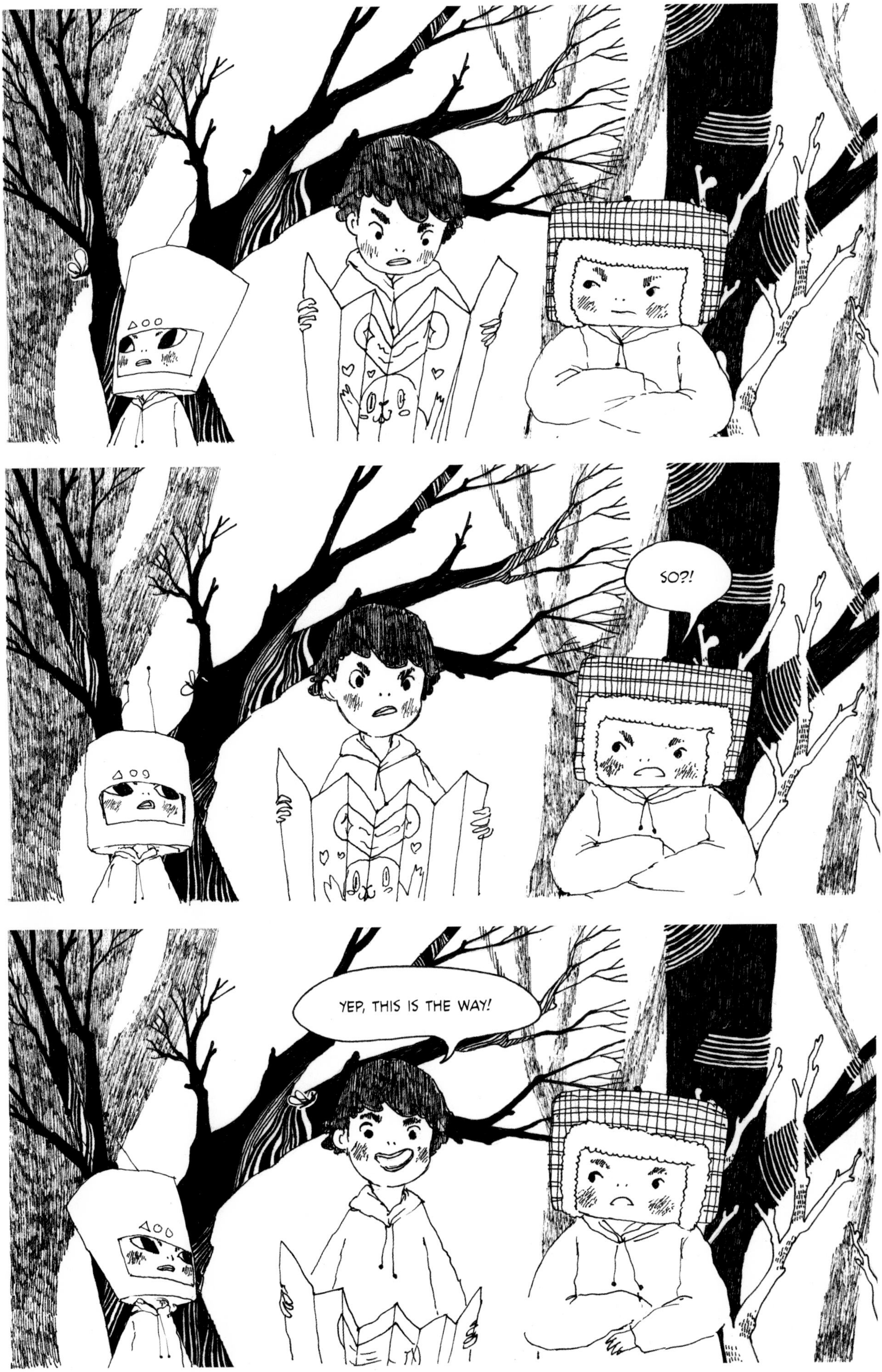
SO?!
YEP, THIS IS THE WAY!

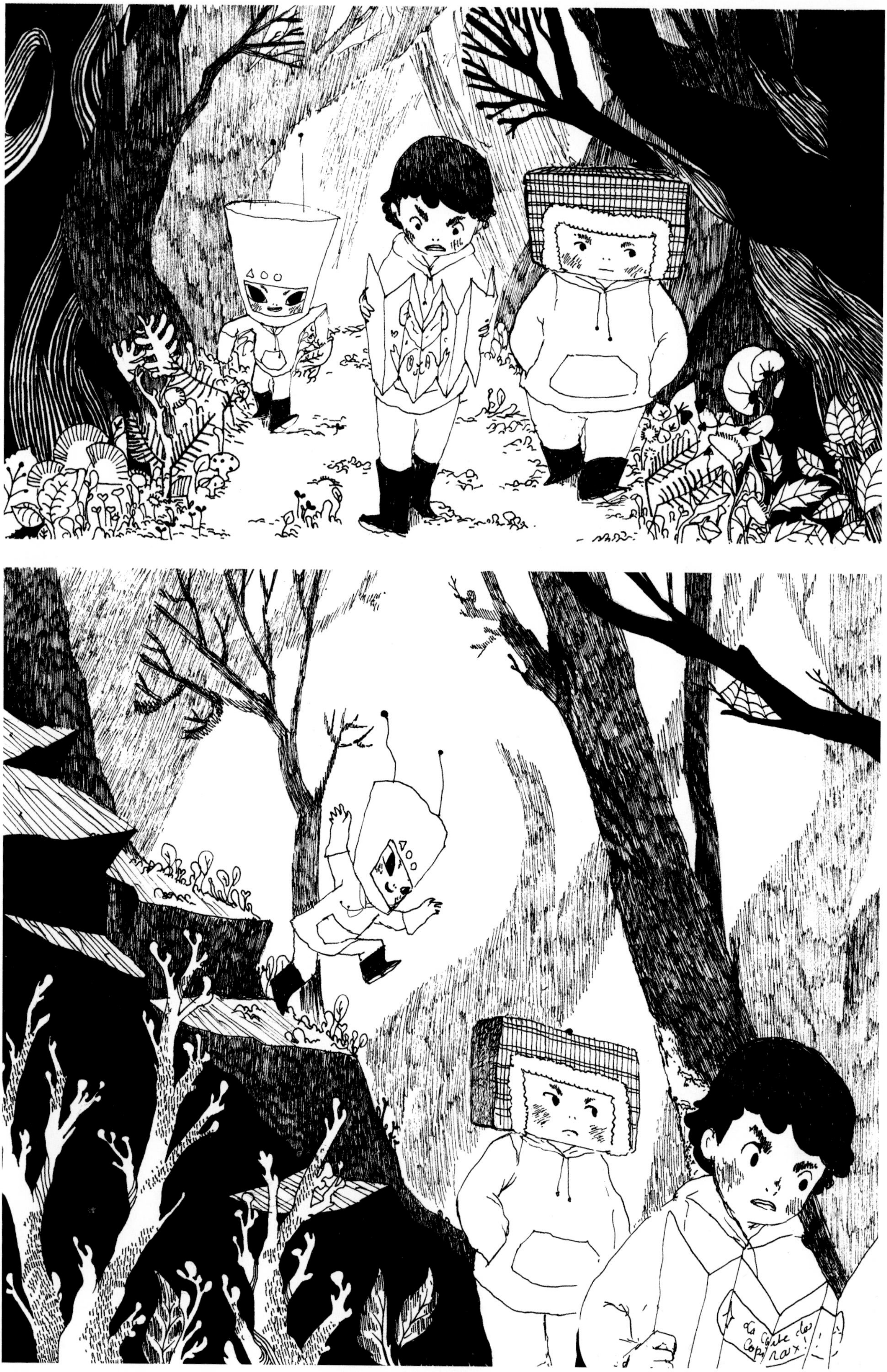

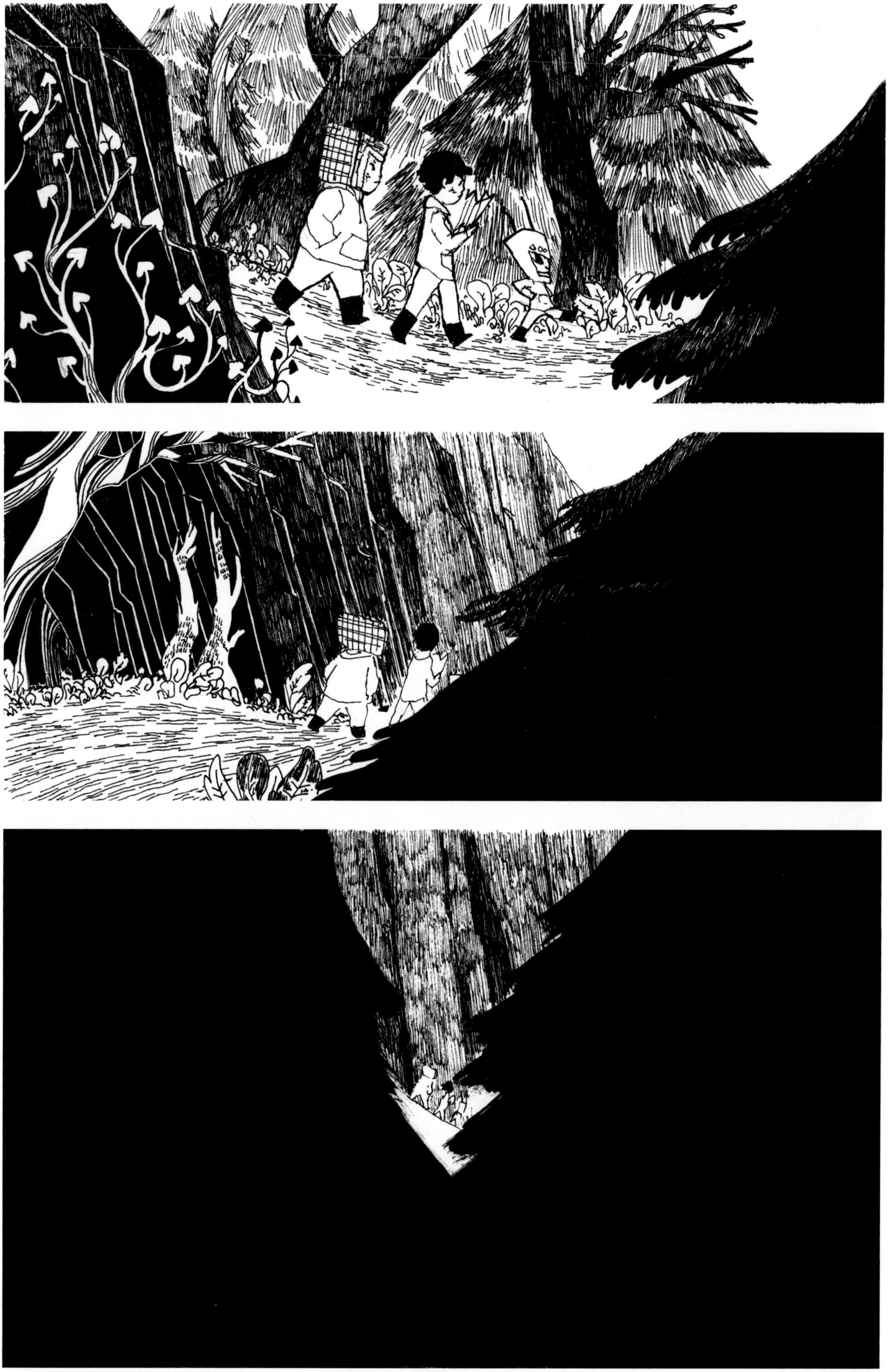

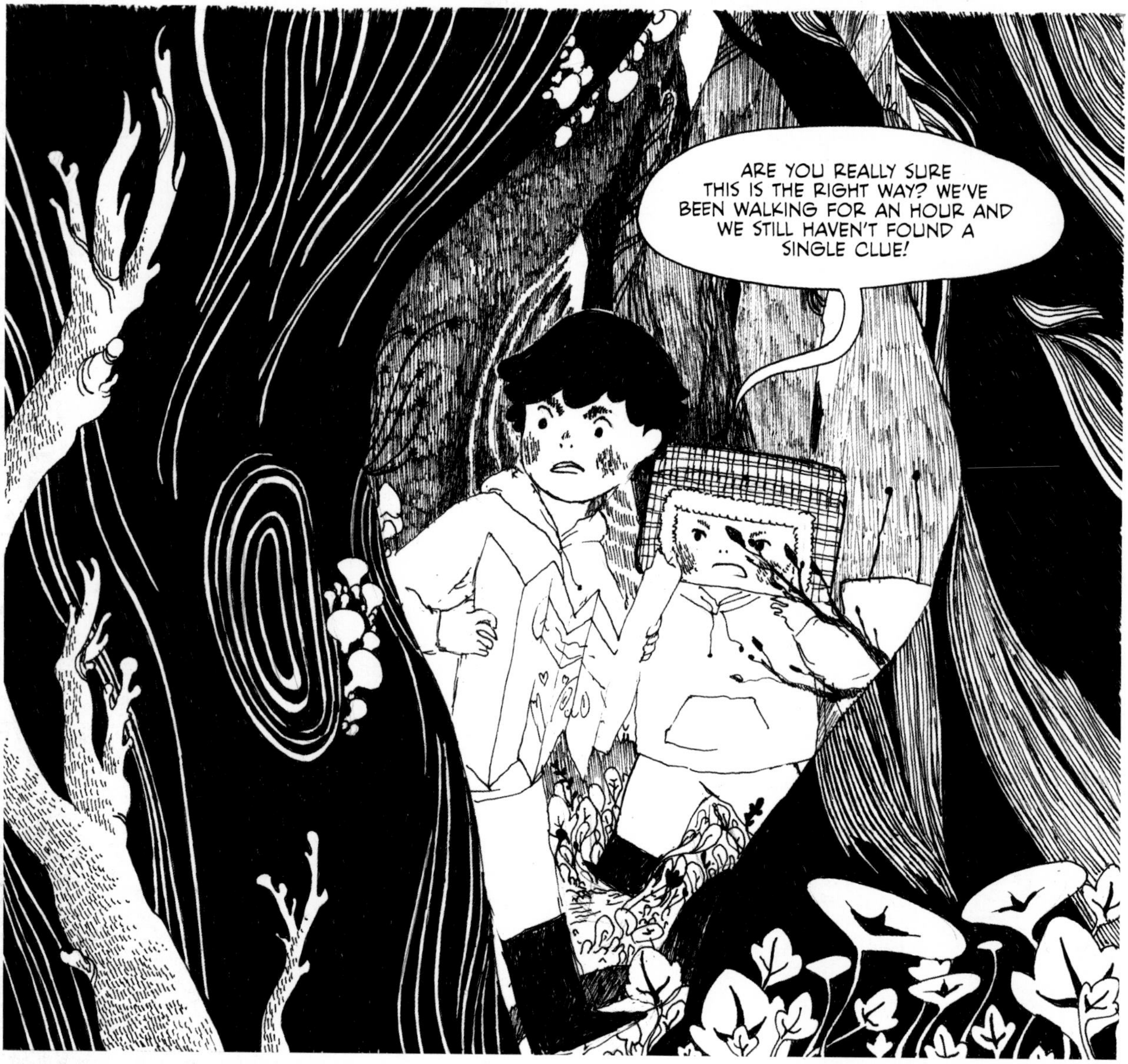
ARE YOU REALLY SURE THIS IS THE RIGHT WAY? WE'VE BEEN WALKING FOR AN HOUR AND WE STILL HAVEN'T FOUND A SINGLE CLUE!

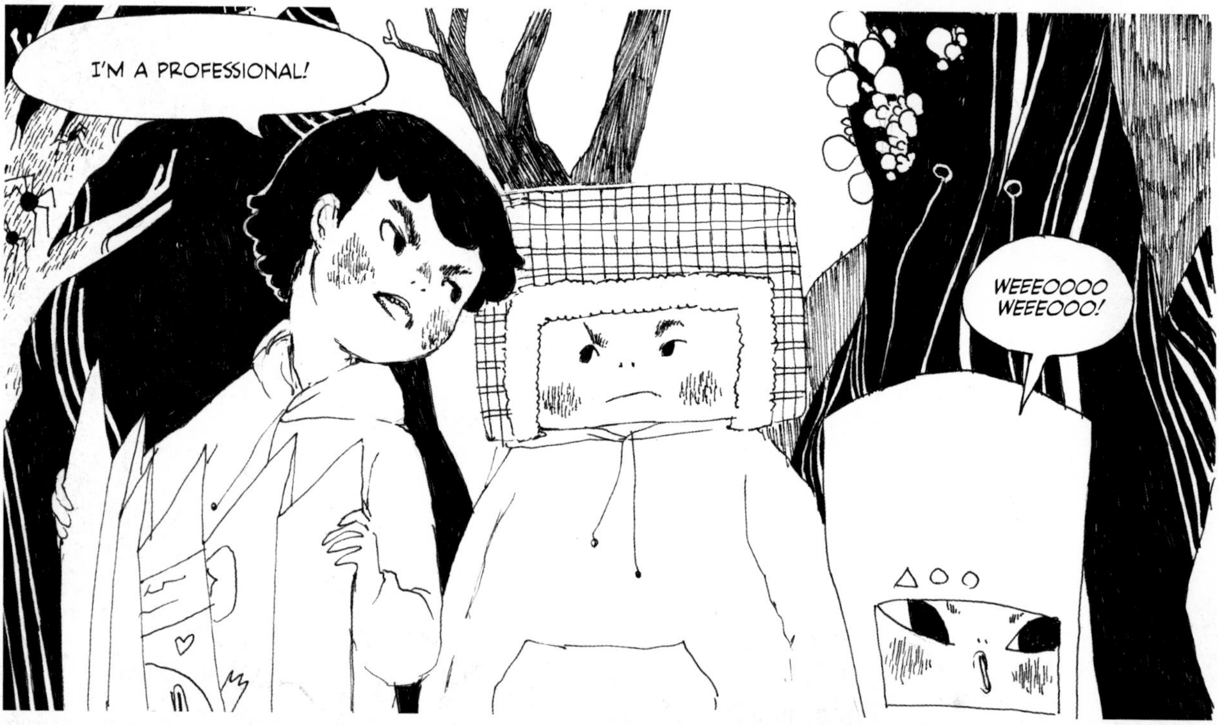
I'M A PROFESSIONAL!
WEEEOOOO WEEEOOO!

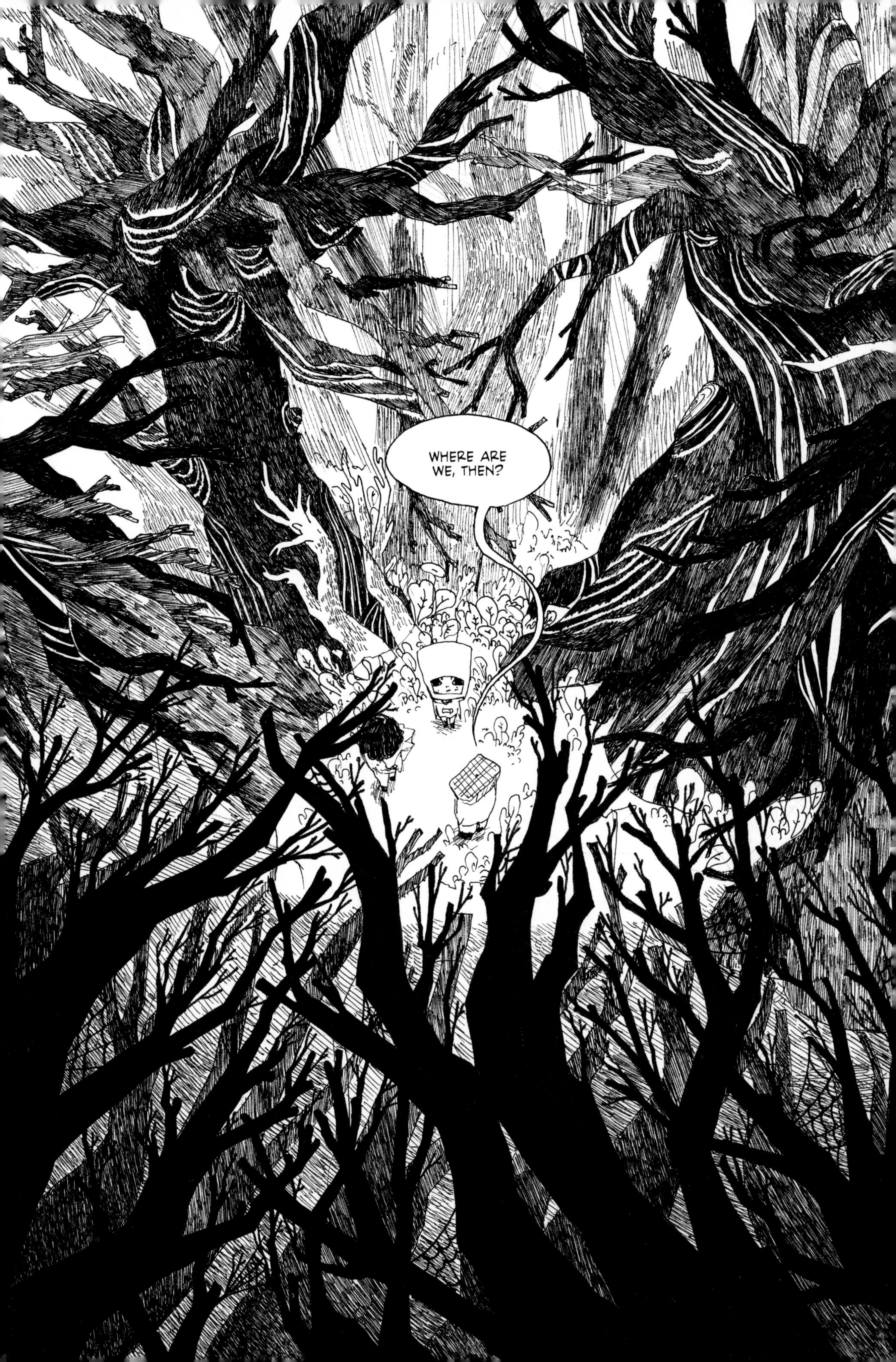
WHERE ARE WE, THEN?

UMM...

ACCORDING TO THE MAP, WE NEED TO FOLLOW THE "PATH OF HAPPY TREES DISGUISED AS BOBCATS"... SO TREES WITH MARKS!

HIYA!

THERE ARE SOME MARKS HERE, BUT I DON'T THINK...

NICE!

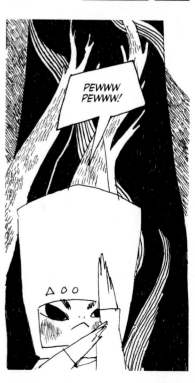

PEWWW PEWWW!

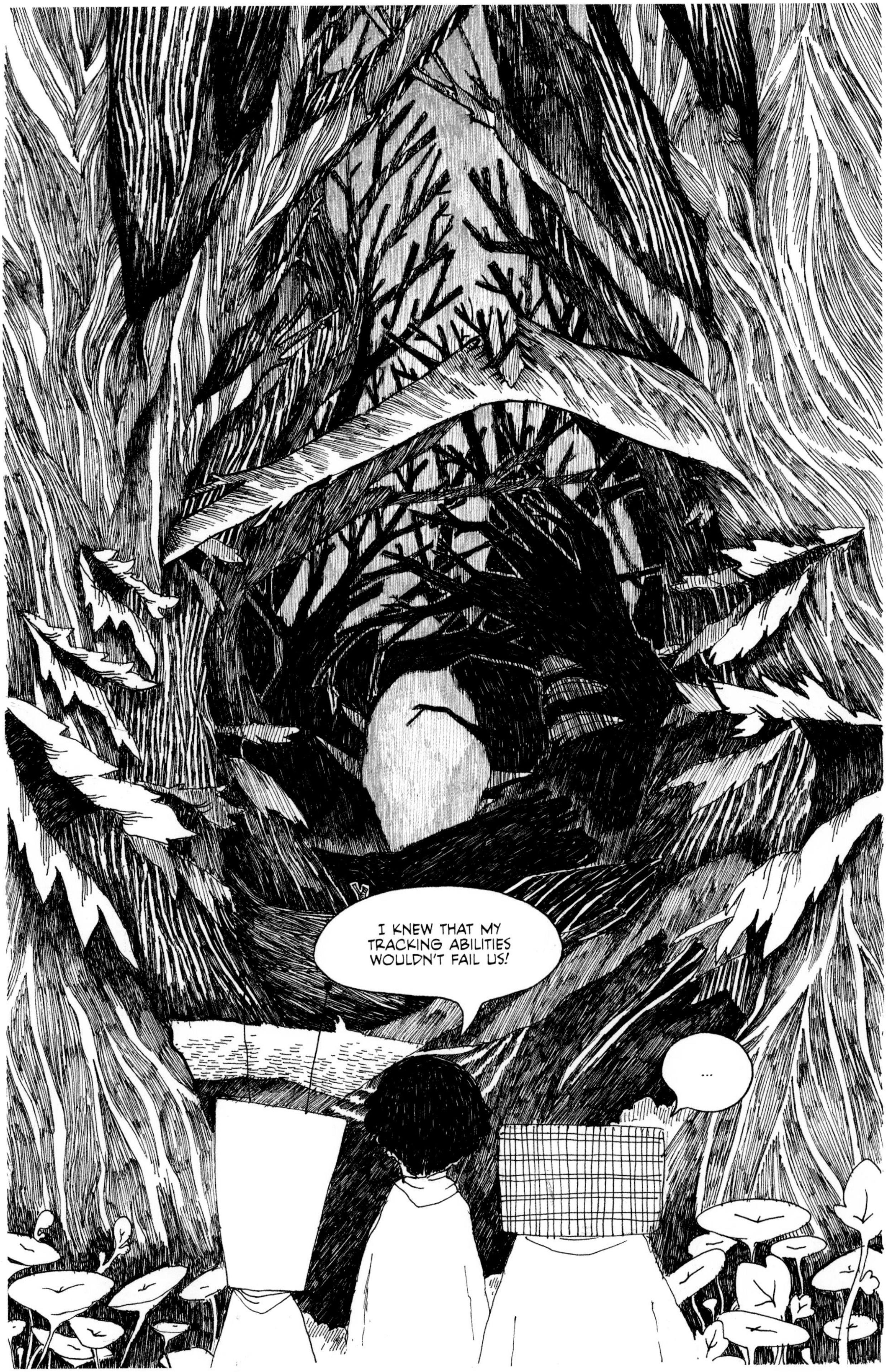
I KNEW THAT MY
TRACKING ABILITIES
WOULDN'T FAIL US!
...

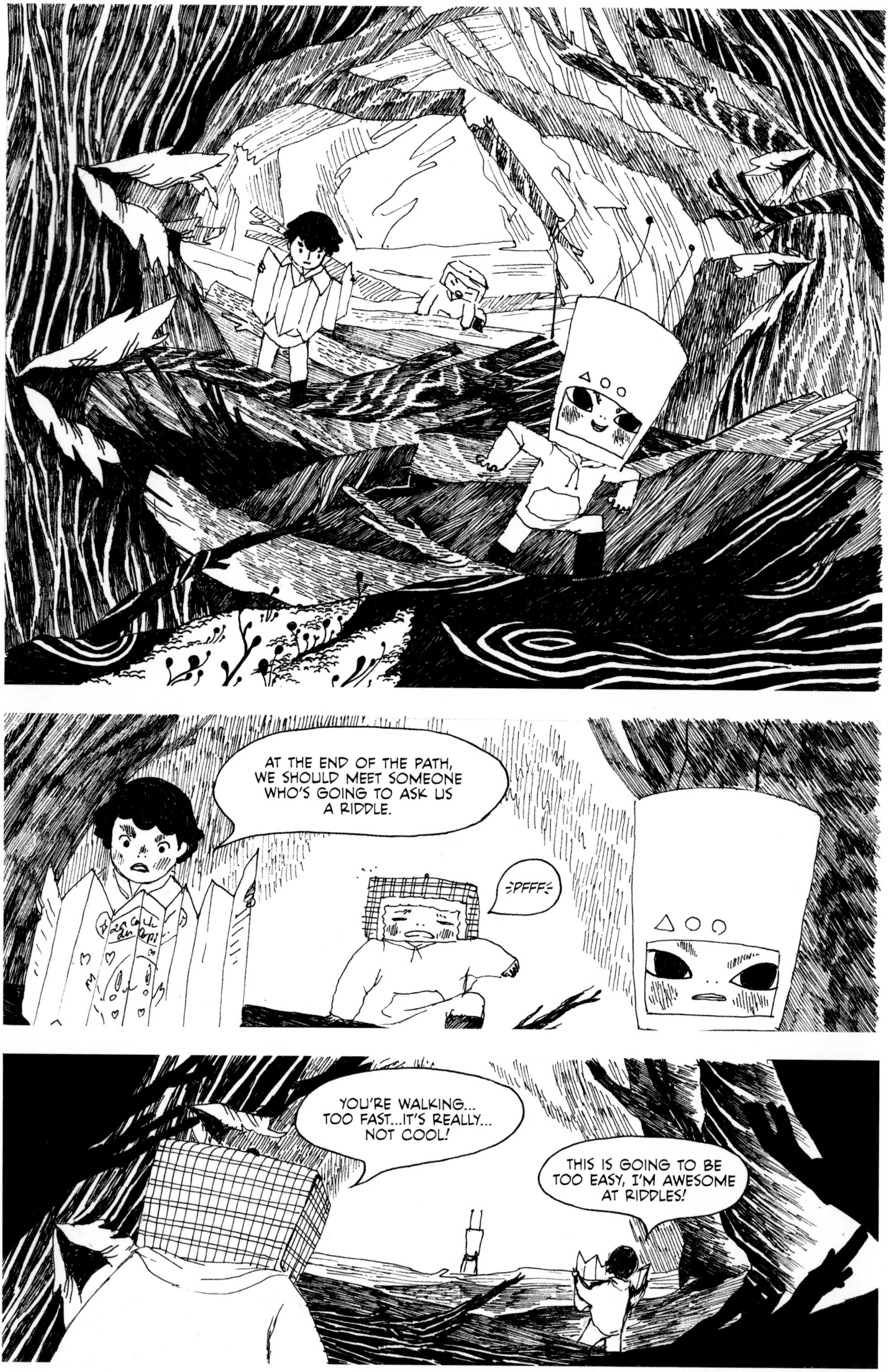
AT THE END OF THE PATH, WE SHOULD MEET SOMEONE WHO'S GOING TO ASK US A RIDDLE.
PFFF
YOU'RE WALKING... TOO FAST...IT'S REALLY... NOT COOL!
THIS IS GOING TO BE TOO EASY, I'M AWESOME AT RIDDLES!

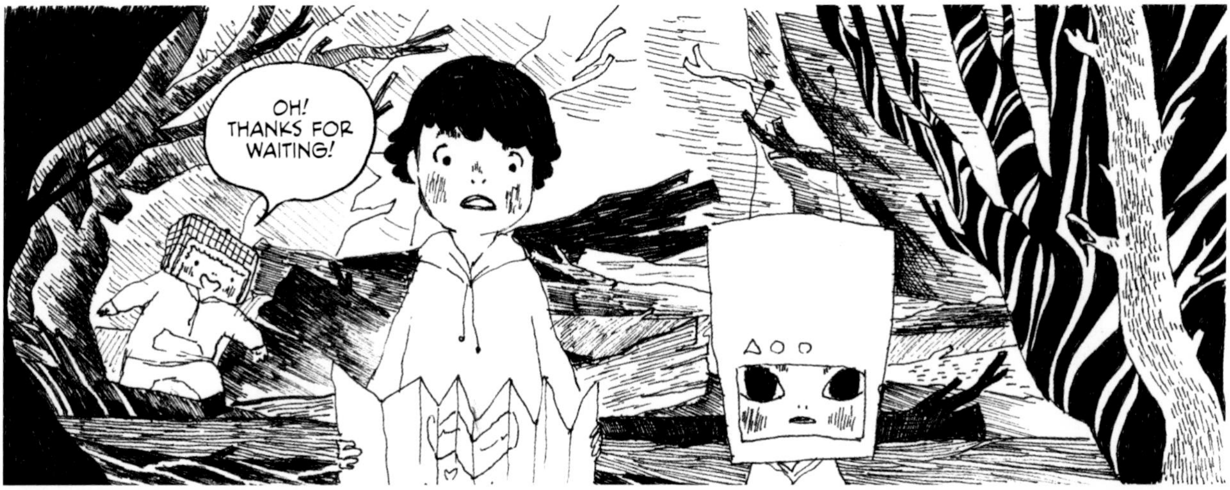
OH! THANKS FOR WAITING!

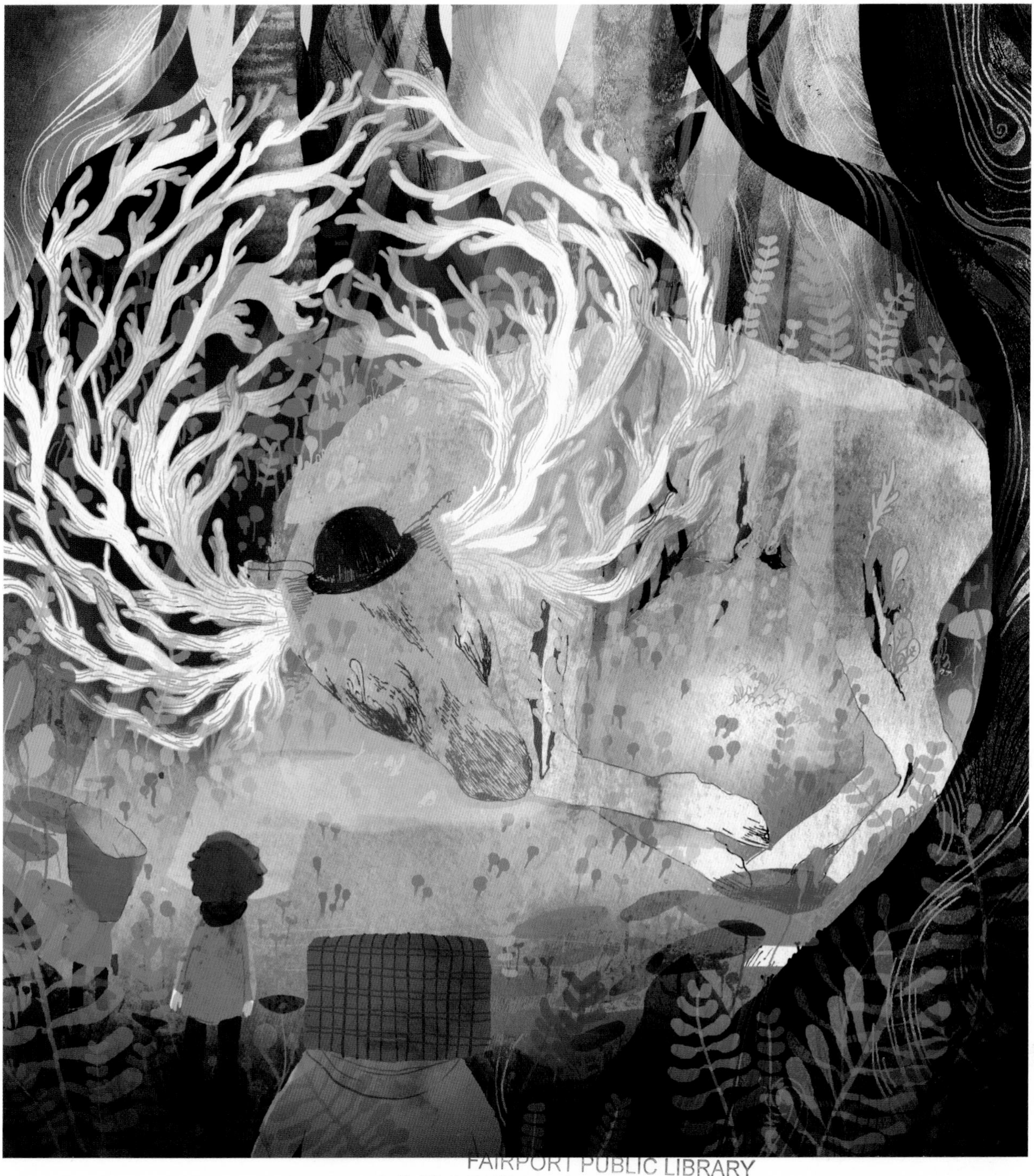

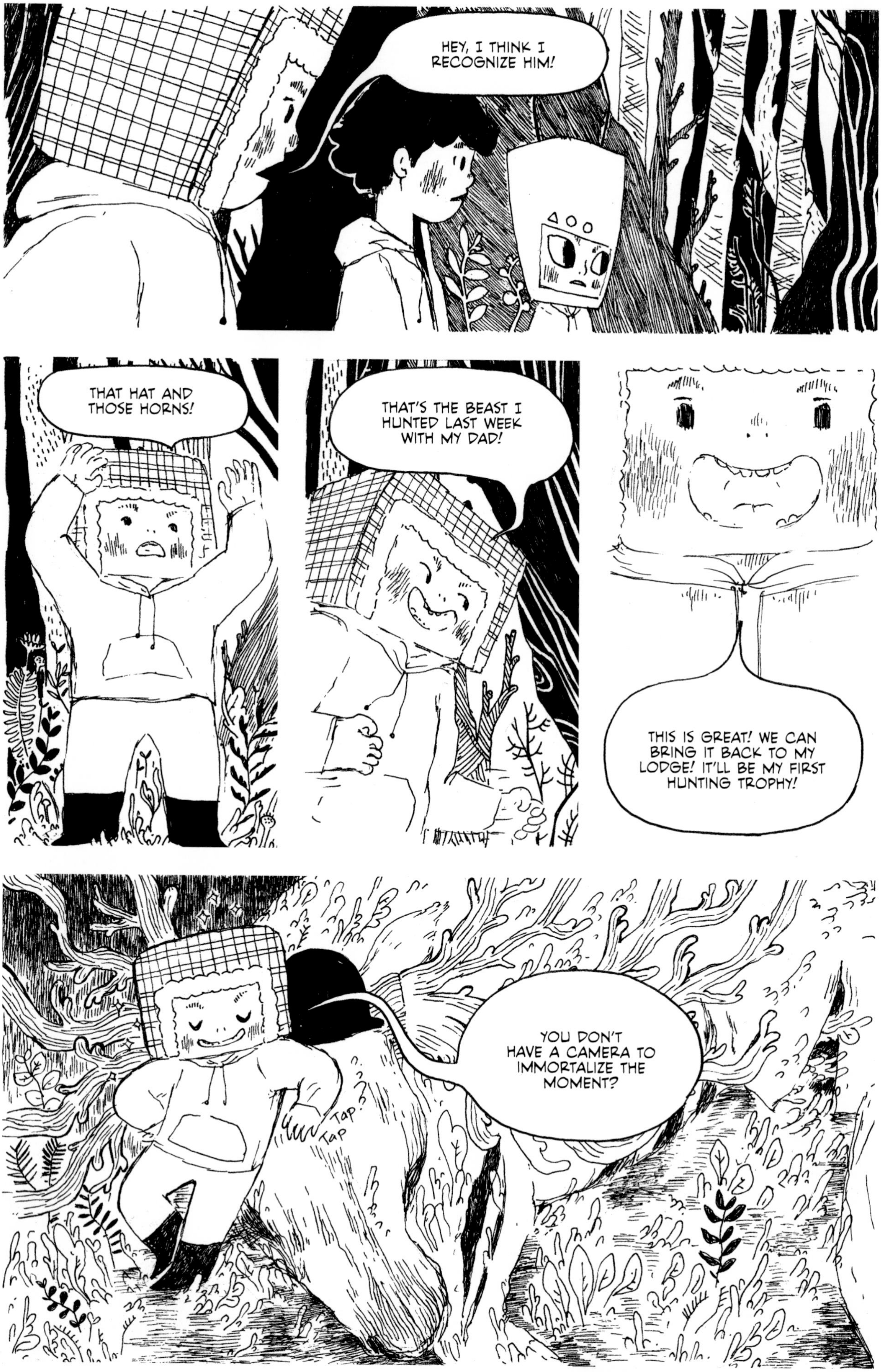
HEY, I THINK I RECOGNIZE HIM!
THAT HAT AND THOSE HORNS!
THAT'S THE BEAST I HUNTED LAST WEEK WITH MY DAD!
THIS IS GREAT! WE CAN BRING IT BACK TO MY LODGE! IT'LL BE MY FIRST HUNTING TROPHY!
Tap Tap
YOU DON'T HAVE A CAMERA TO IMMORTALIZE THE MOMENT?

=PFF= I CAN'T BELIEVE YOU!
THERE'S NO WAY YOU HUNTED SOMETHING LIKE THAT!
YOU'RE JUST JEALOUS!
AS IF!

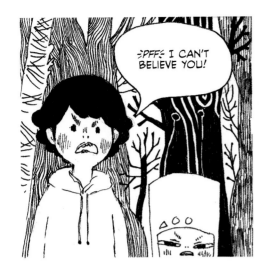

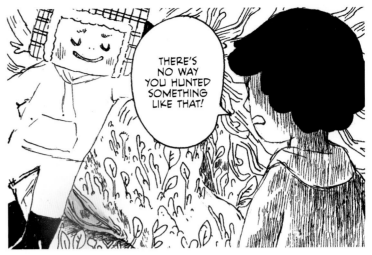

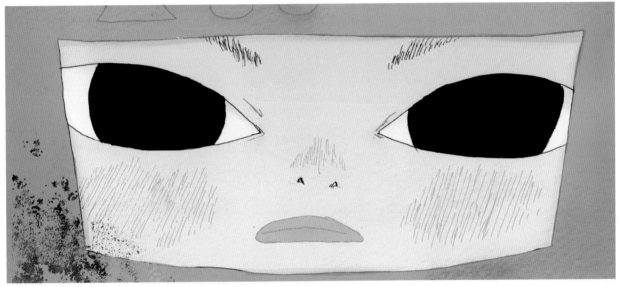

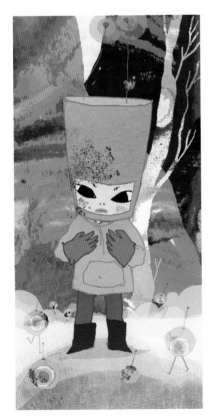

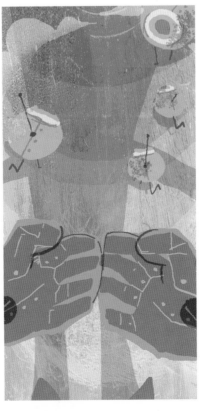

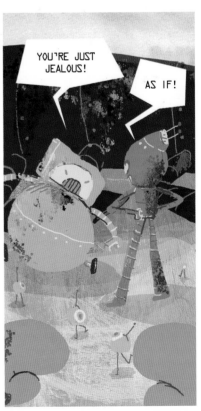

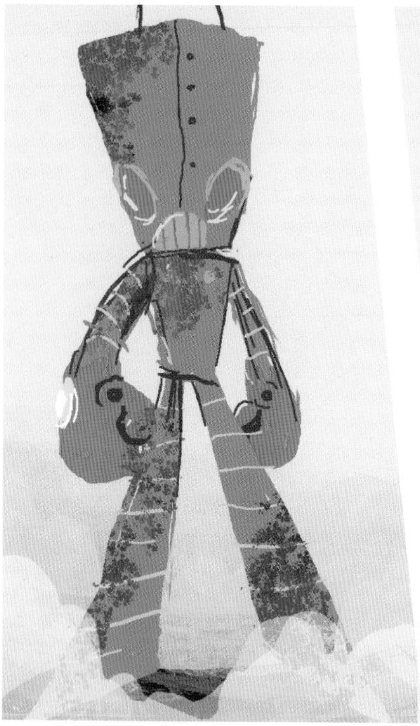

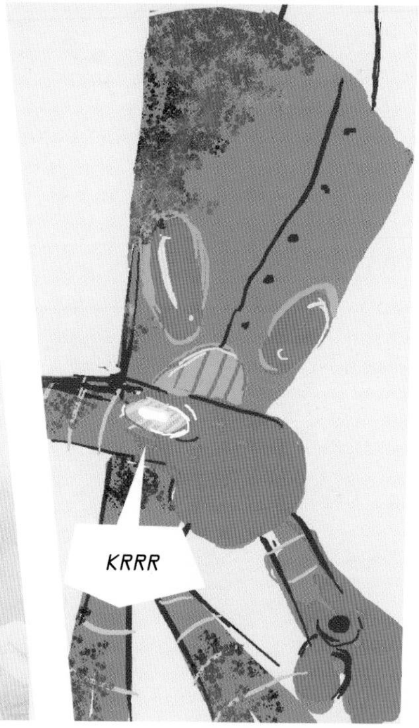
KRRR

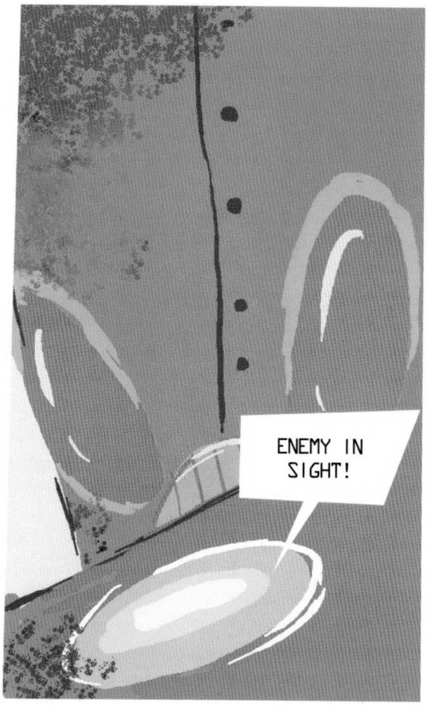
ENEMY IN SIGHT!

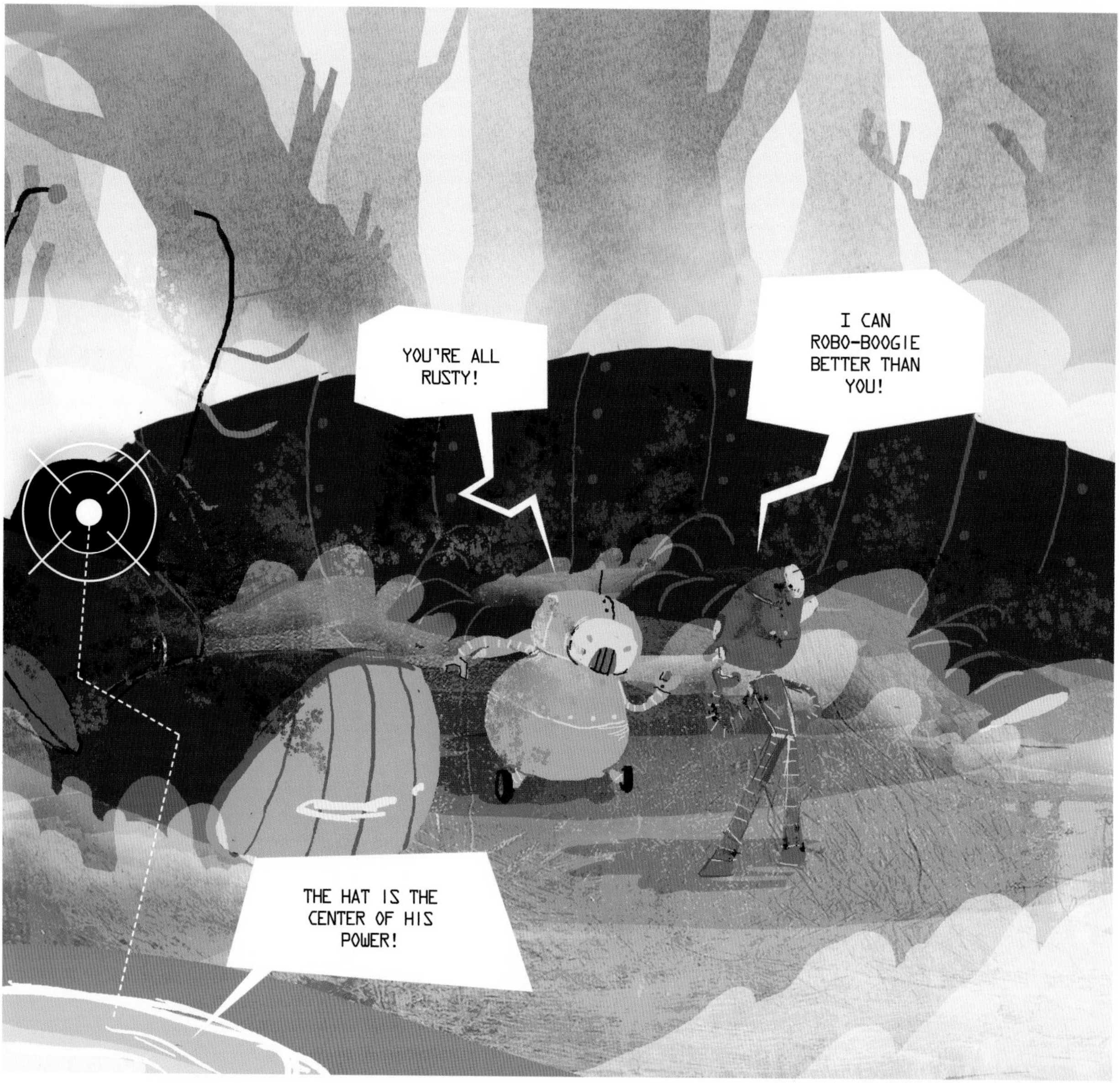
YOU'RE ALL RUSTY!
I CAN ROBO-BOOGIE BETTER THAN YOU!
THE HAT IS THE CENTER OF HIS POWER!

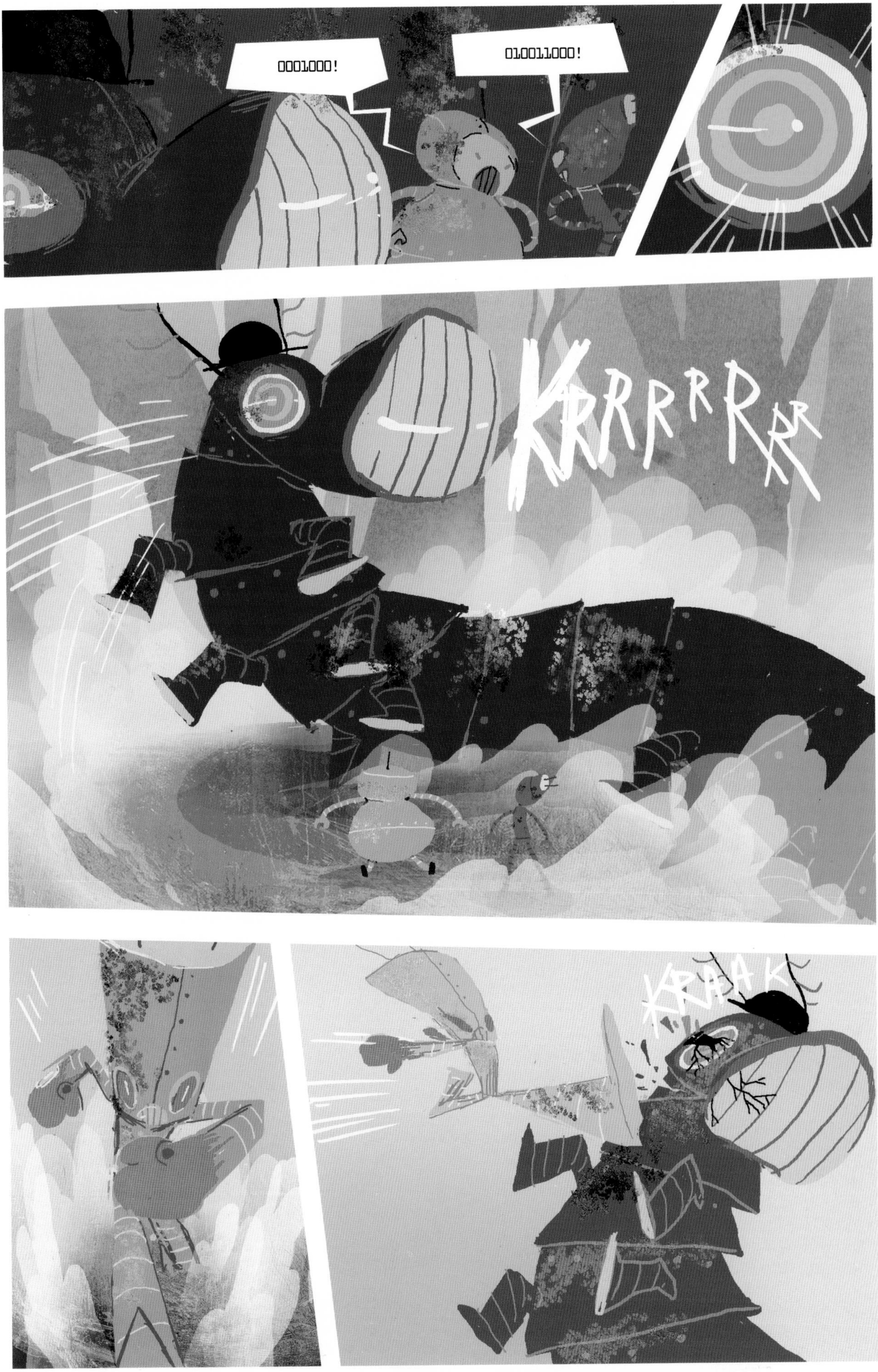
0001000!
010011000!
KRRRRRRR
KRAAK

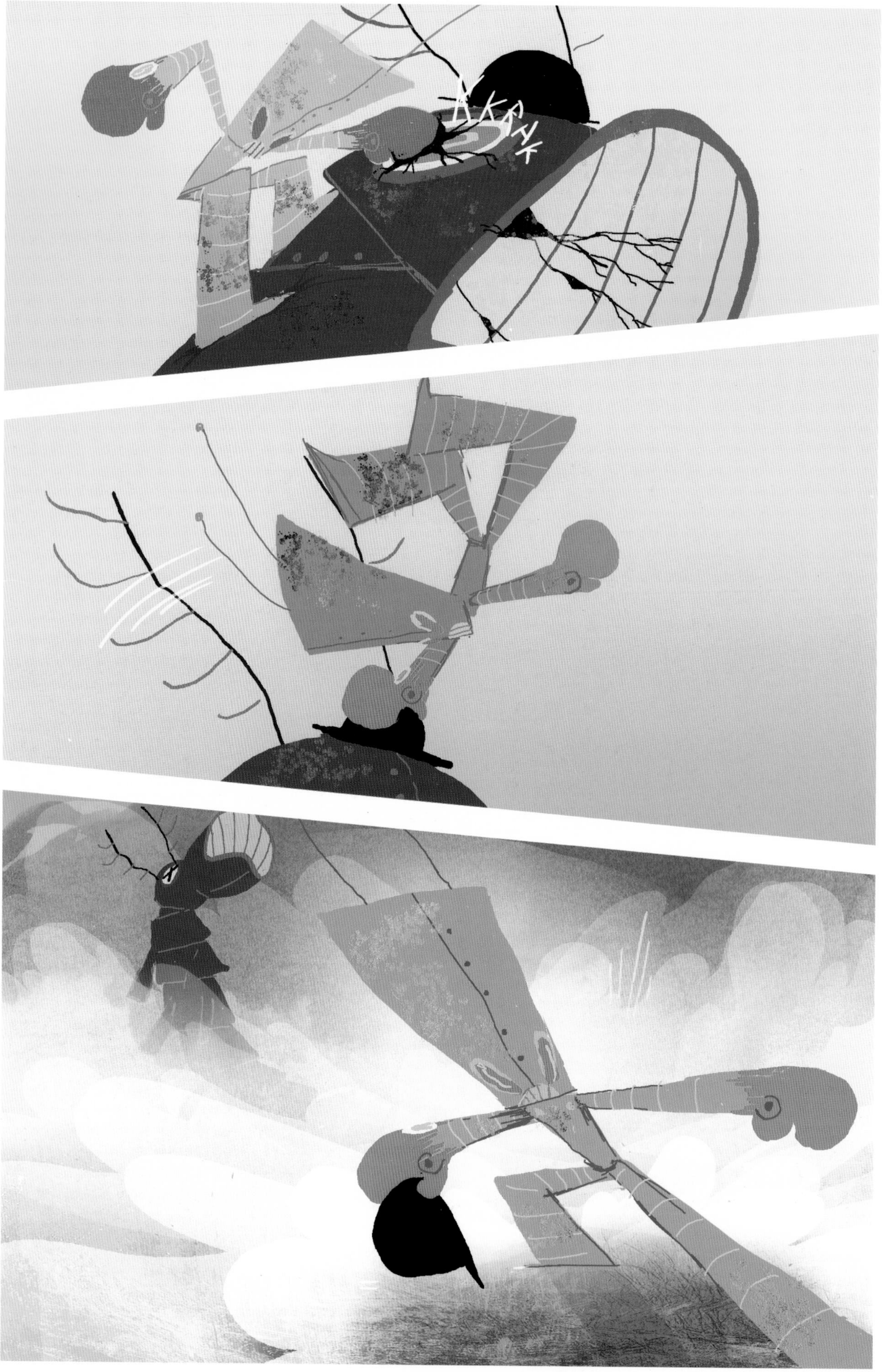

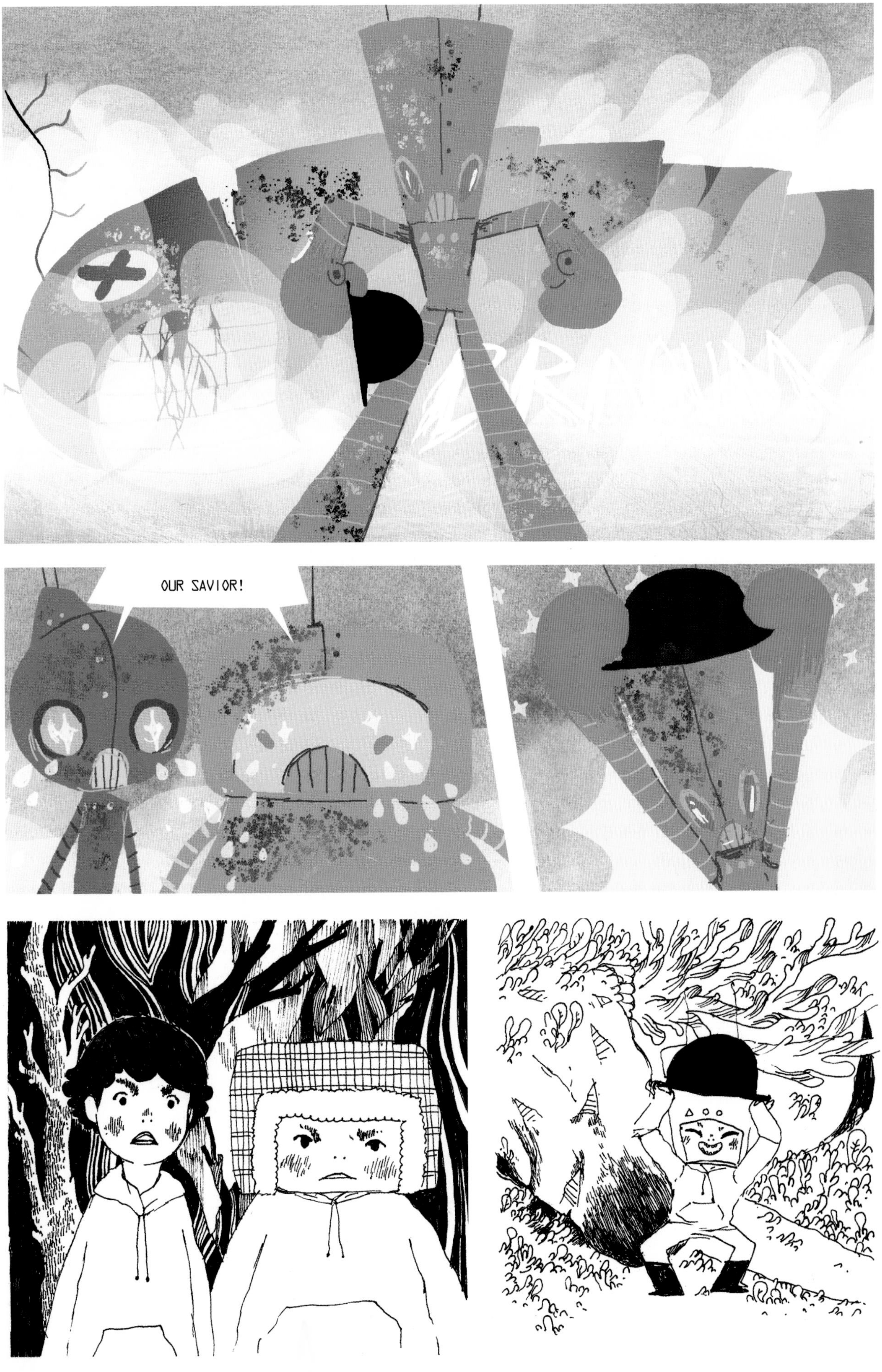
OUR SAVIOR!

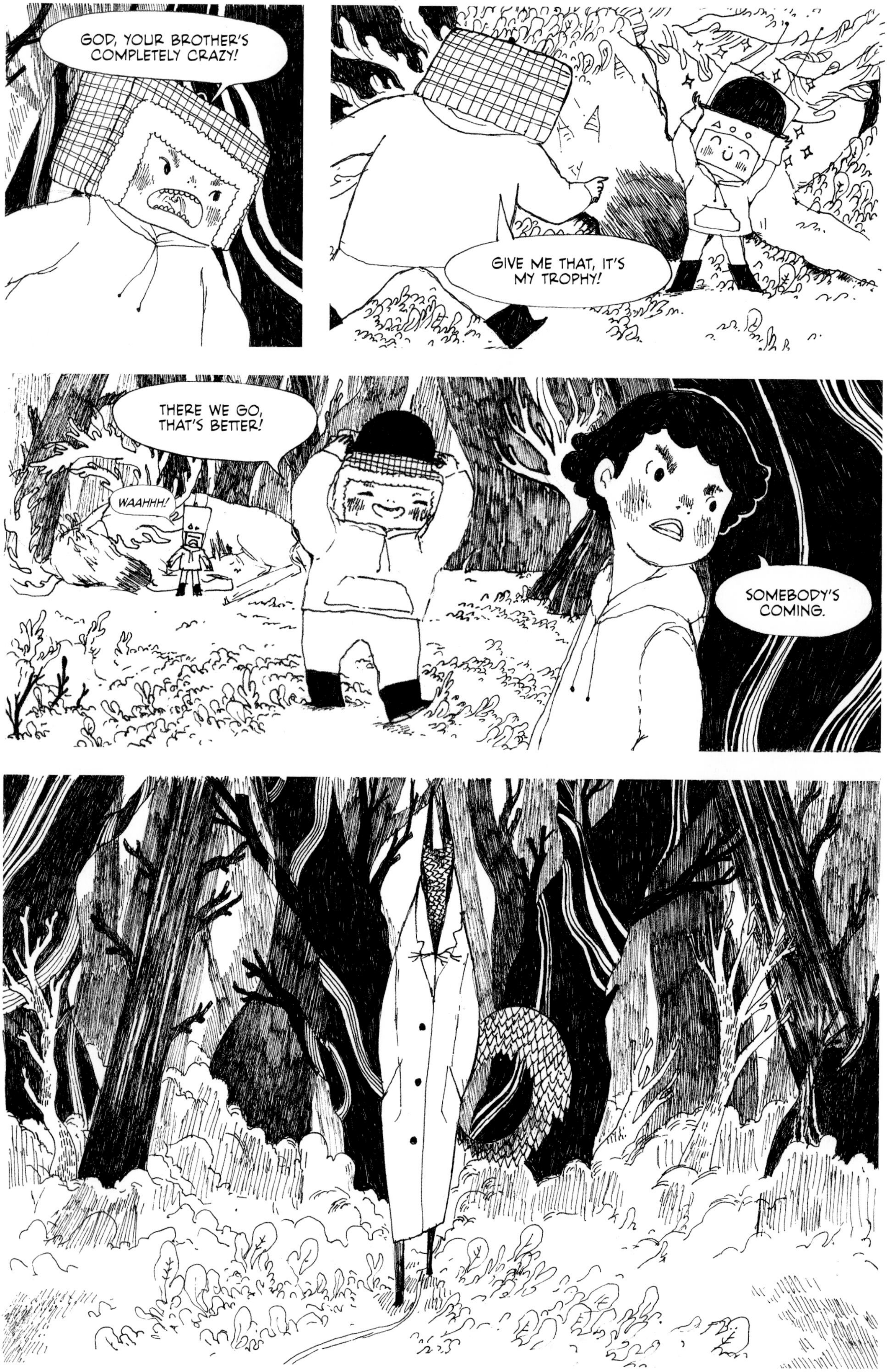

GOD, YOUR BROTHER'S COMPLETELY CRAZY!
GIVE ME THAT, IT'S MY TROPHY!
THERE WE GO, THAT'S BETTER!
WAAHHH!
SOMEBODY'S COMING.

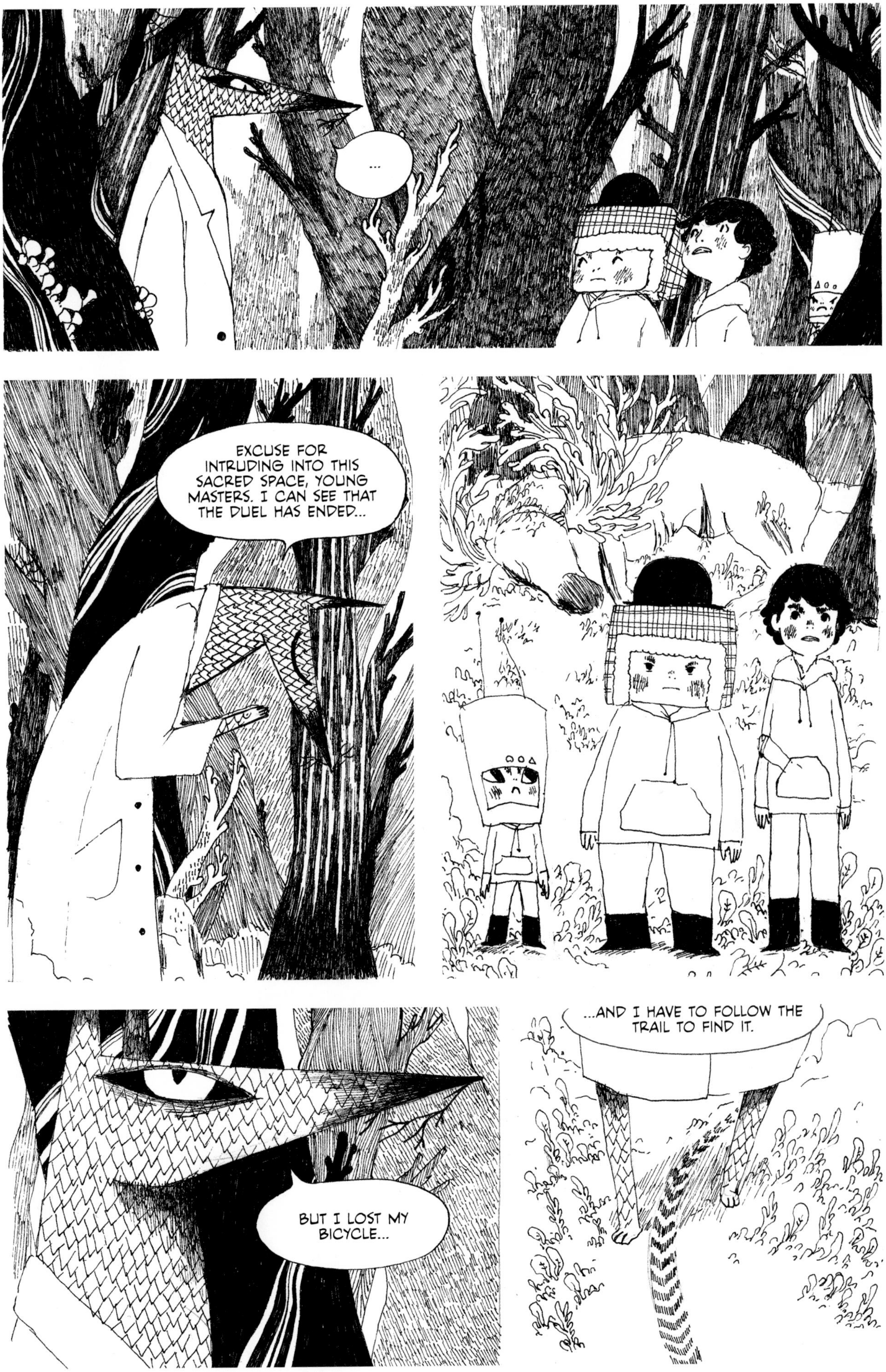
...
EXCUSE FOR INTRUDING INTO THIS SACRED SPACE, YOUNG MASTERS. I CAN SEE THAT THE DUEL HAS ENDED...
BUT I LOST MY BICYCLE...
...AND I HAVE TO FOLLOW THE TRAIL TO FIND IT.

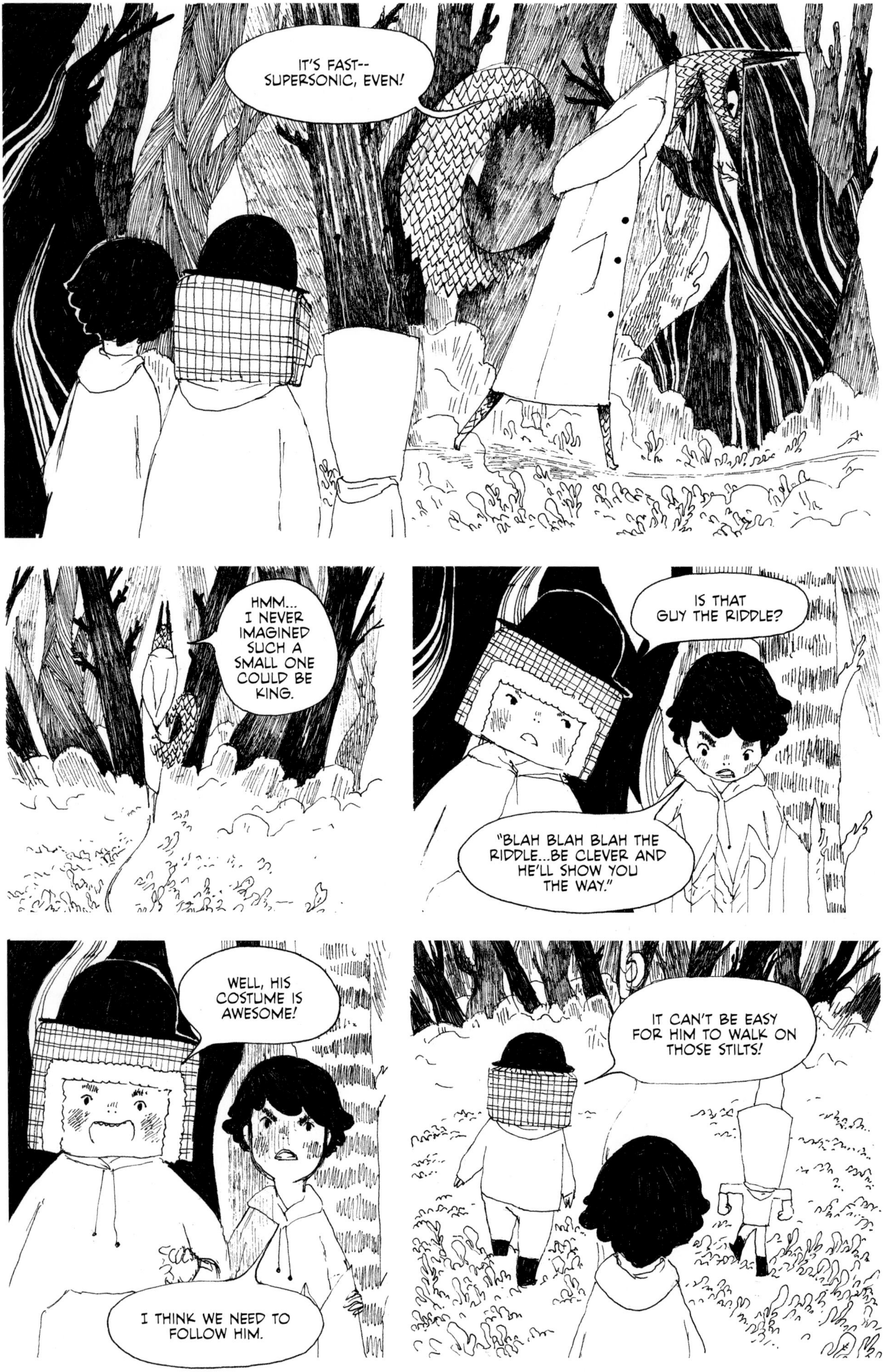
IT'S FAST--
SUPERSONIC, EVEN!
HMM... I NEVER IMAGINED SUCH A SMALL ONE COULD BE KING.
IS THAT GUY THE RIDDLE?
"BLAH BLAH BLAH THE RIDDLE...BE CLEVER AND HE'LL SHOW YOU THE WAY."
WELL, HIS COSTUME IS AWESOME!
I THINK WE NEED TO FOLLOW HIM.
IT CAN'T BE EASY FOR HIM TO WALK ON THOSE STILTS!

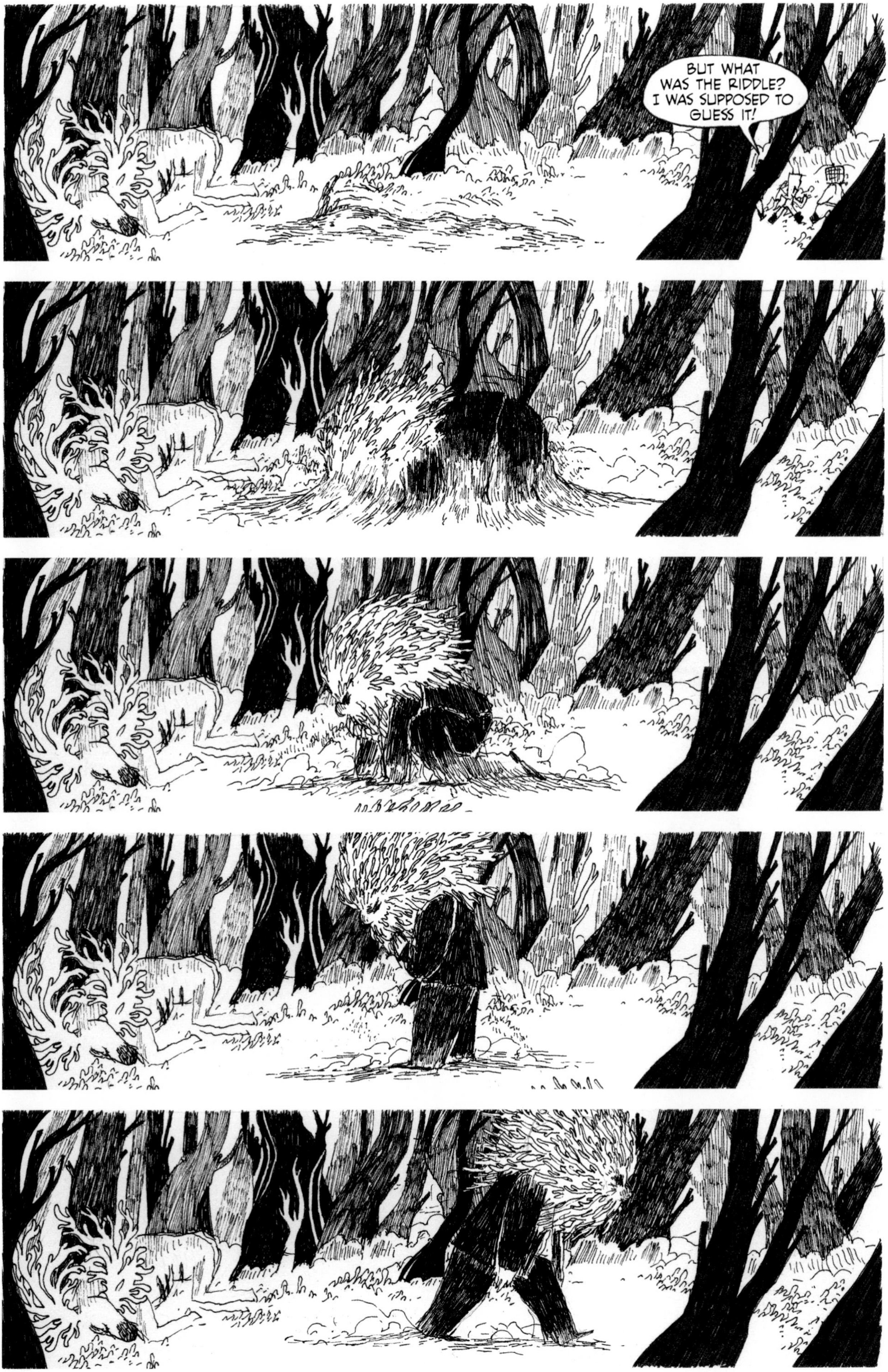
BUT WHAT WAS THE RIDDLE? I WAS SUPPOSED TO GUESS IT!

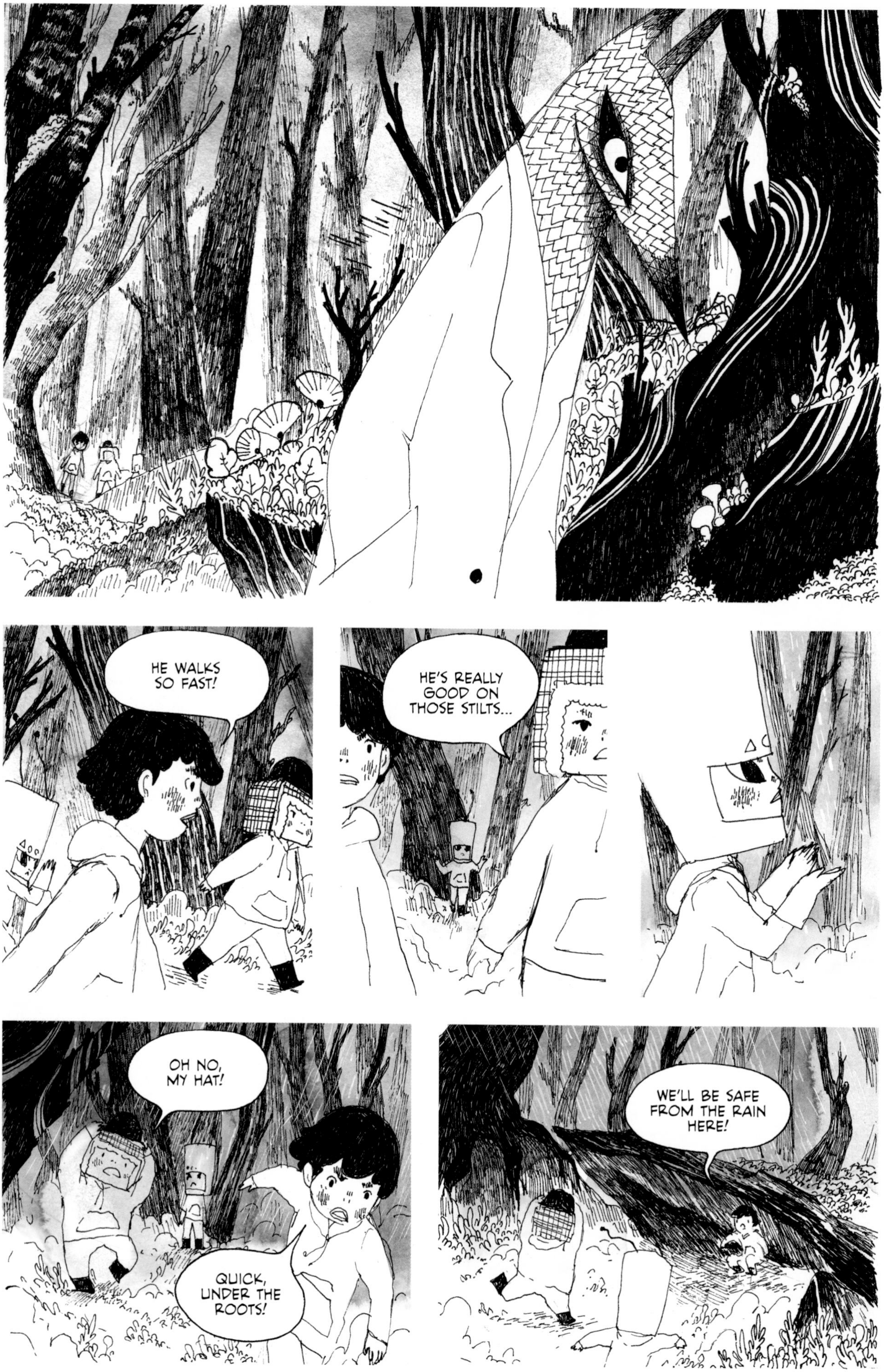
HE WALKS SO FAST!
HE'S REALLY GOOD ON THOSE STILTS...
OH NO, MY HAT!
QUICK, UNDER THE ROOTS!
WE'LL BE SAFE FROM THE RAIN HERE!

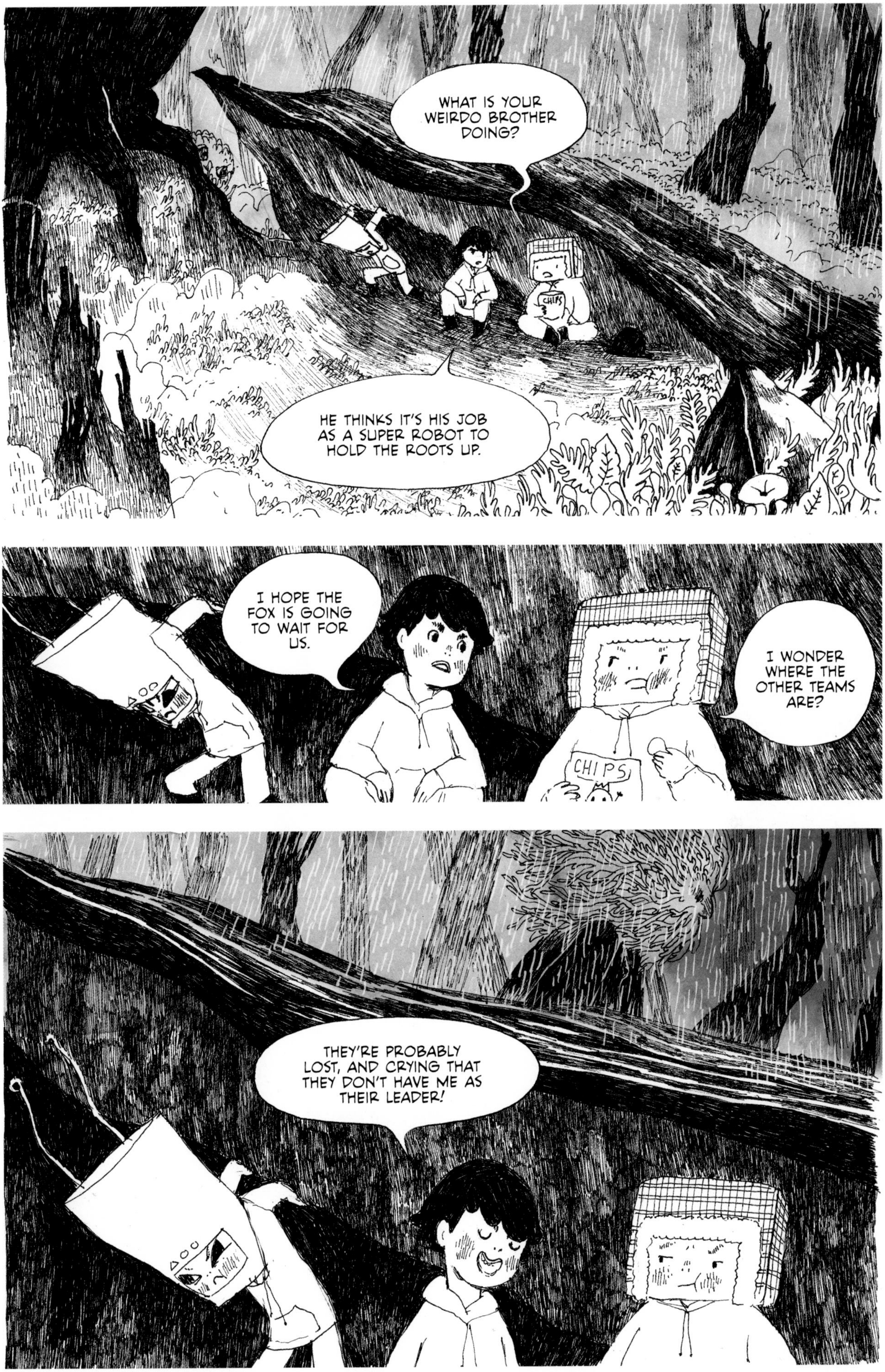
WHAT IS YOUR WEIRDO BROTHER DOING?
HE THINKS IT'S HIS JOB AS A SUPER ROBOT TO HOLD THE ROOTS UP.
CHIPS
I HOPE THE FOX IS GOING TO WAIT FOR US.
I WONDER WHERE THE OTHER TEAMS ARE?
CHIPS
THEY'RE PROBABLY LOST, AND CRYING THAT THEY DON'T HAVE ME AS THEIR LEADER!

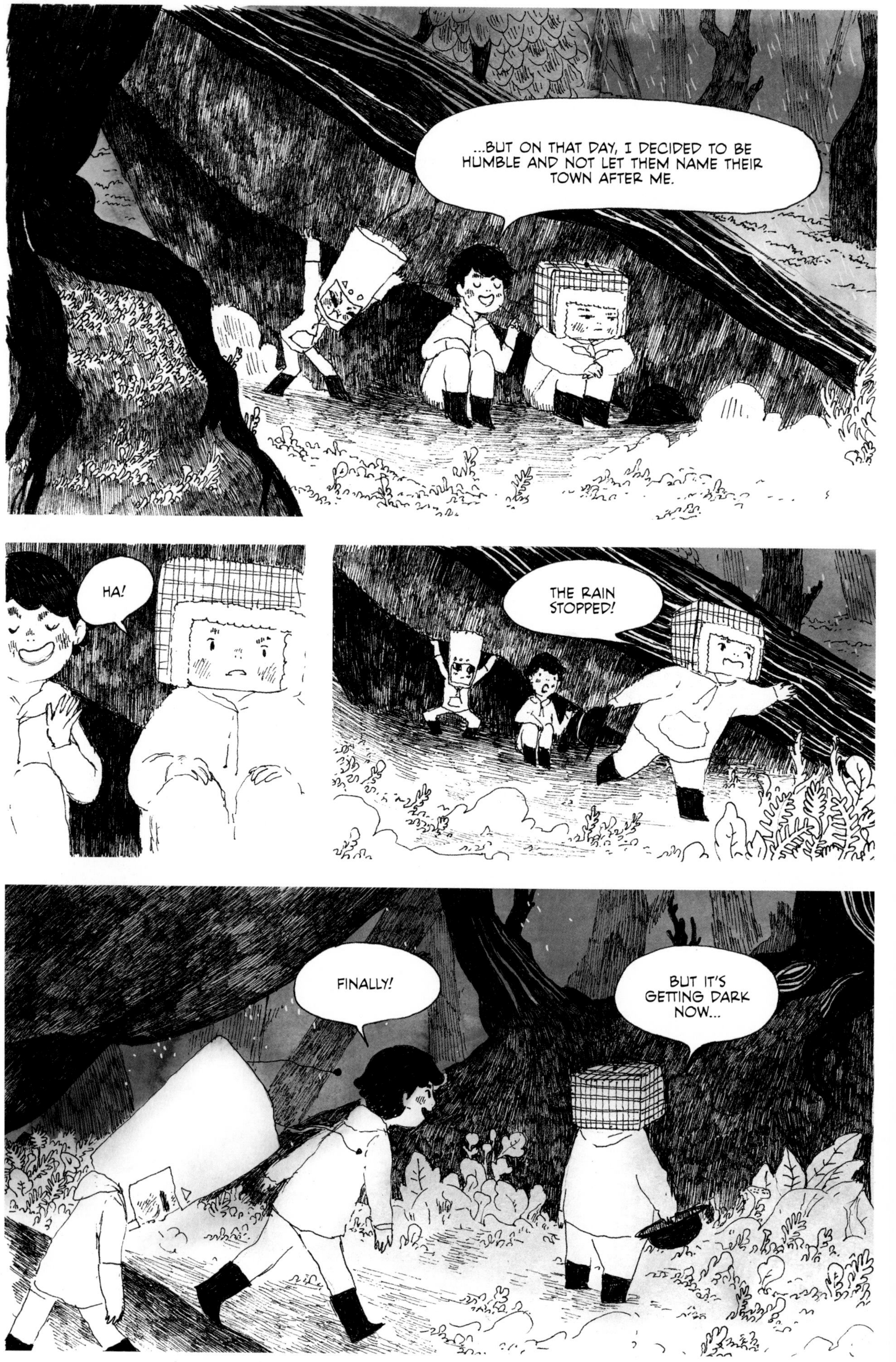
...BUT ON THAT DAY, I DECIDED TO BE HUMBLE AND NOT LET THEM NAME THEIR TOWN AFTER ME.
HA!
THE RAIN STOPPED!
FINALLY!
BUT IT'S GETTING DARK NOW...

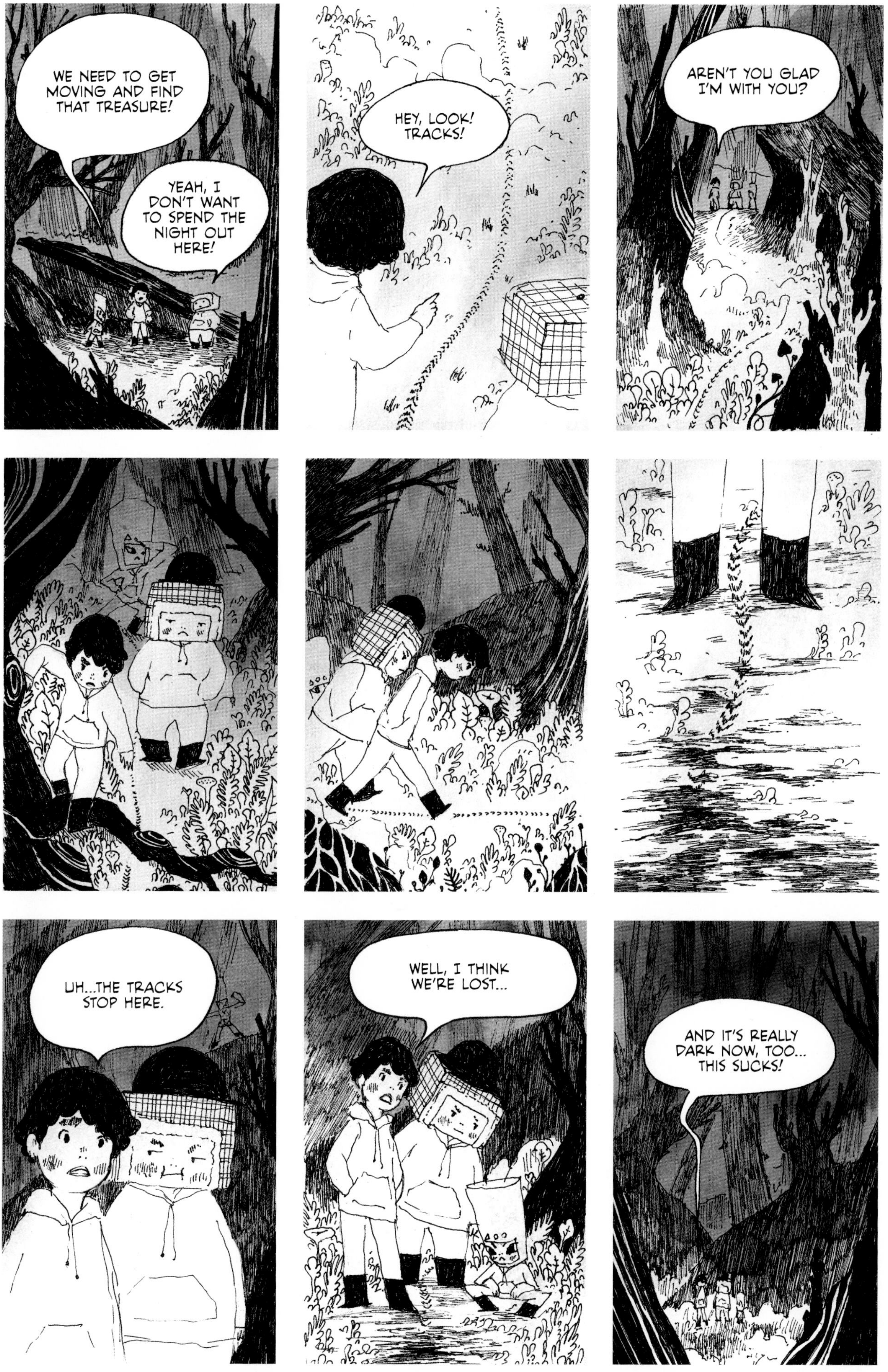
WE NEED TO GET MOVING AND FIND THAT TREASURE!
YEAH, I DON'T WANT TO SPEND THE NIGHT OUT HERE!
HEY, LOOK! TRACKS!
AREN'T YOU GLAD I'M WITH YOU?
UH...THE TRACKS STOP HERE.
WELL, I THINK WE'RE LOST...
AND IT'S REALLY DARK NOW, TOO... THIS SUCKS!

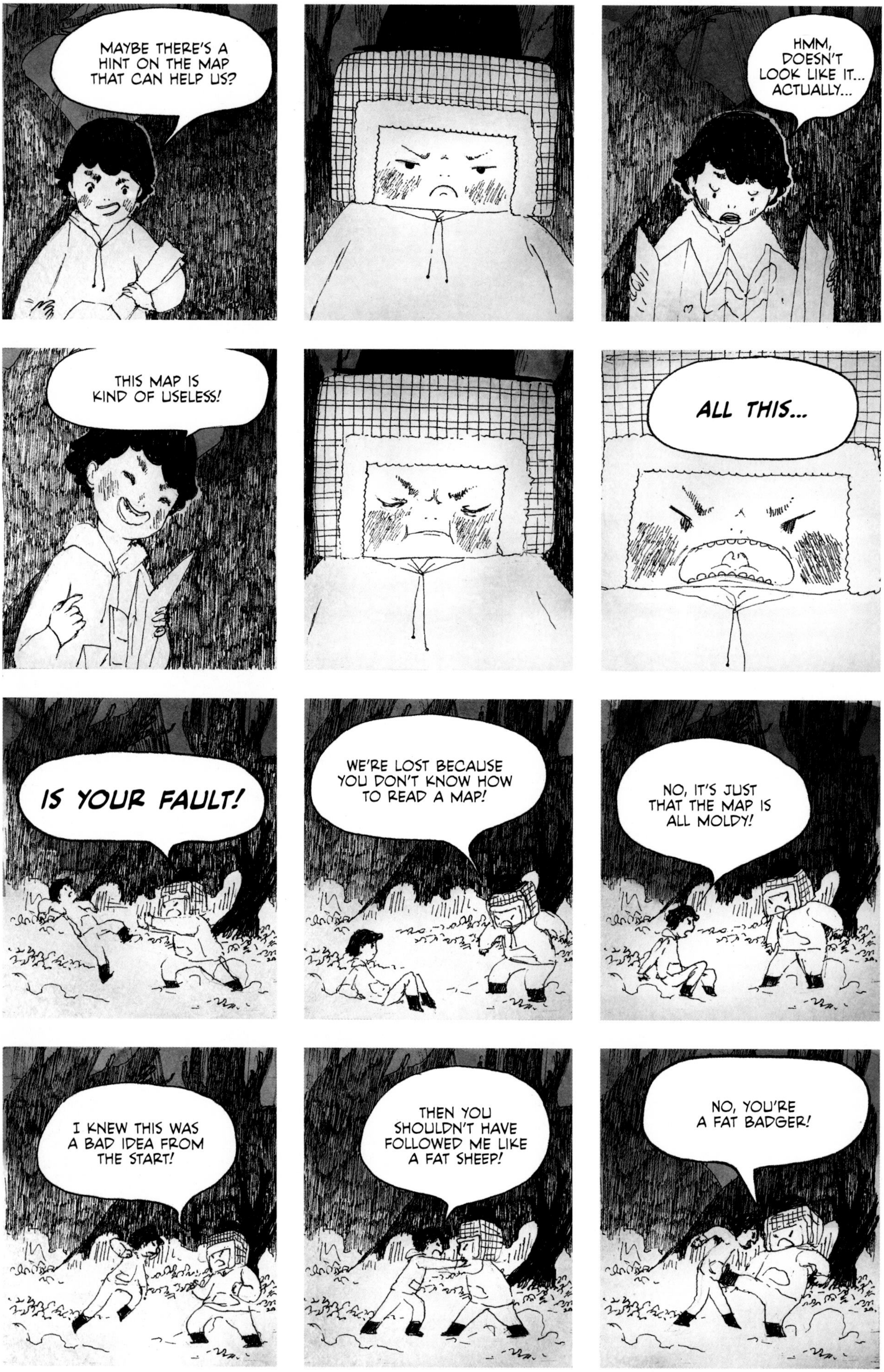
MAYBE THERE'S A HINT ON THE MAP THAT CAN HELP US?
HMM, DOESN'T LOOK LIKE IT... ACTUALLY...
THIS MAP IS KIND OF USELESS!
ALL THIS...
IS YOUR FAULT!
WE'RE LOST BECAUSE YOU DON'T KNOW HOW TO READ A MAP!
NO, IT'S JUST THAT THE MAP IS ALL MOLDY!
I KNEW THIS WAS A BAD IDEA FROM THE START!
THEN YOU SHOULDN'T HAVE FOLLOWED ME LIKE A FAT SHEEP!
NO, YOU'RE A FAT BADGER!

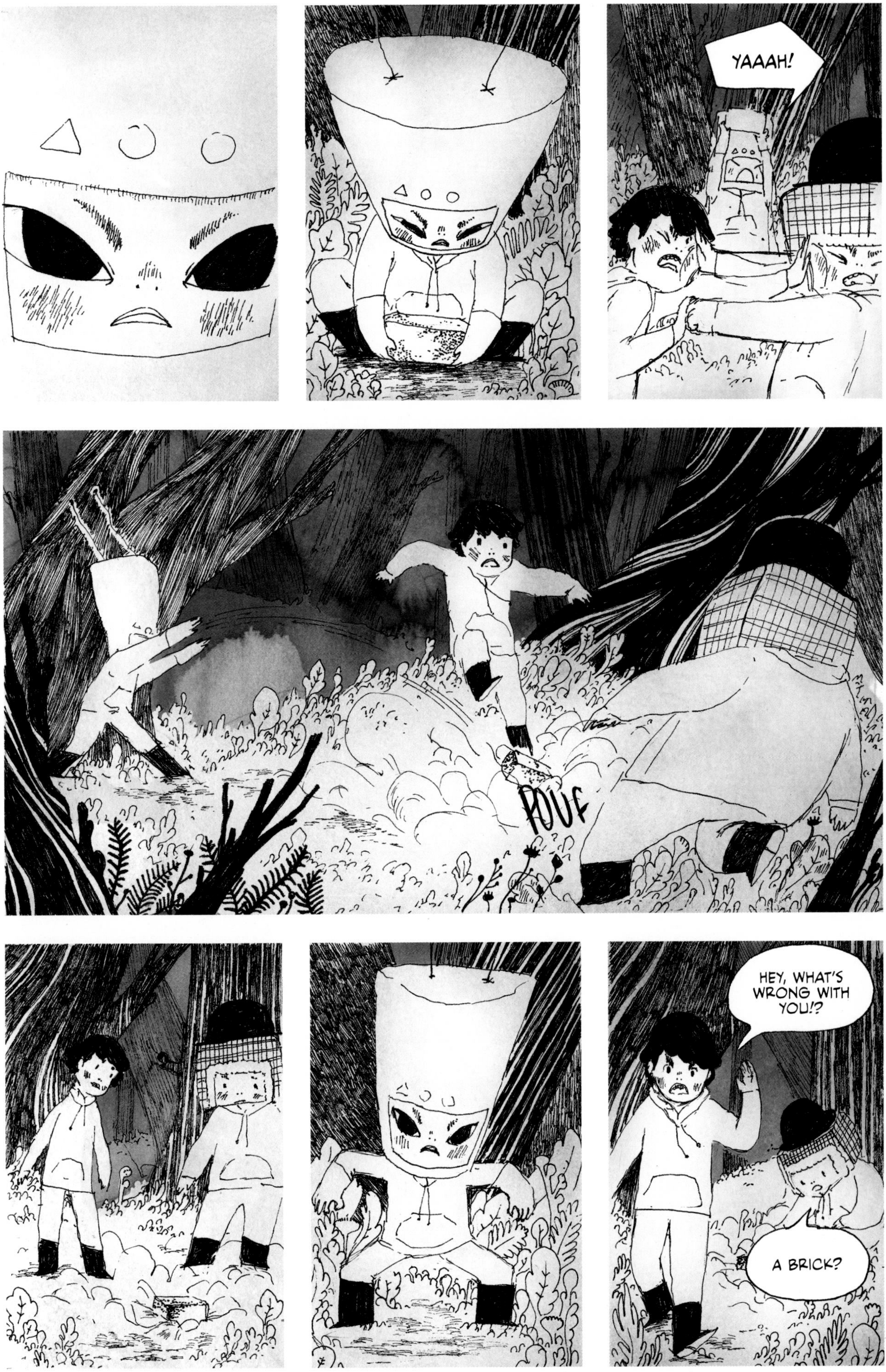
YAAAH!
POUF
HEY, WHAT'S WRONG WITH YOU!?
A BRICK?

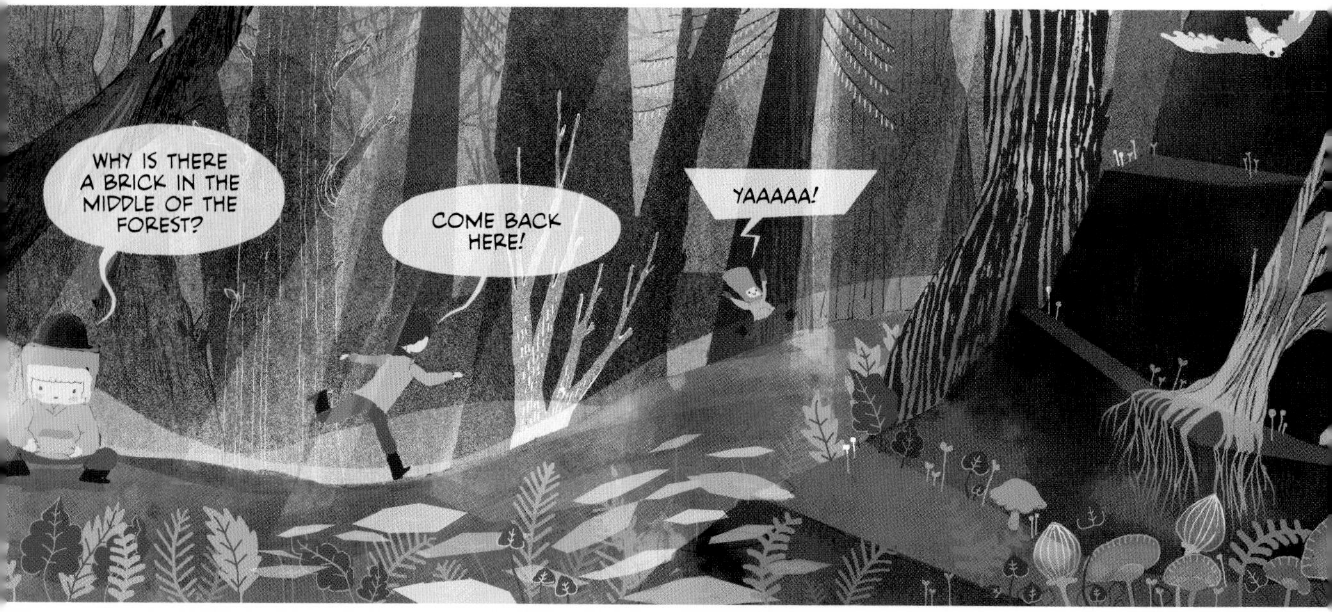
WHY IS THERE A BRICK IN THE MIDDLE OF THE FOREST?
COME BACK HERE!
YAAAAA!

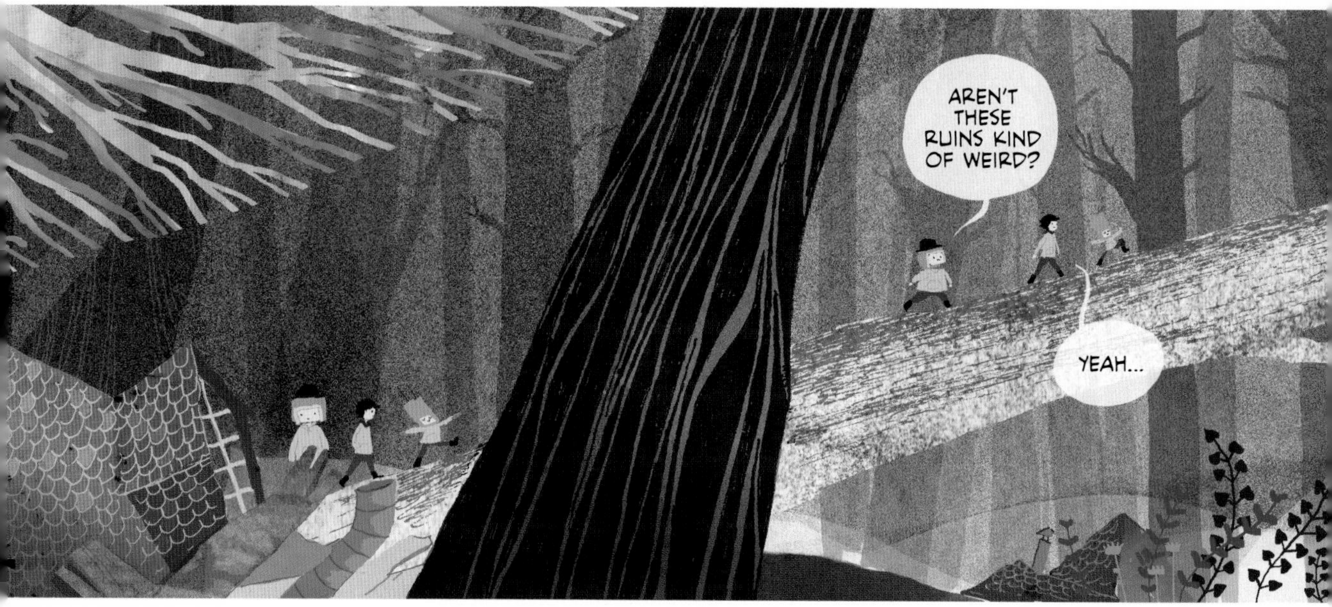
AREN'T THESE RUINS KIND OF WEIRD?
YEAH...

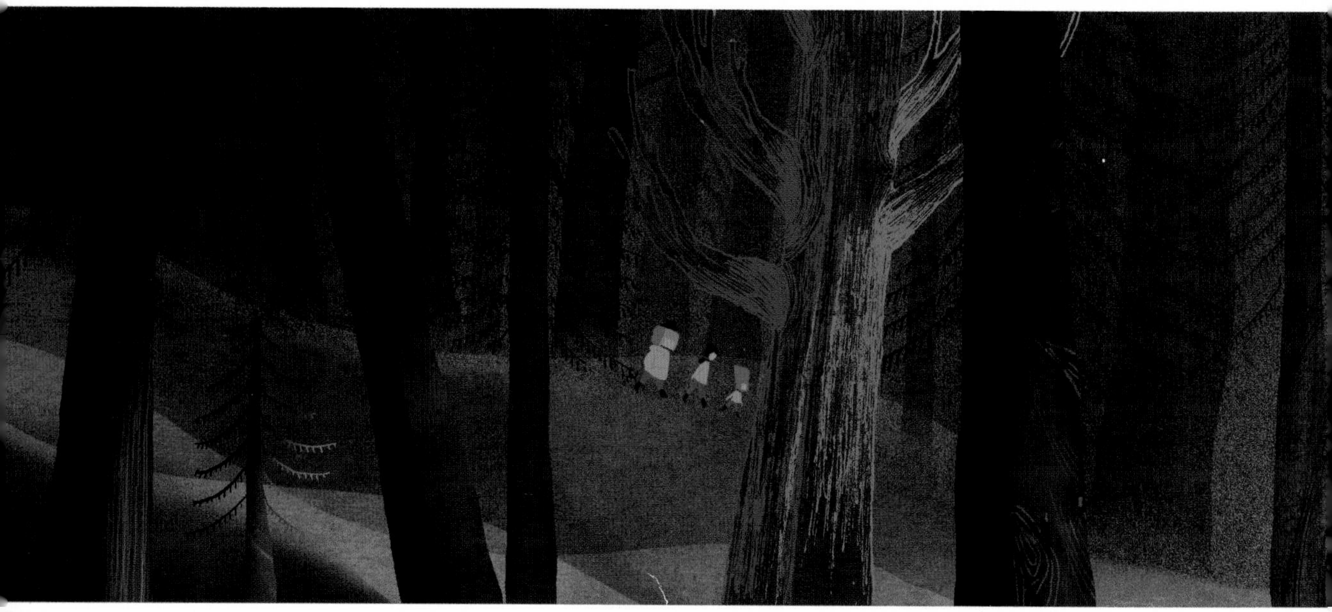

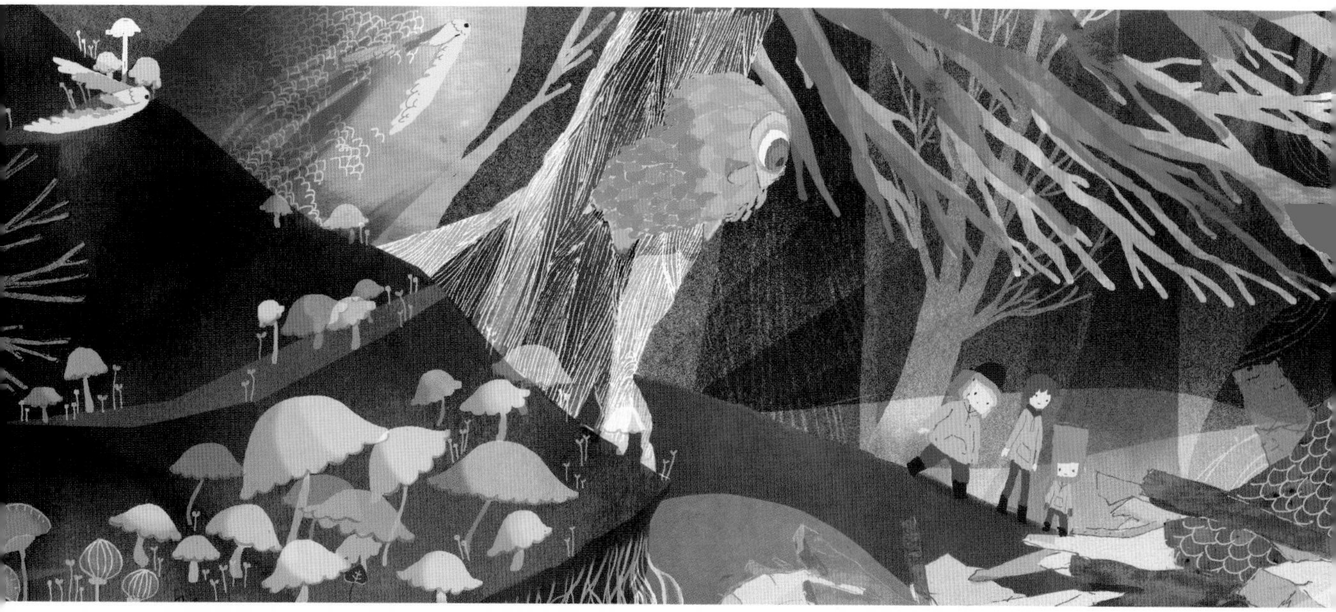

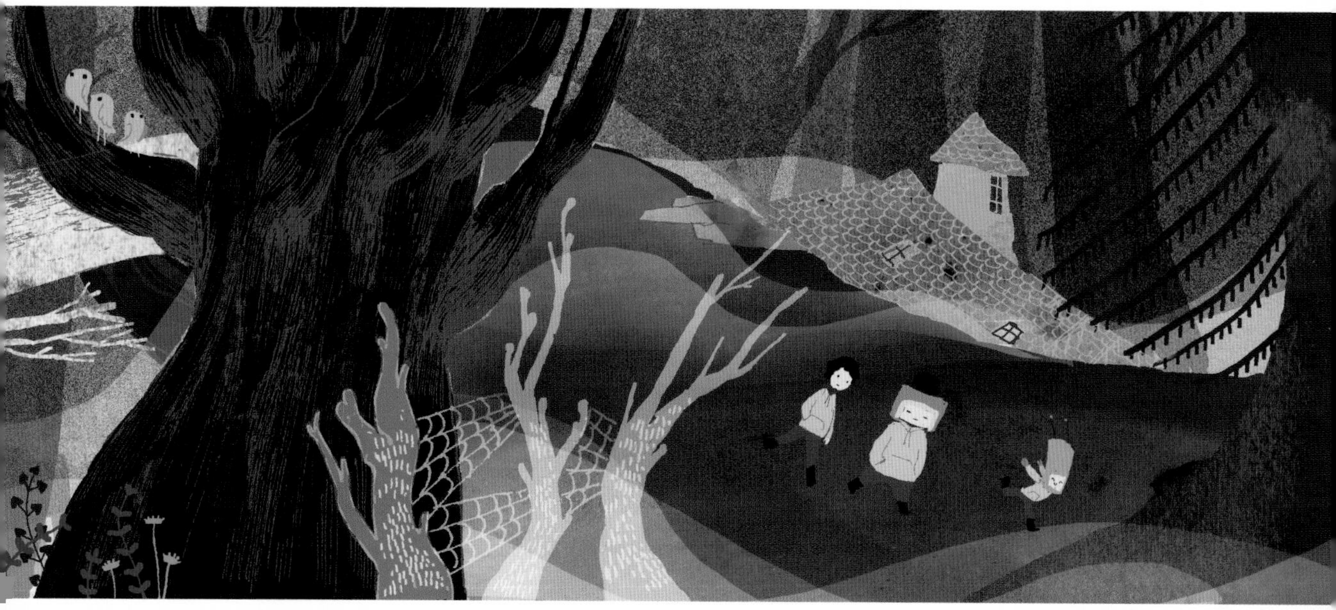

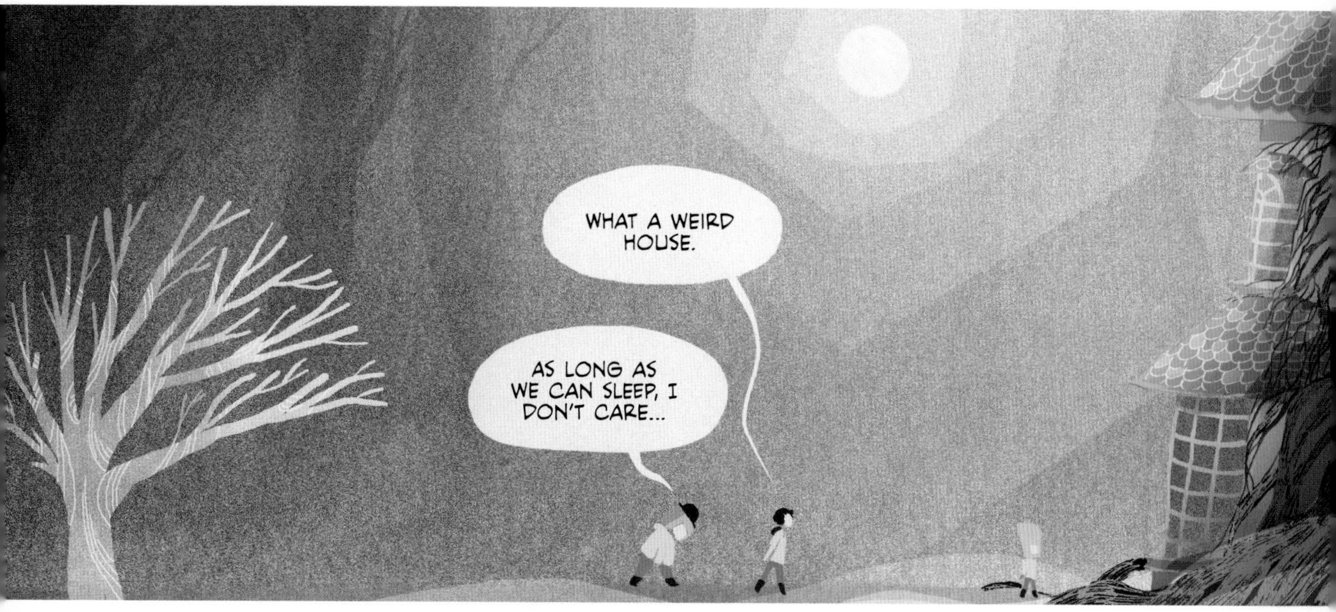
WHAT A WEIRD HOUSE.
AS LONG AS WE CAN SLEEP, I DON'T CARE...

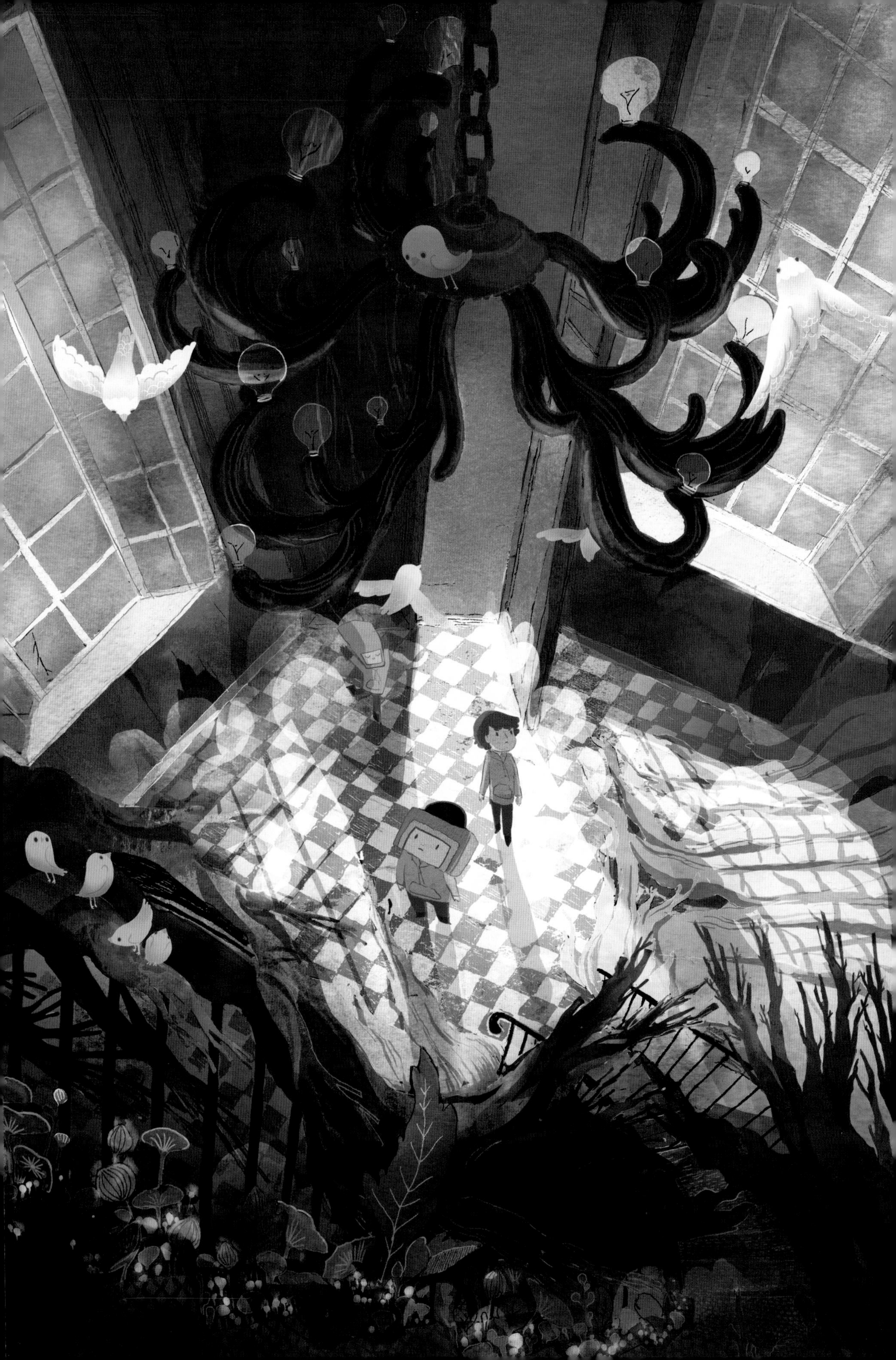

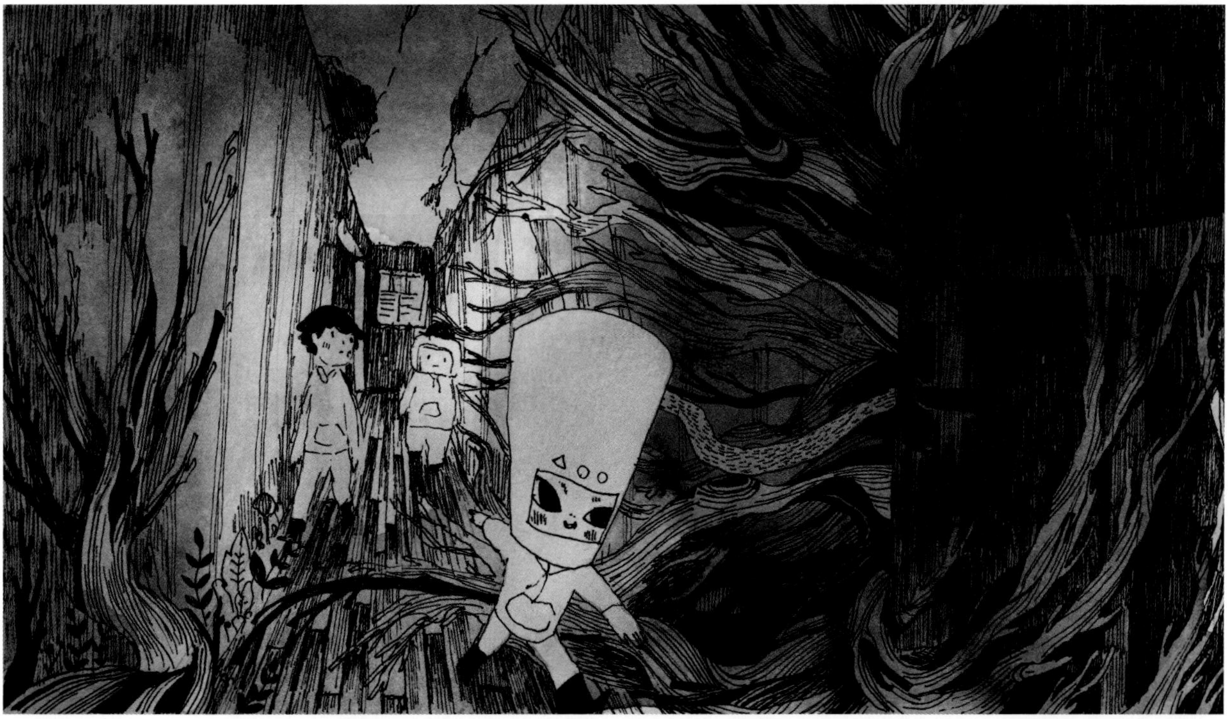

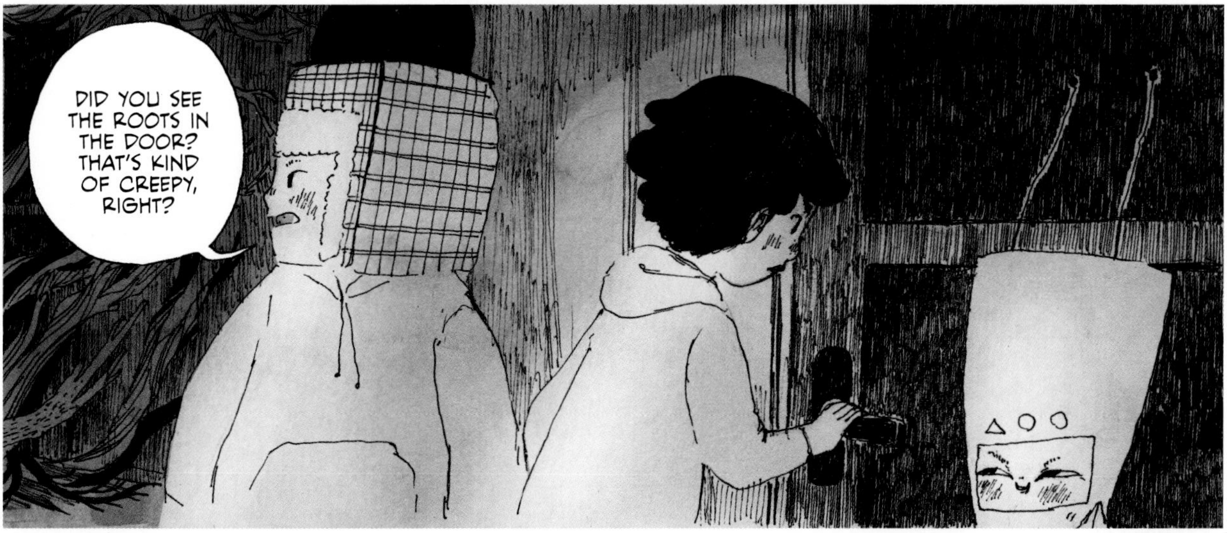
DID YOU SEE THE ROOTS IN THE DOOR? THAT'S KIND OF CREEPY, RIGHT?

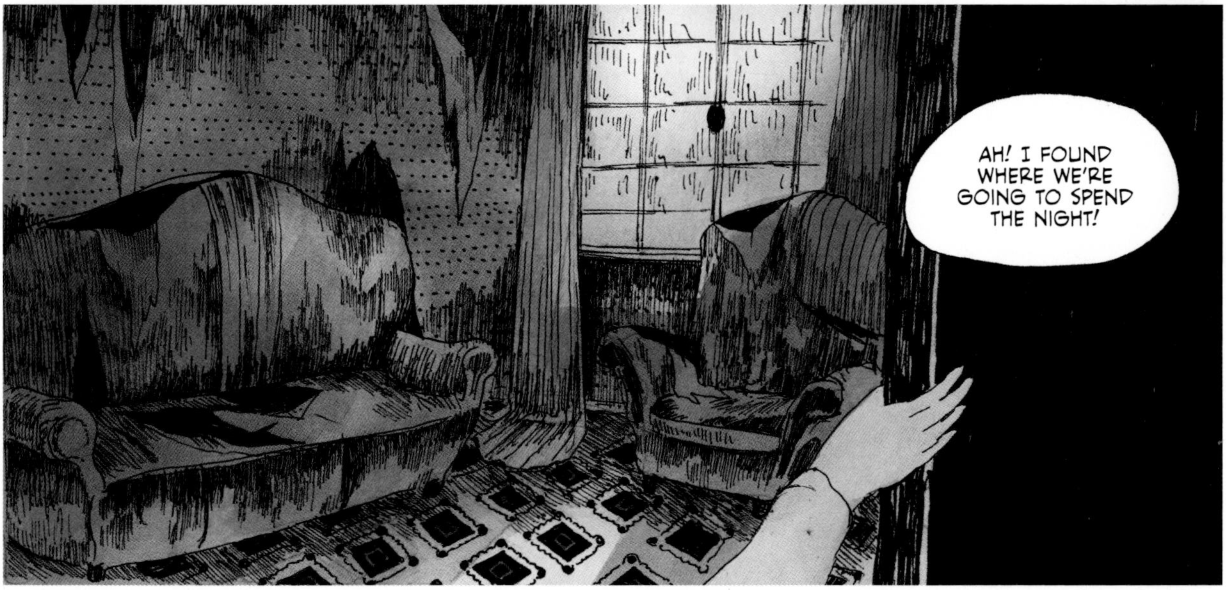
AH! I FOUND WHERE WE'RE GOING TO SPEND THE NIGHT!

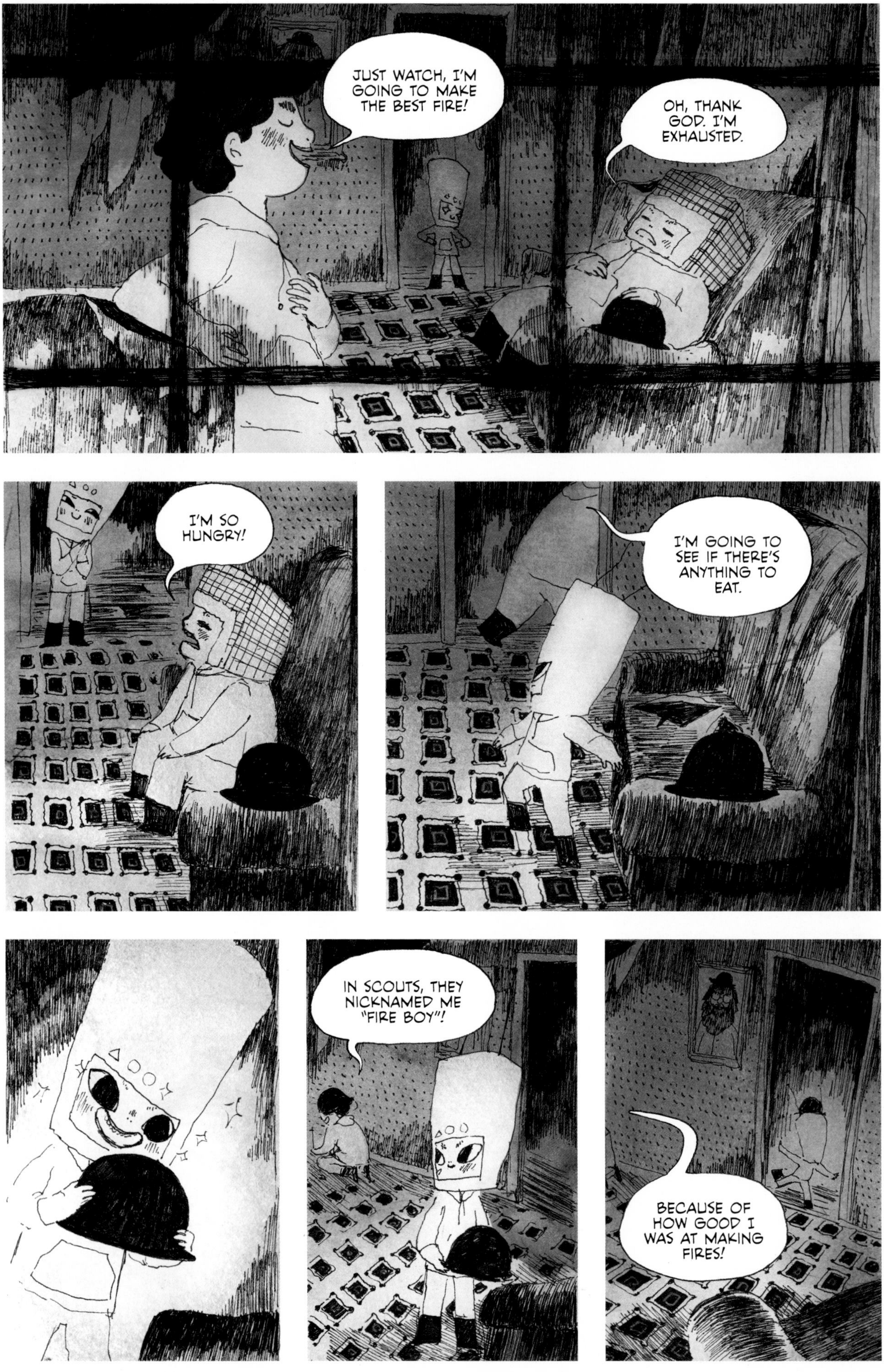
JUST WATCH, I'M GOING TO MAKE THE BEST FIRE!
OH, THANK GOD. I'M EXHAUSTED.
I'M SO HUNGRY!
I'M GOING TO SEE IF THERE'S ANYTHING TO EAT.
IN SCOUTS, THEY NICKNAMED ME "FIRE BOY"!
BECAUSE OF HOW GOOD I WAS AT MAKING FIRES!

GOOD JOB!
YOU HAVE TO HIDE IT IN A SAFE PLACE NOW!
BEHIND THIS DOOR...
...IT'LL BE SAFE!
?
BACK UP, IT'S OPENING!
NiiiiiH

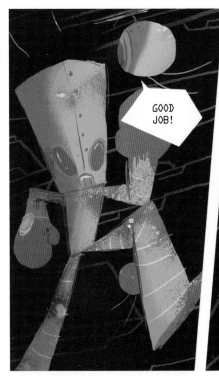

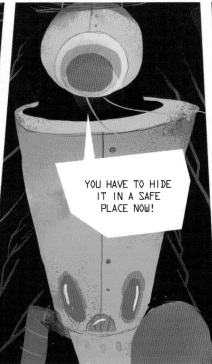

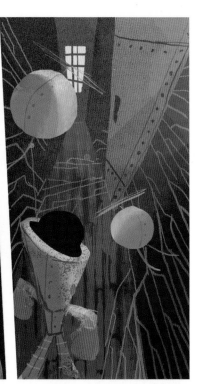

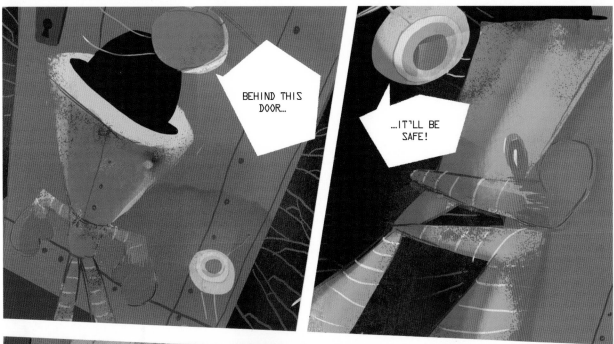

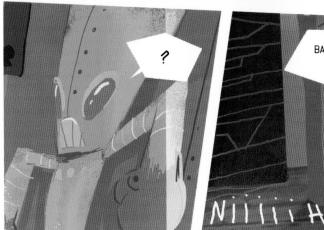

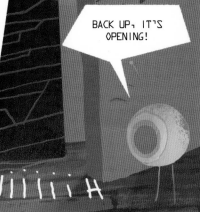

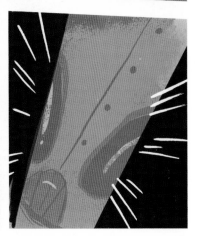

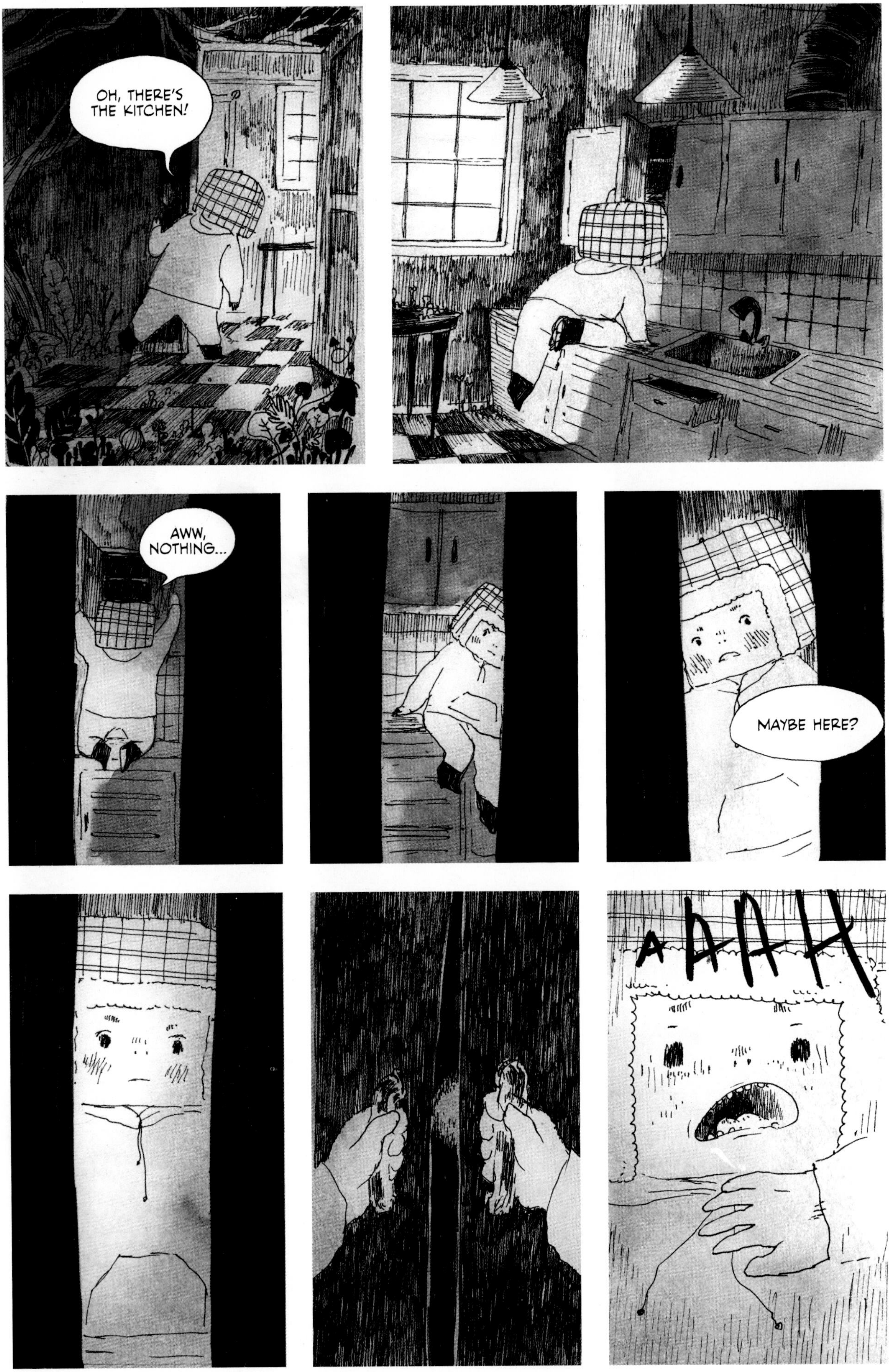
OH, THERE'S THE KITCHEN!
AWW, NOTHING...
MAYBE HERE?
AAAH

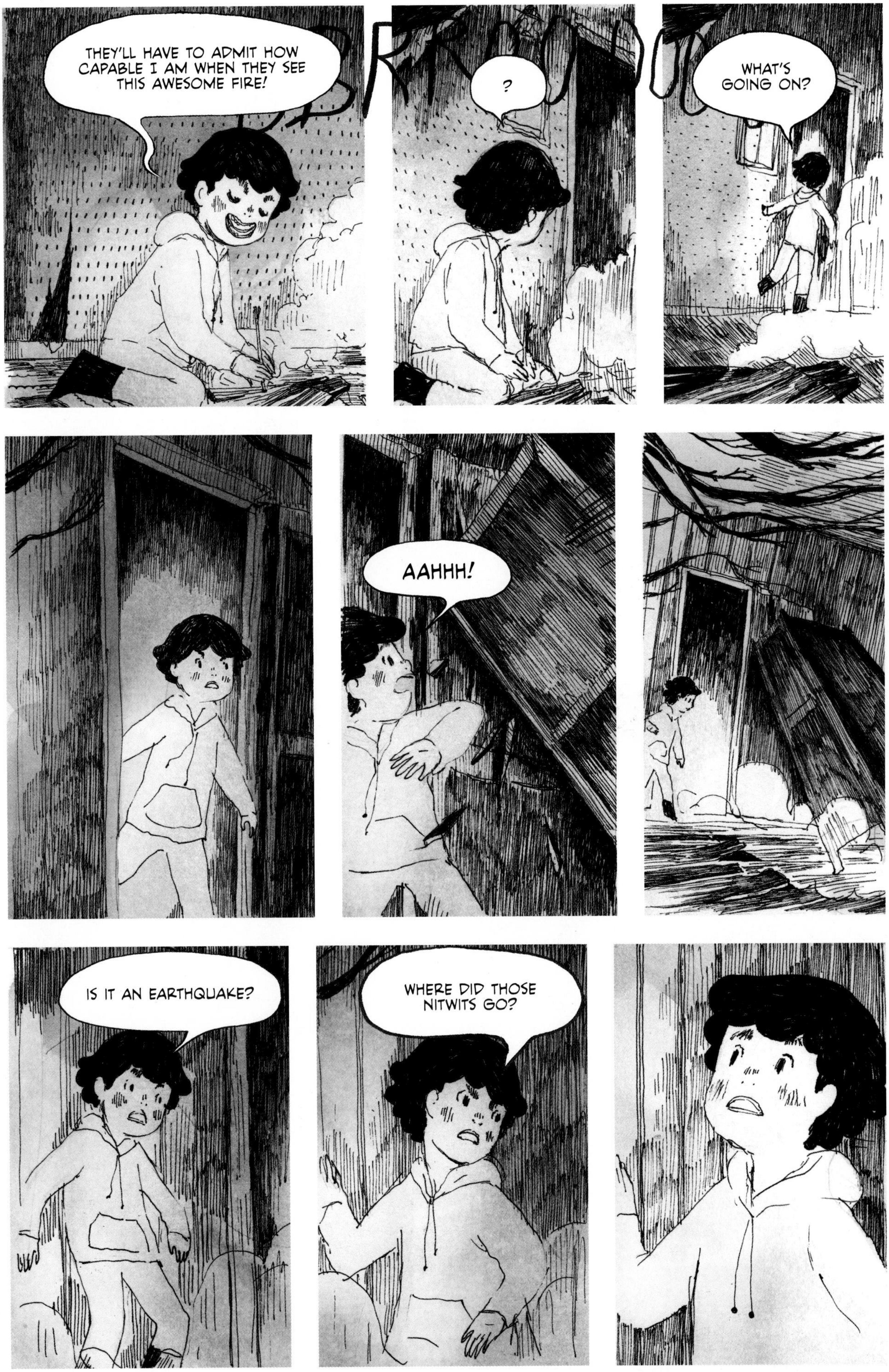
THEY'LL HAVE TO ADMIT HOW CAPABLE I AM WHEN THEY SEE THIS AWESOME FIRE!
?
WHAT'S GOING ON?
AAHHH!
IS IT AN EARTHQUAKE?
WHERE DID THOSE NITWITS GO?

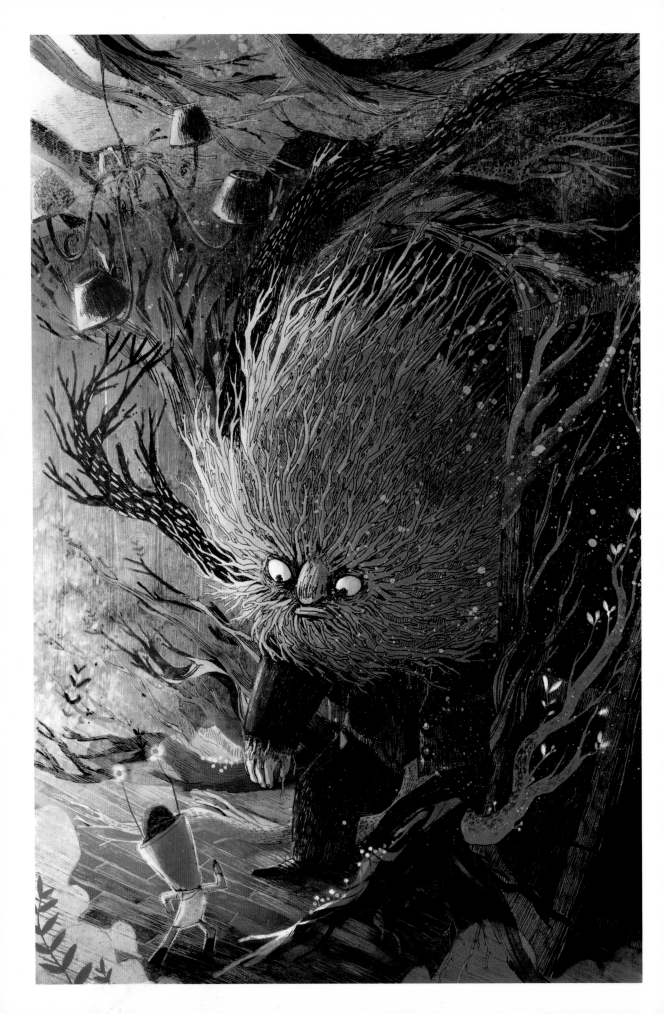

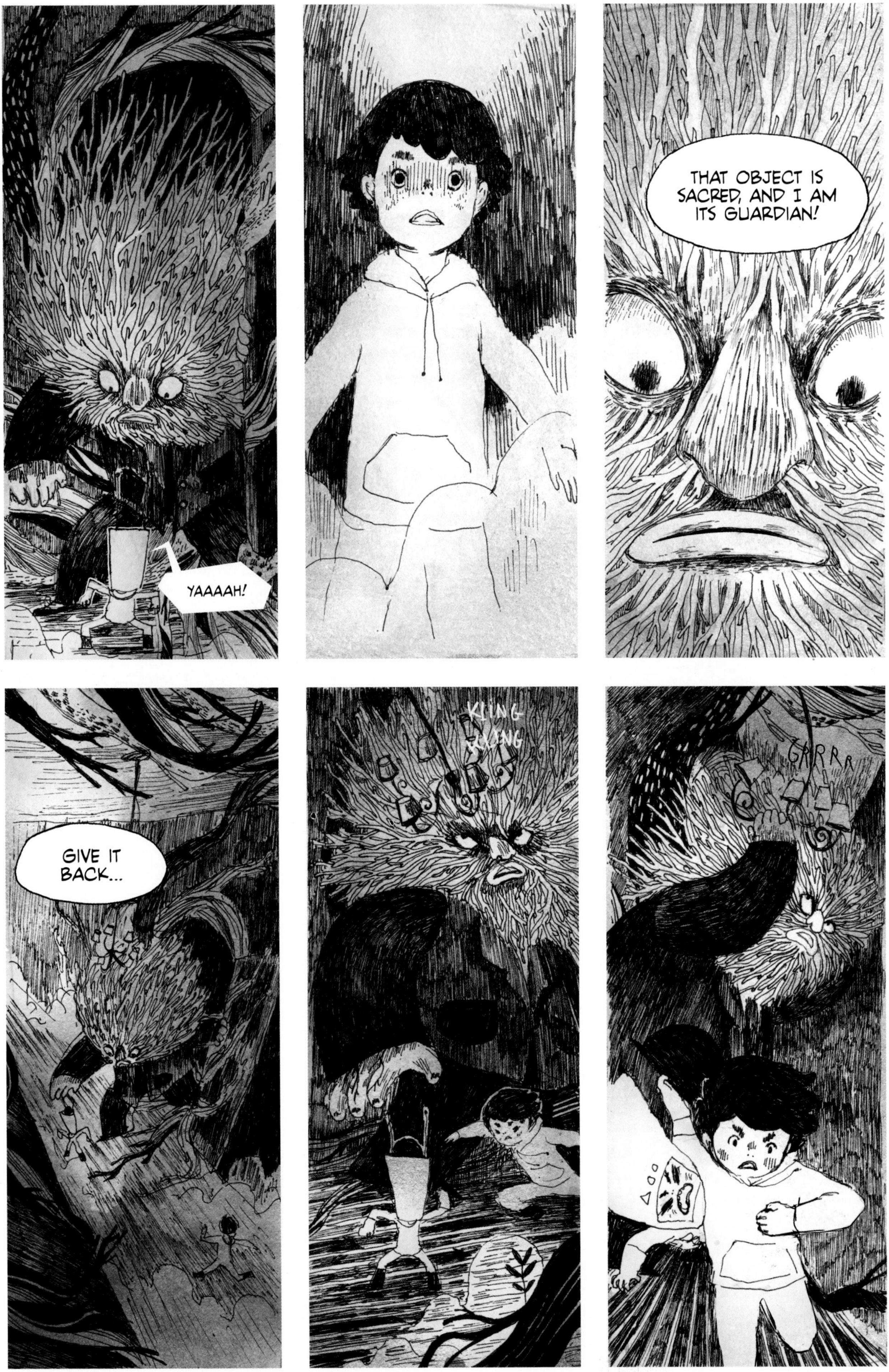
YAAAAH!
THAT OBJECT IS SACRED, AND I AM ITS GUARDIAN!
GIVE IT BACK...
KLING KLING
GRRRR

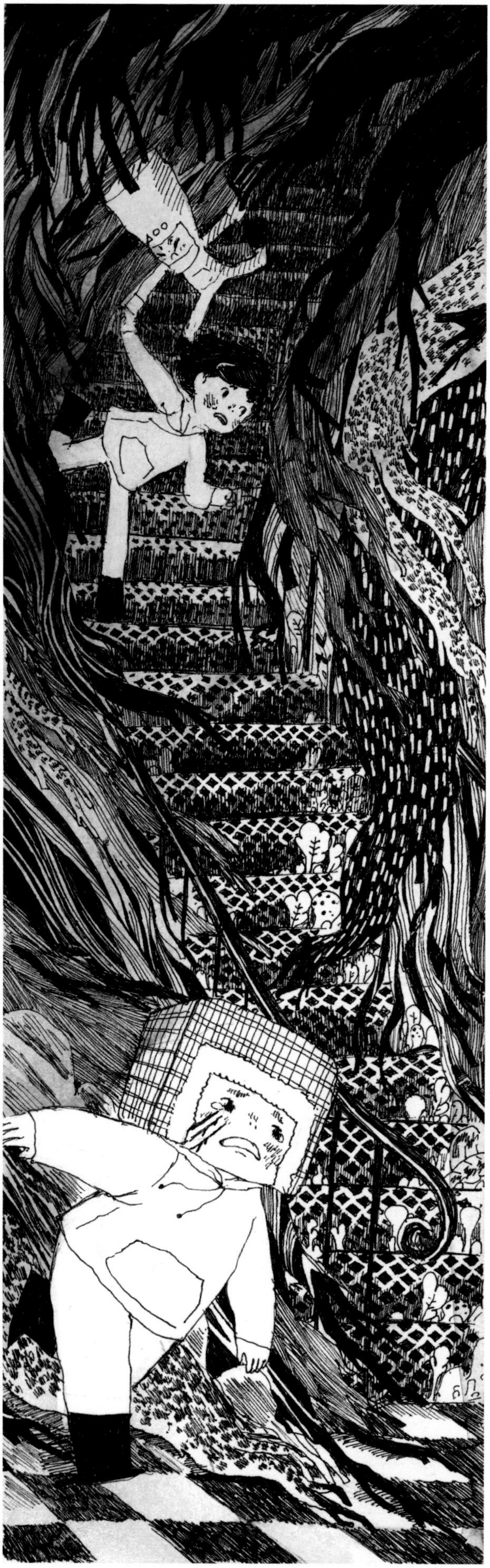
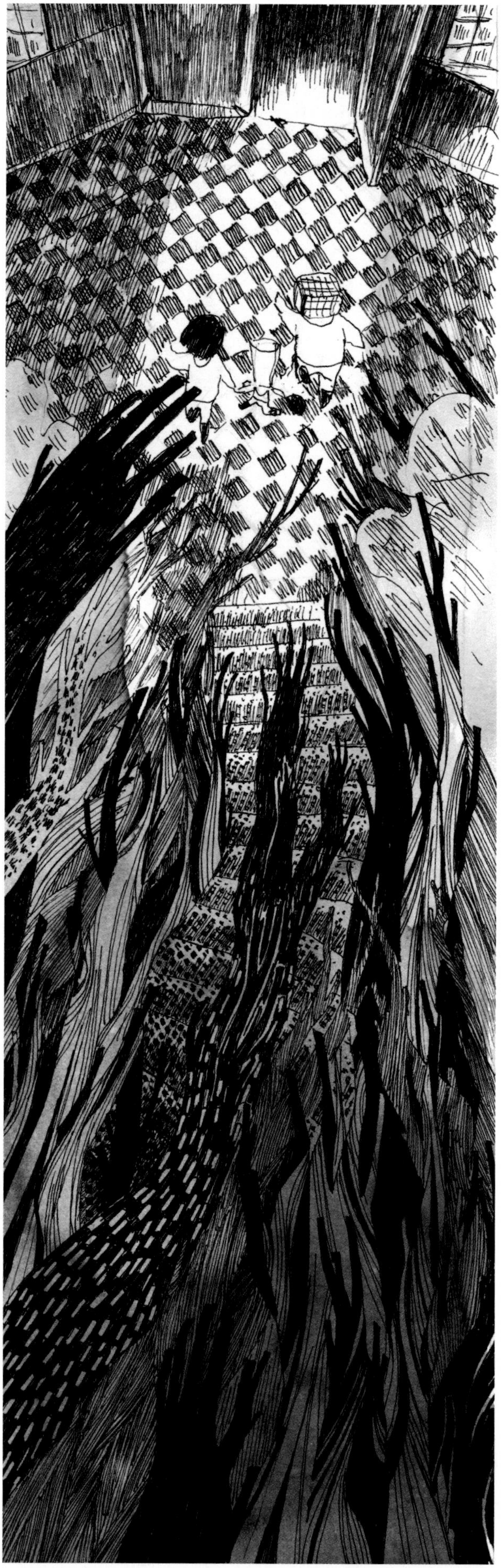

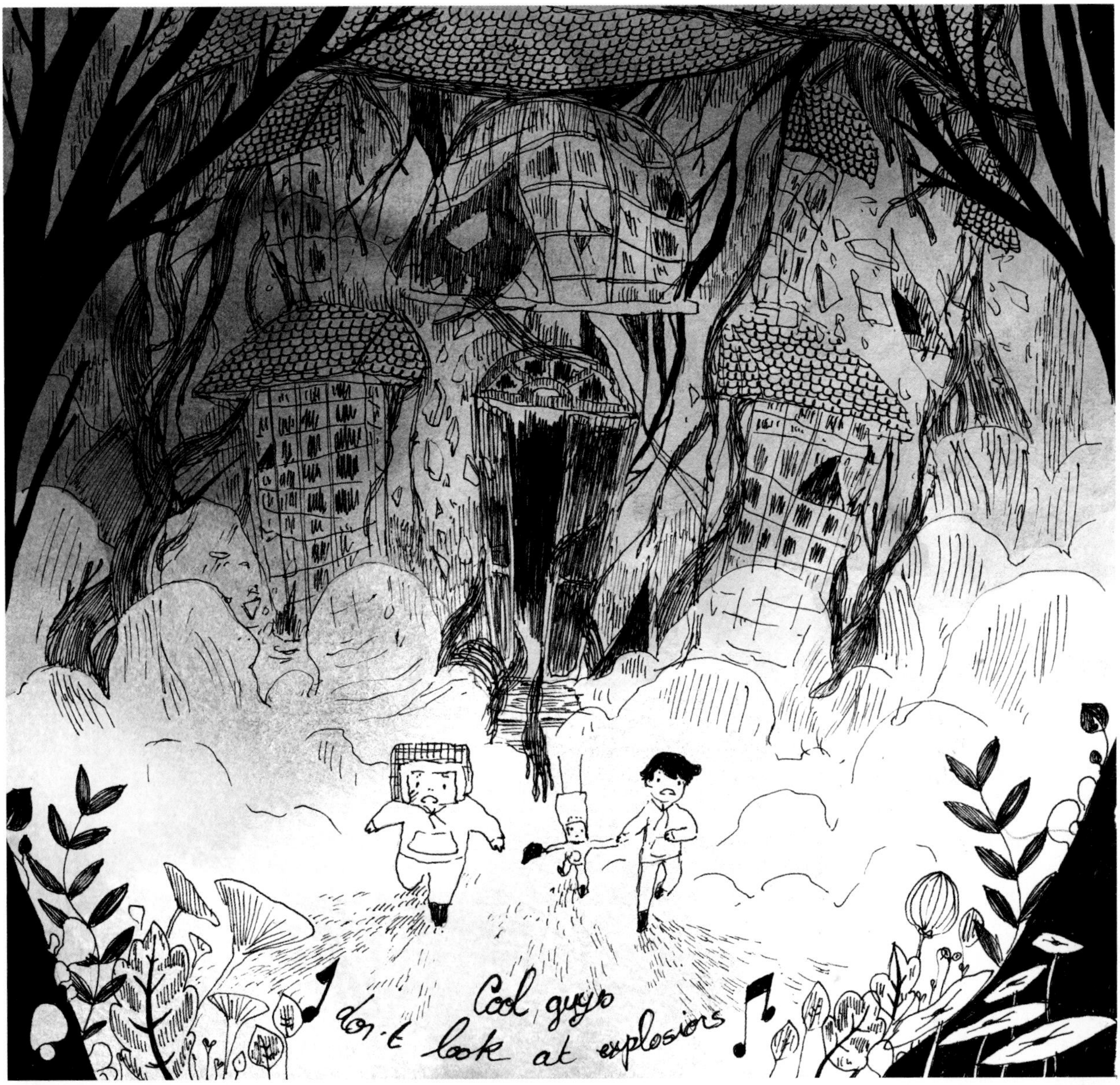
Cool guys
don't look at explosions

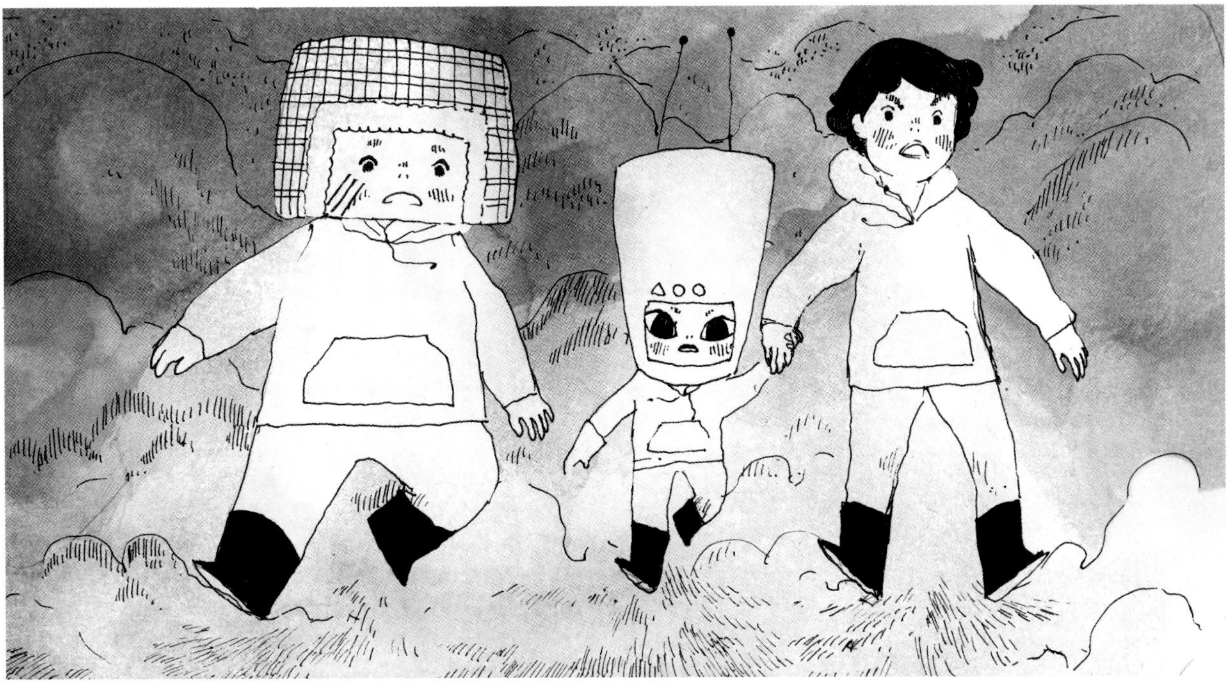

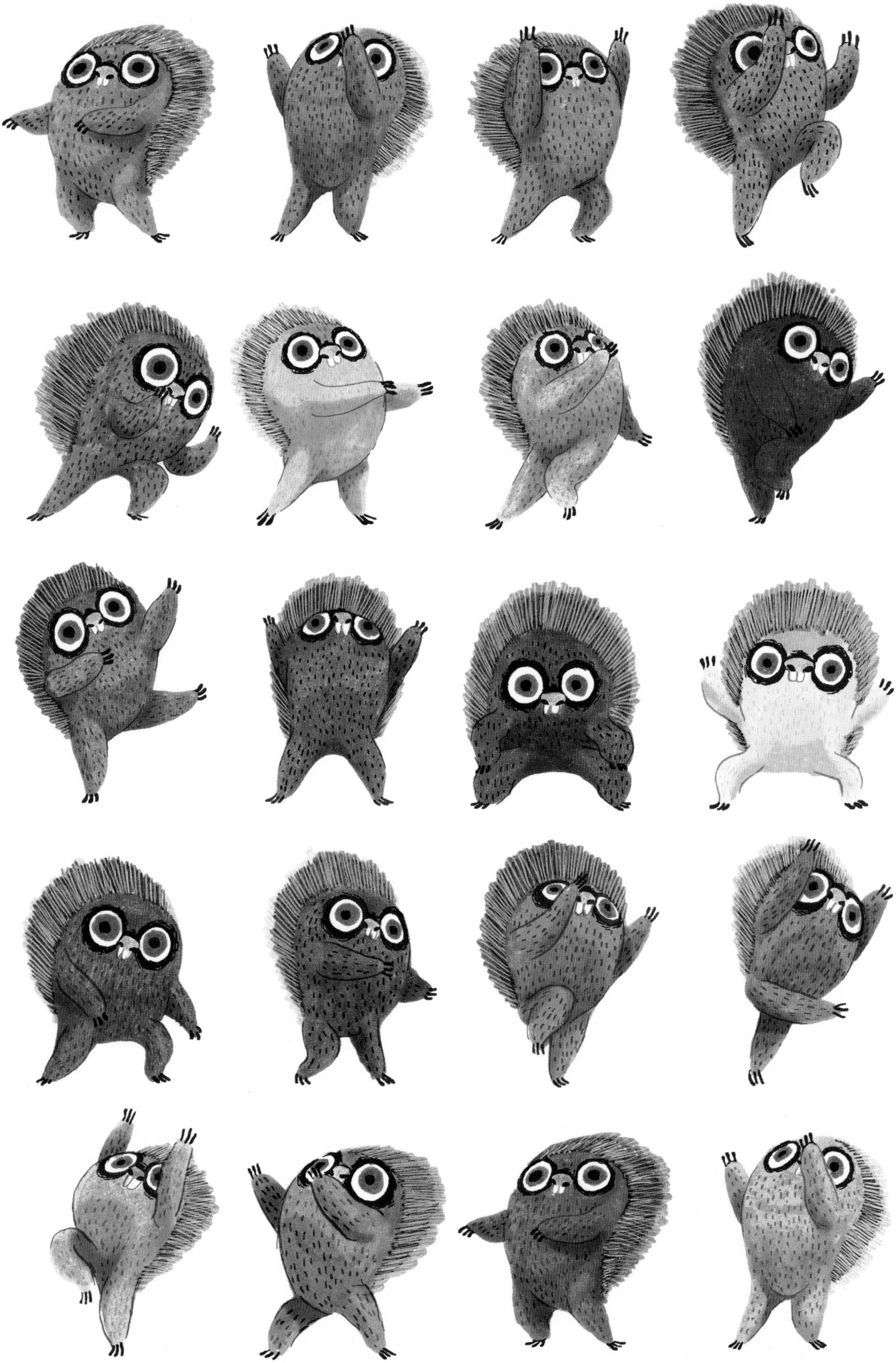

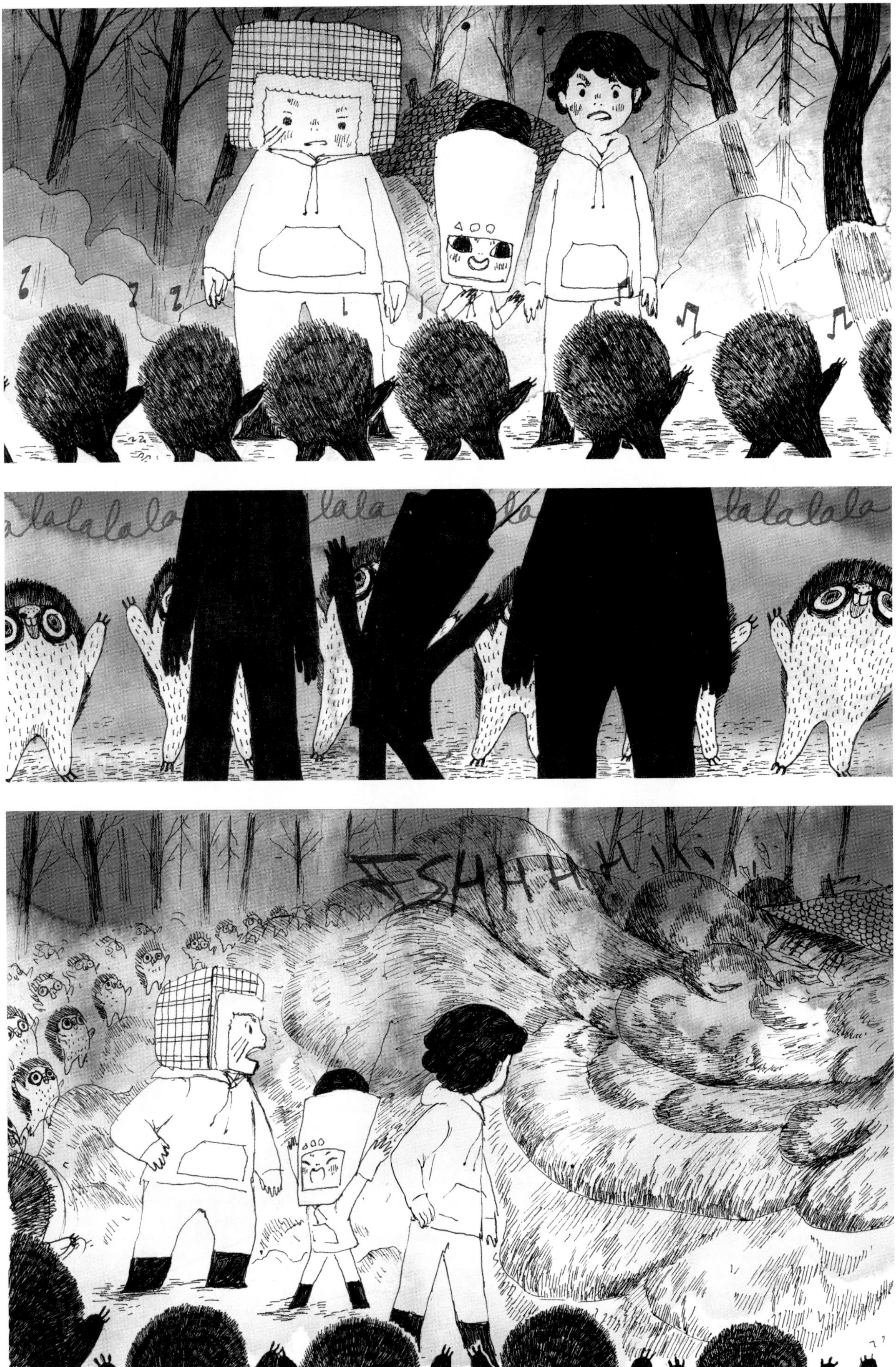
lalalala lala la lalalala
TSHHHiki

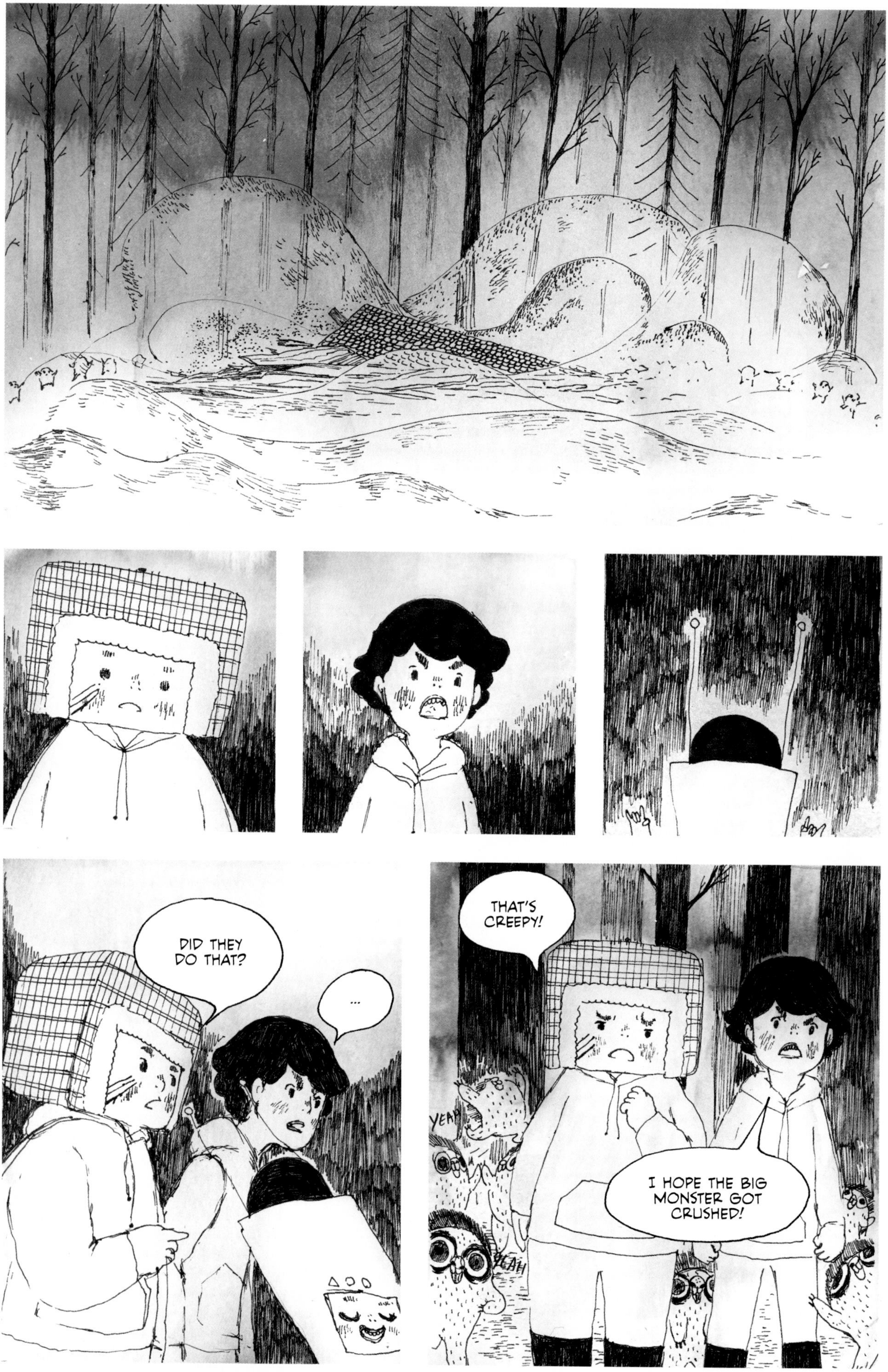
DID THEY DO THAT?
...
THAT'S CREEPY!
I HOPE THE BIG MONSTER GOT CRUSHED!

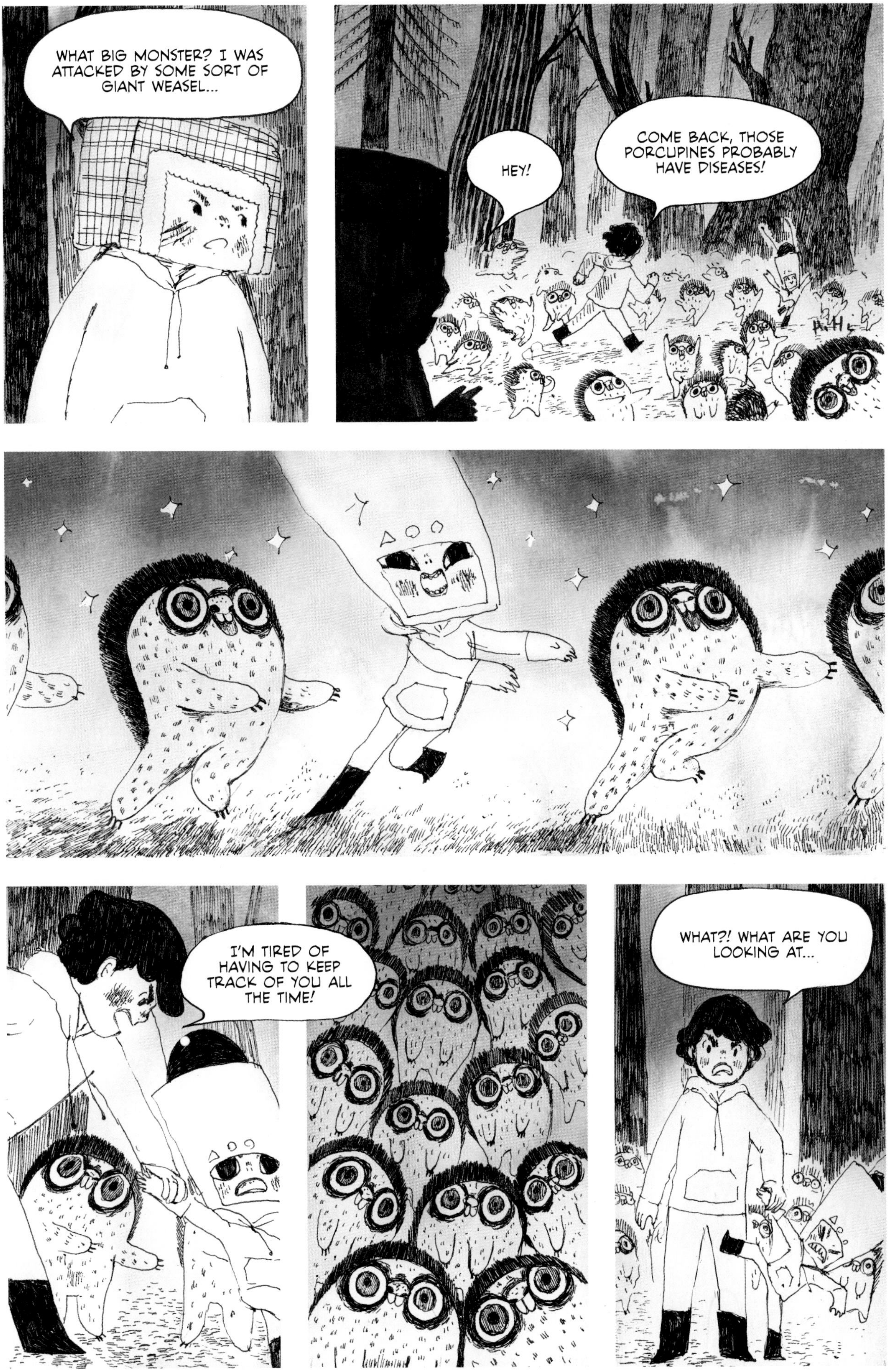
WHAT BIG MONSTER? I WAS ATTACKED BY SOME SORT OF GIANT WEASEL...
HEY!
COME BACK, THOSE PORCUPINES PROBABLY HAVE DISEASES!
I'M TIRED OF HAVING TO KEEP TRACK OF YOU ALL THE TIME!
WHAT?! WHAT ARE YOU LOOKING AT...

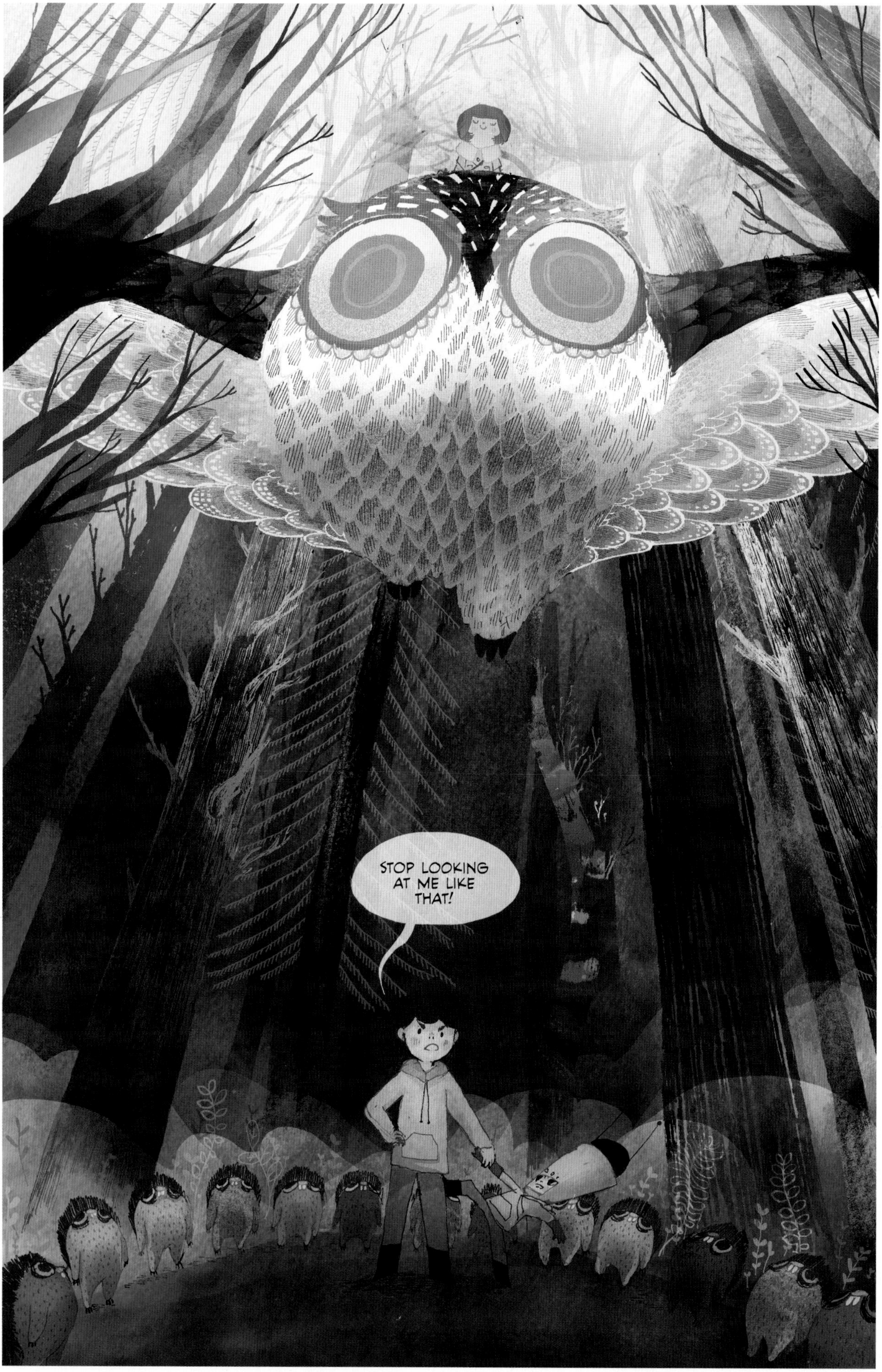
STOP LOOKING AT ME LIKE THAT!

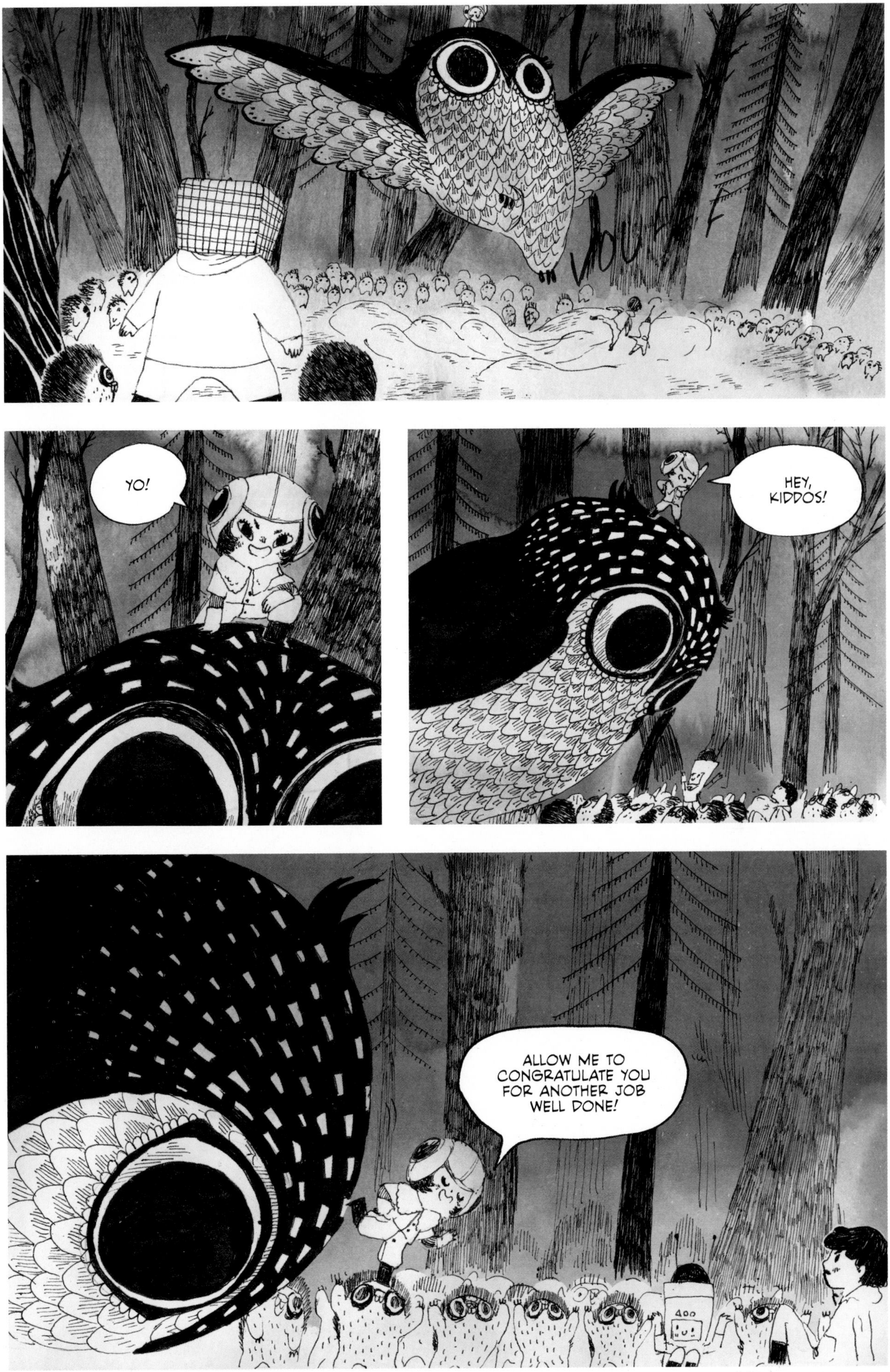
YO!
HEY, KIDDOS!
ALLOW ME TO CONGRATULATE YOU FOR ANOTHER JOB WELL DONE!

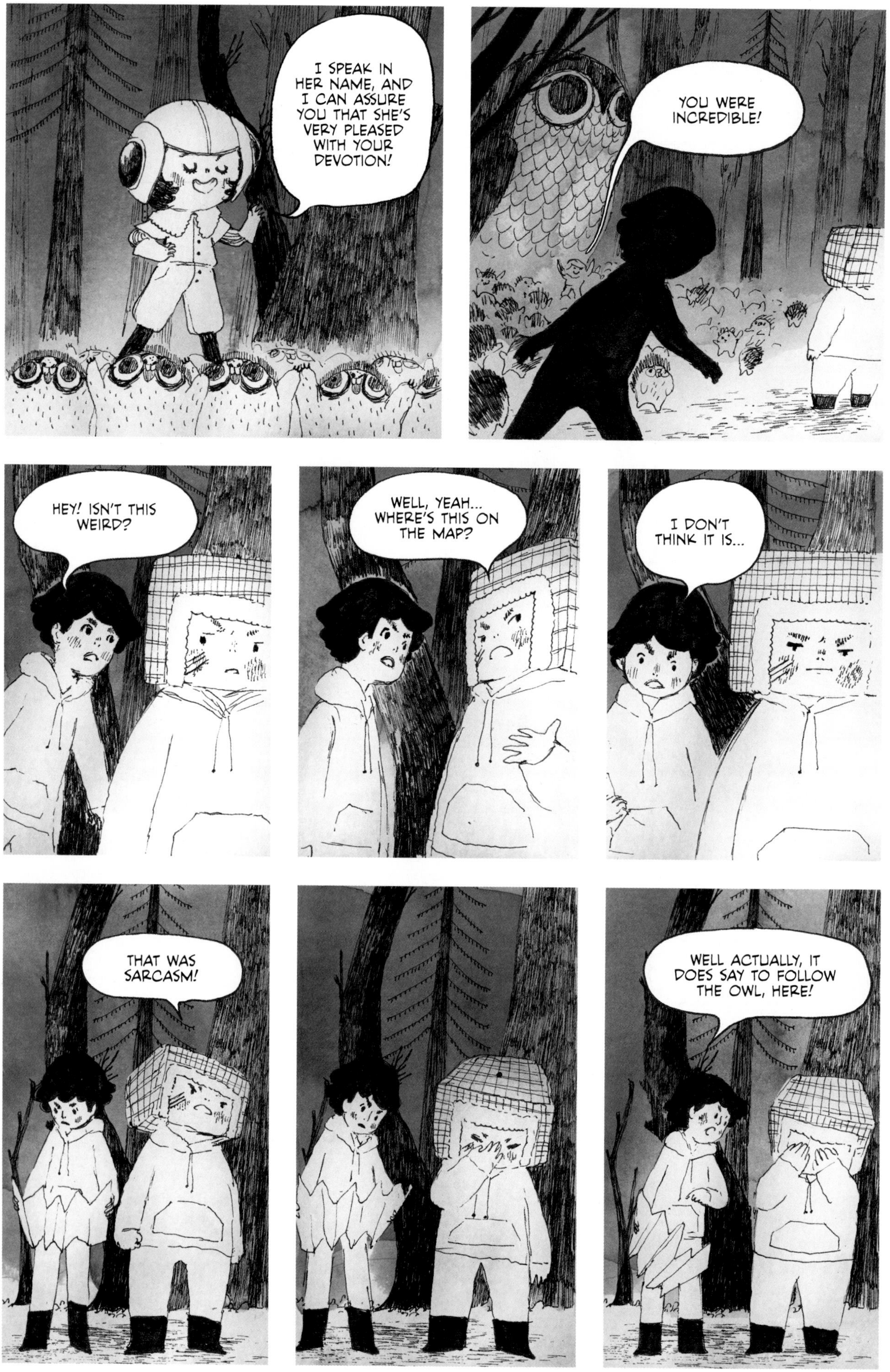
I SPEAK IN HER NAME, AND I CAN ASSURE YOU THAT SHE'S VERY PLEASED WITH YOUR DEVOTION!
YOU WERE INCREDIBLE!
HEY! ISN'T THIS WEIRD?
WELL, YEAH... WHERE'S THIS ON THE MAP?
I DON'T THINK IT IS...
THAT WAS SARCASM!
WELL ACTUALLY, IT DOES SAY TO FOLLOW THE OWL, HERE!

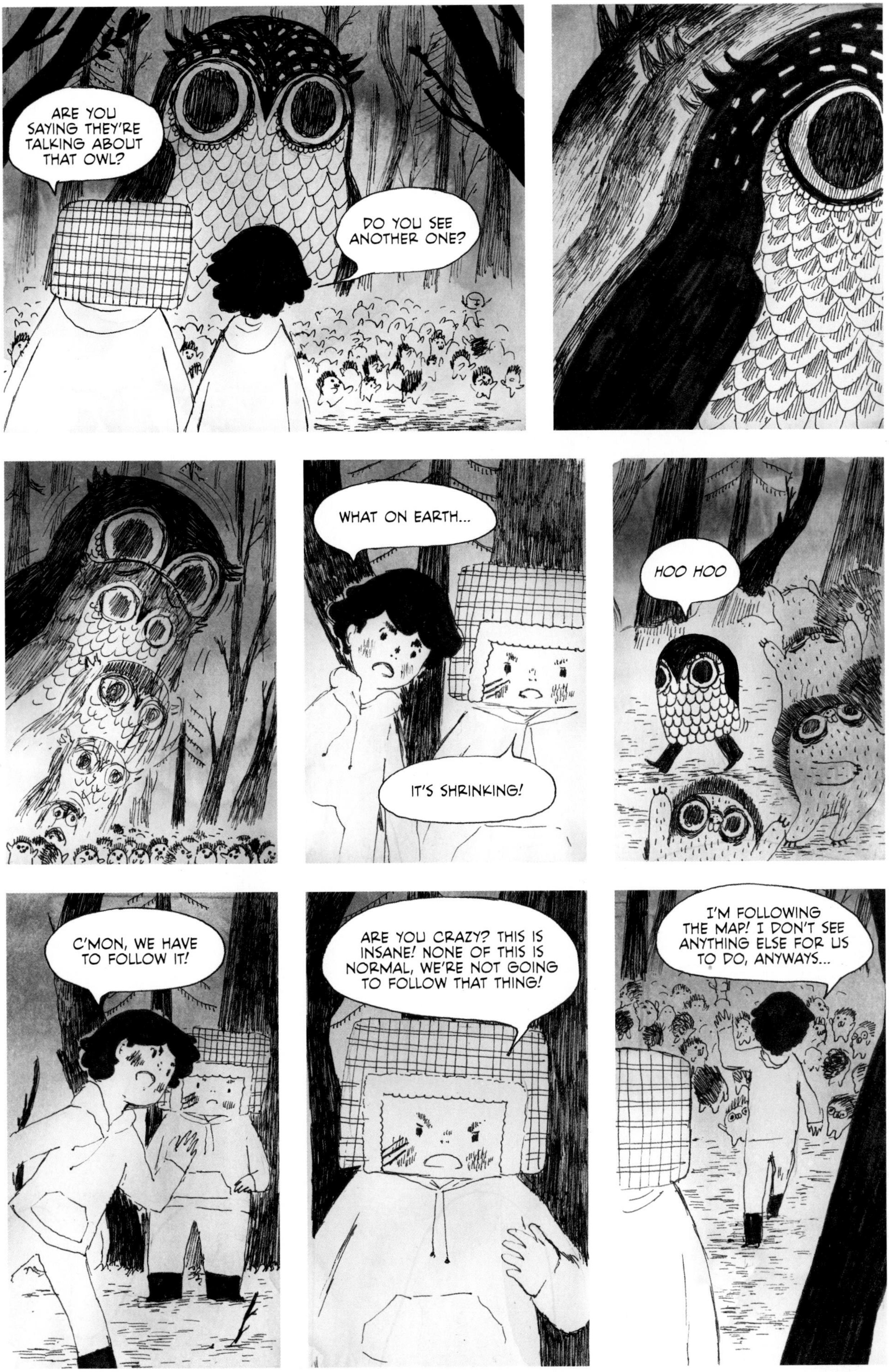
ARE YOU SAYING THEY'RE TALKING ABOUT THAT OWL?
DO YOU SEE ANOTHER ONE?
WHAT ON EARTH...
IT'S SHRINKING!
HOO HOO
C'MON, WE HAVE TO FOLLOW IT!
ARE YOU CRAZY? THIS IS INSANE! NONE OF THIS IS NORMAL, WE'RE NOT GOING TO FOLLOW THAT THING!
I'M FOLLOWING THE MAP! I DON'T SEE ANYTHING ELSE FOR US TO DO, ANYWAYS...

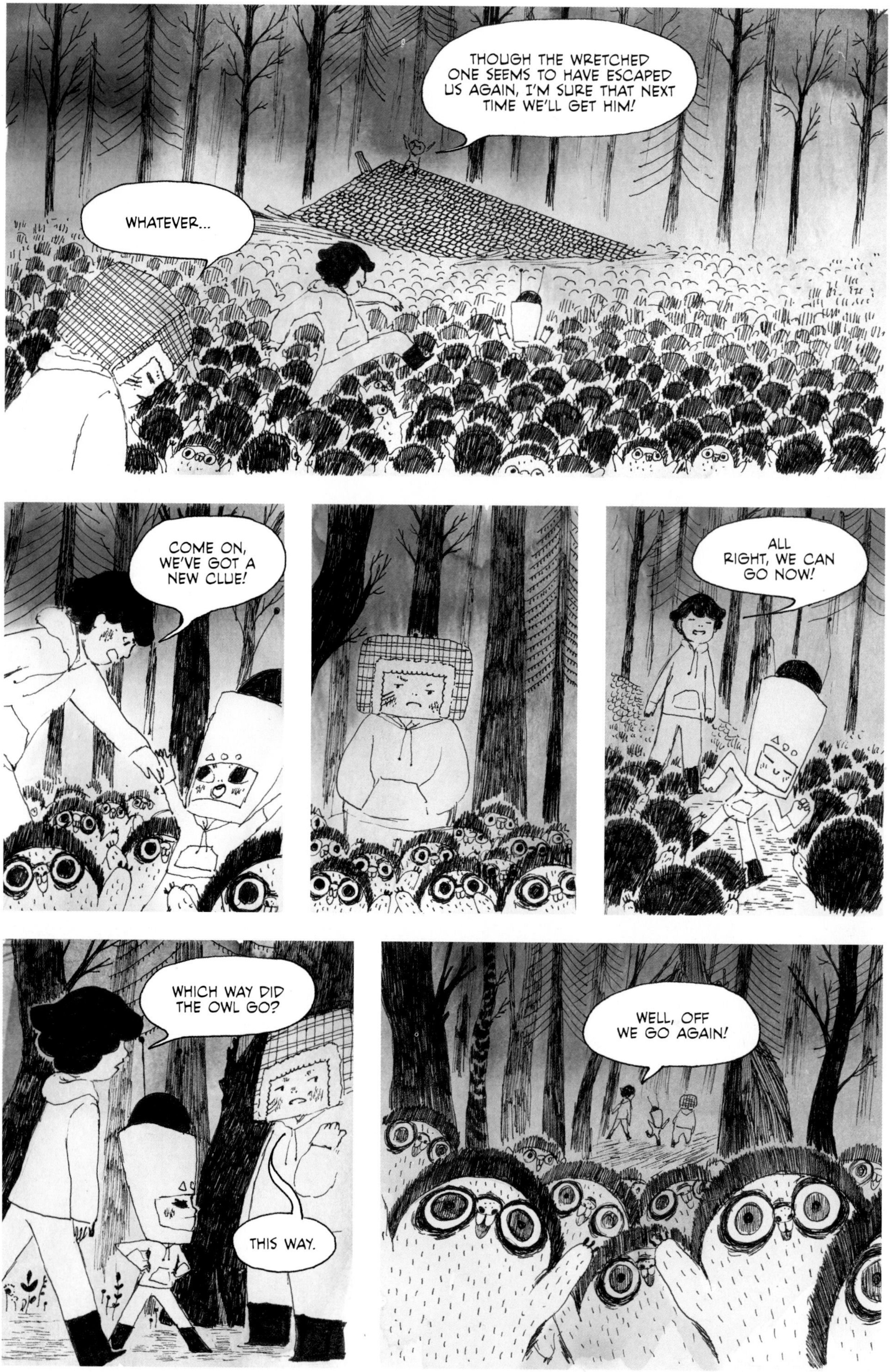
THOUGH THE WRETCHED ONE SEEMS TO HAVE ESCAPED US AGAIN, I'M SURE THAT NEXT TIME WE'LL GET HIM!
WHATEVER...
COME ON, WE'VE GOT A NEW CLUE!
ALL RIGHT, WE CAN GO NOW!
WHICH WAY DID THE OWL GO?
THIS WAY.
WELL, OFF WE GO AGAIN!

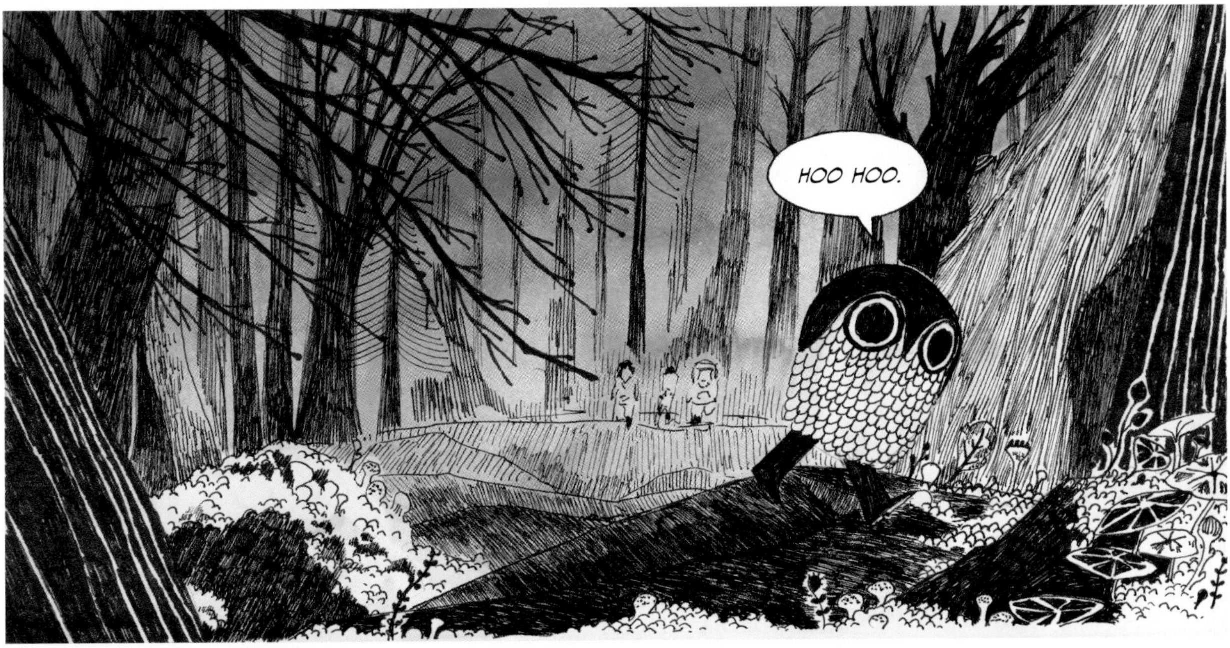
HOO HOO.

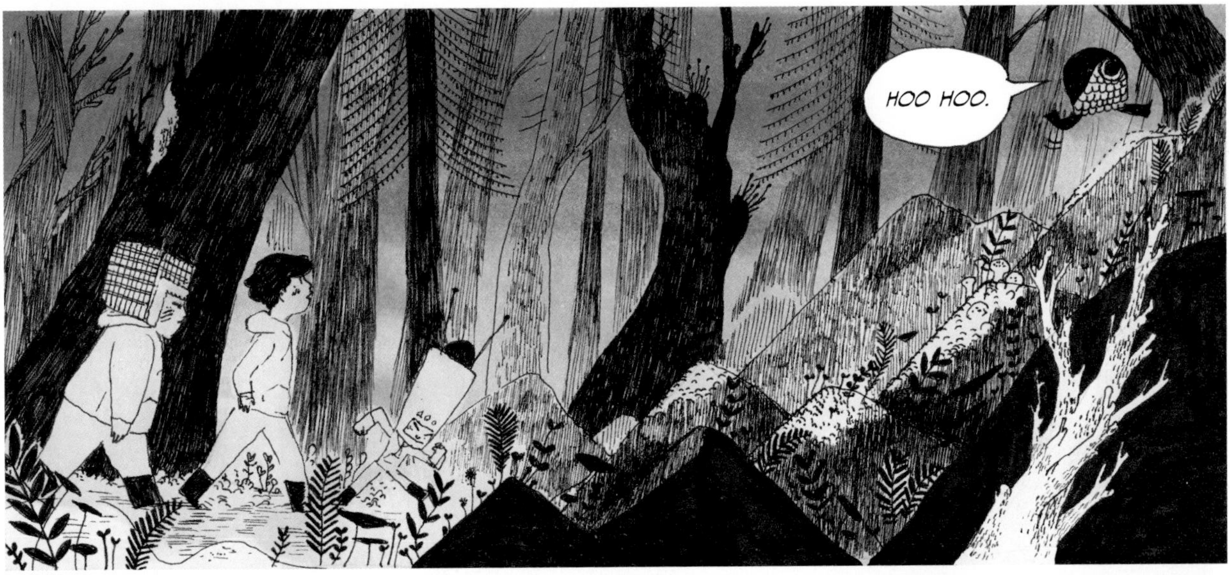
HOO HOO.

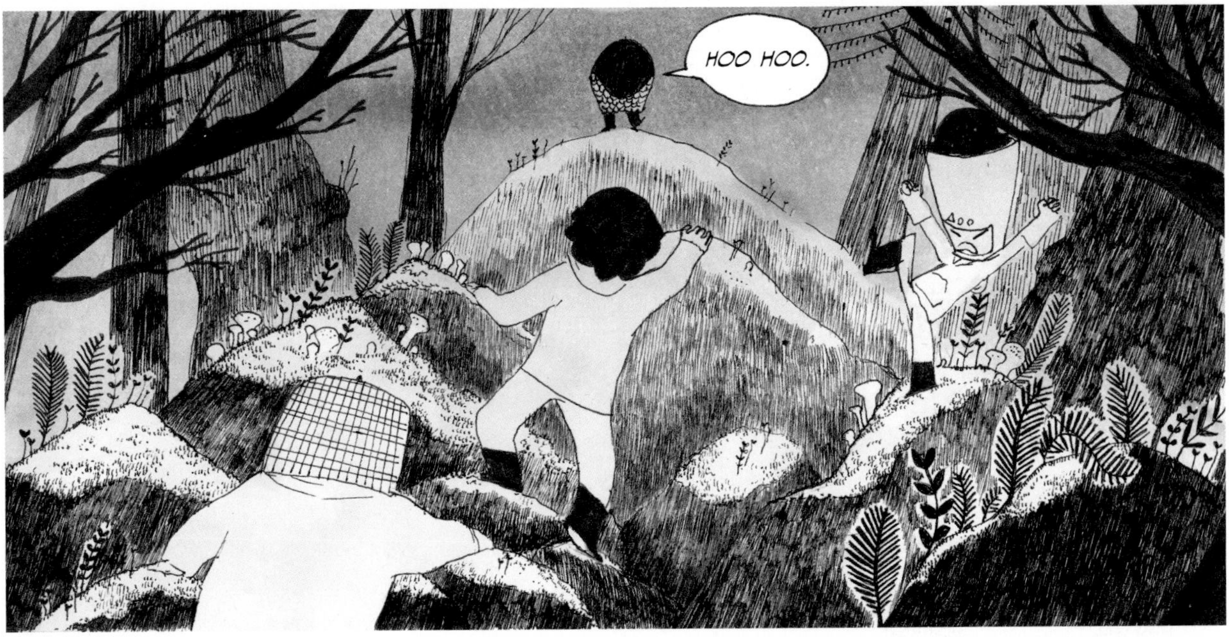
HOO HOO.

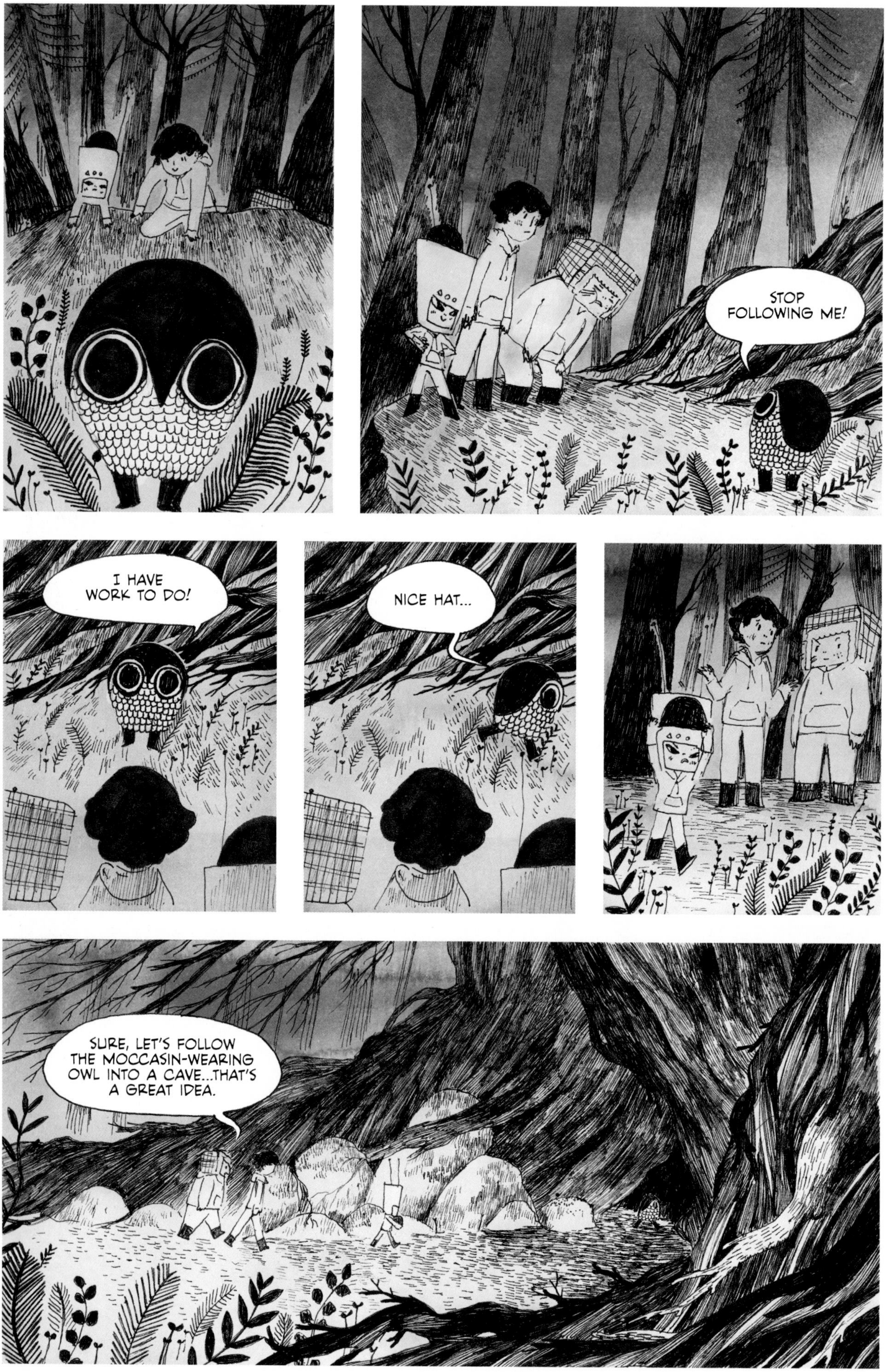
STOP FOLLOWING ME!
I HAVE WORK TO DO!
NICE HAT...
SURE, LET'S FOLLOW THE MOCCASIN-WEARING OWL INTO A CAVE...THAT'S A GREAT IDEA.

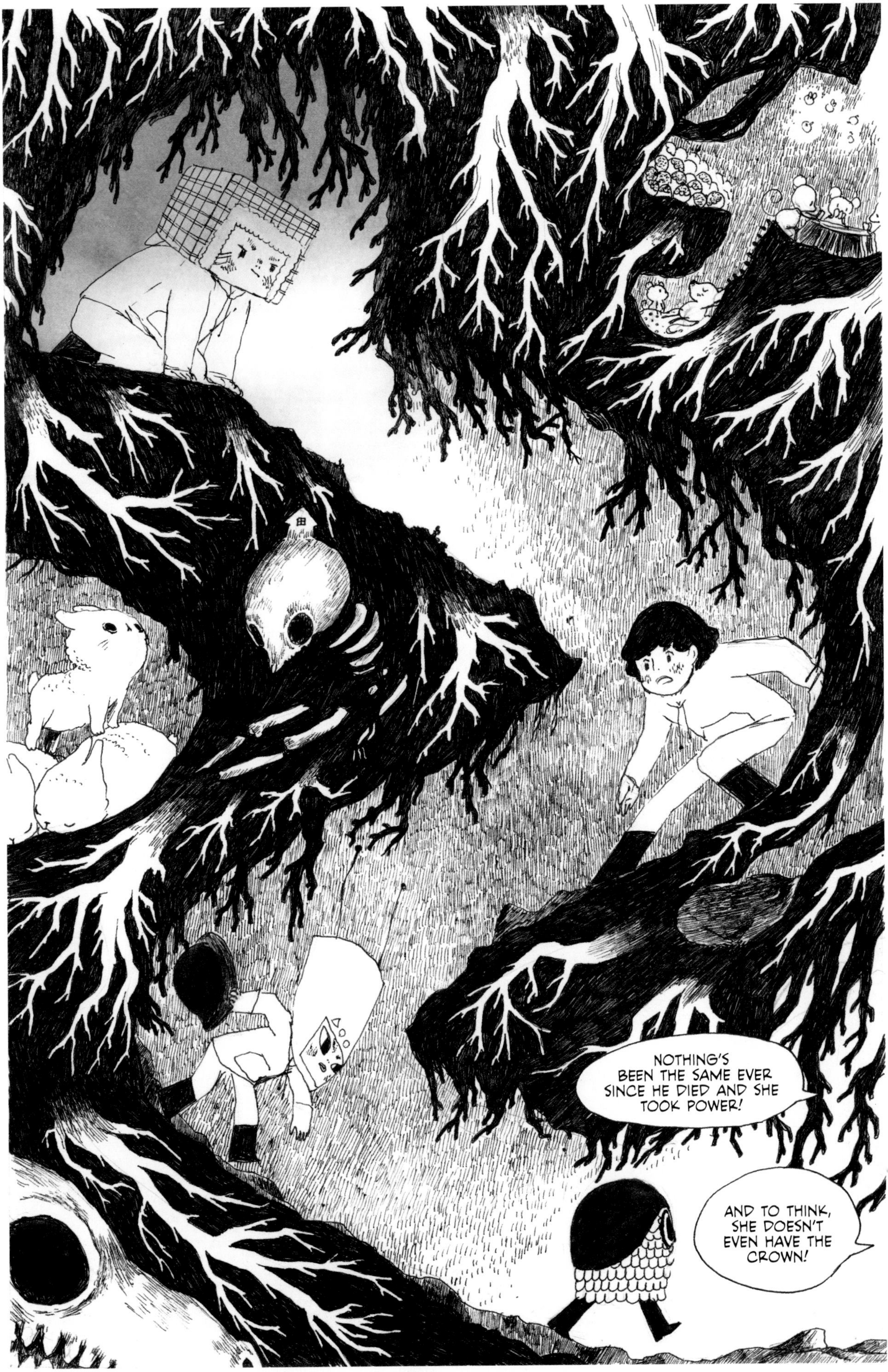
NOTHING'S BEEN THE SAME EVER SINCE HE DIED AND SHE TOOK POWER!
AND TO THINK, SHE DOESN'T EVEN HAVE THE CROWN!

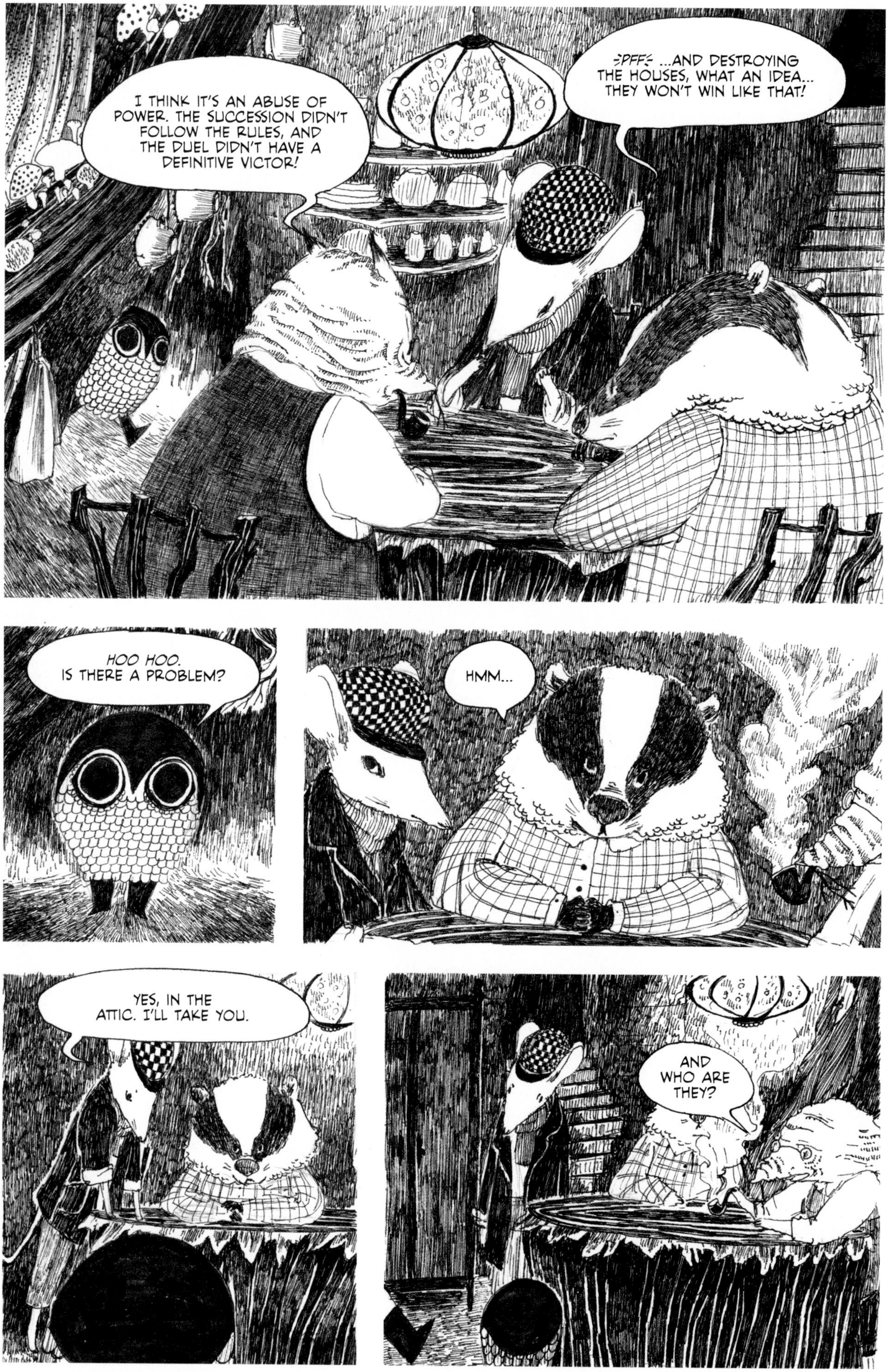
I THINK IT'S AN ABUSE OF POWER. THE SUCCESSION DIDN'T FOLLOW THE RULES, AND THE DUEL DIDN'T HAVE A DEFINITIVE VICTOR!
PFF ...AND DESTROYING THE HOUSES, WHAT AN IDEA... THEY WON'T WIN LIKE THAT!
HOO HOO. IS THERE A PROBLEM?
HMM...
YES, IN THE ATTIC. I'LL TAKE YOU.
AND WHO ARE THEY?

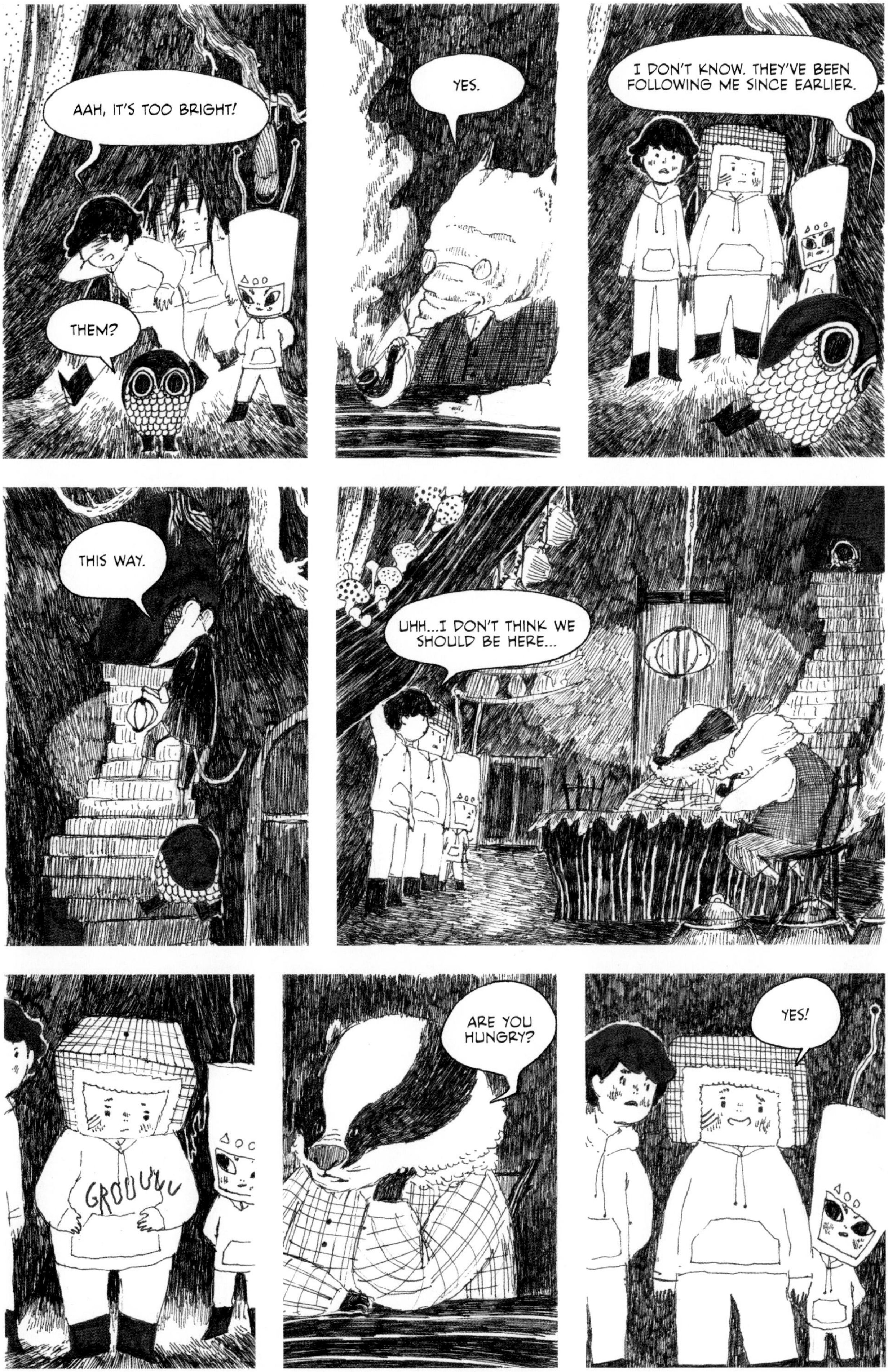
AAH, IT'S TOO BRIGHT!
THEM?
YES.
I DON'T KNOW. THEY'VE BEEN FOLLOWING ME SINCE EARLIER.
THIS WAY.
UHH...I DON'T THINK WE SHOULD BE HERE...
GROUUUU
ARE YOU HUNGRY?
YES!

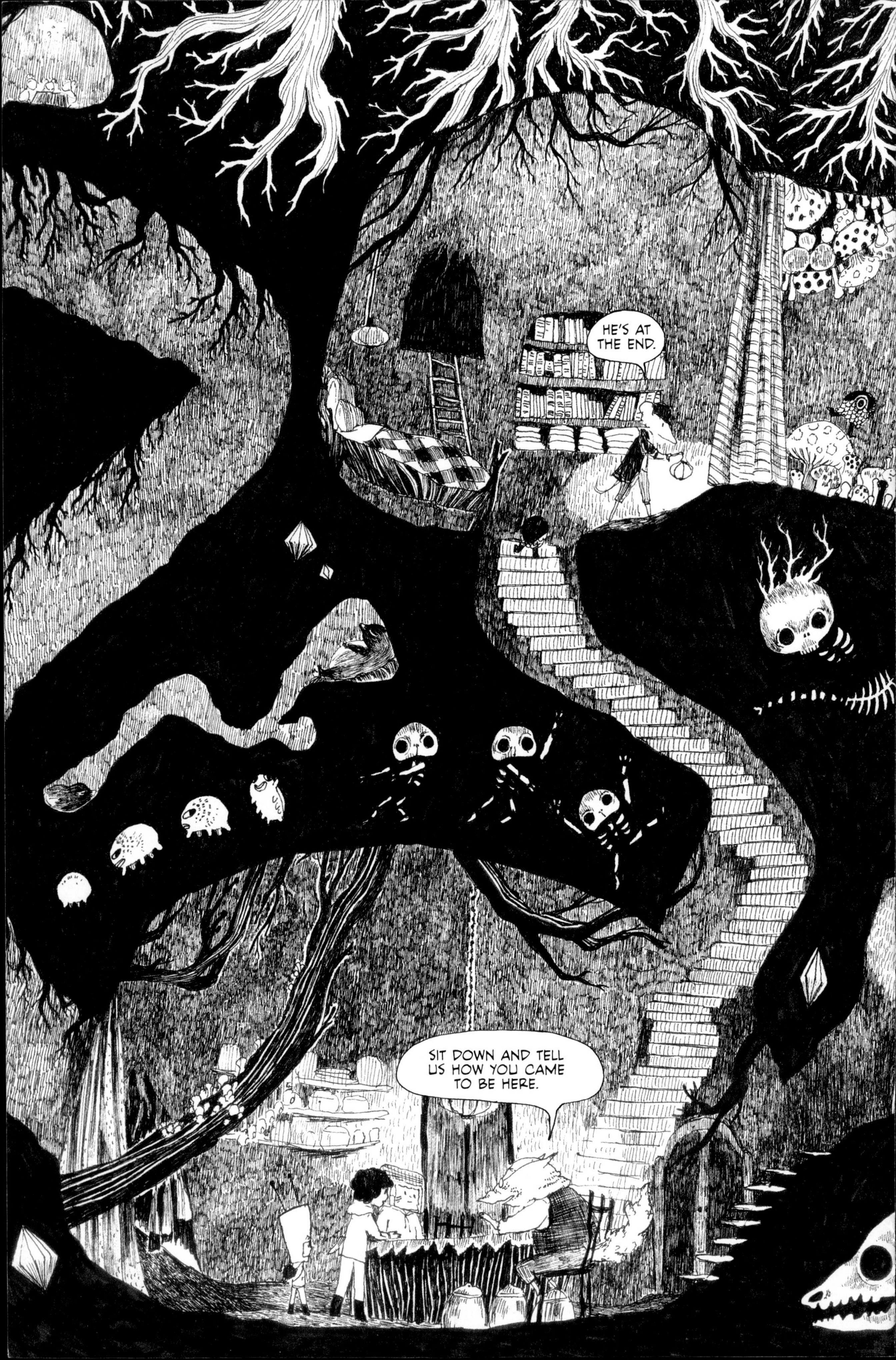
HE'S AT THE END.
SIT DOWN AND TELL US HOW YOU CAME TO BE HERE.

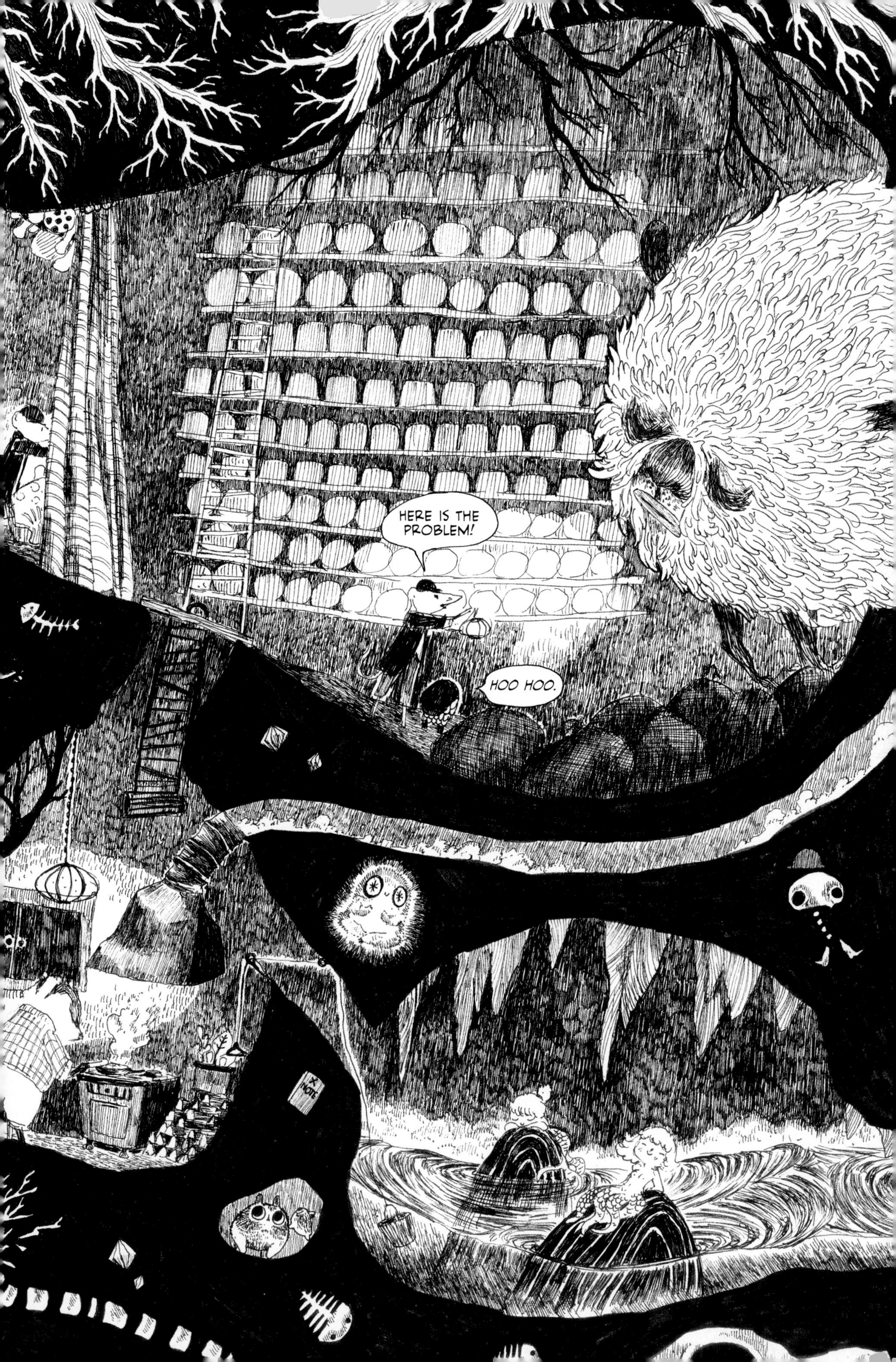
HERE IS THE PROBLEM!
HOO HOO.

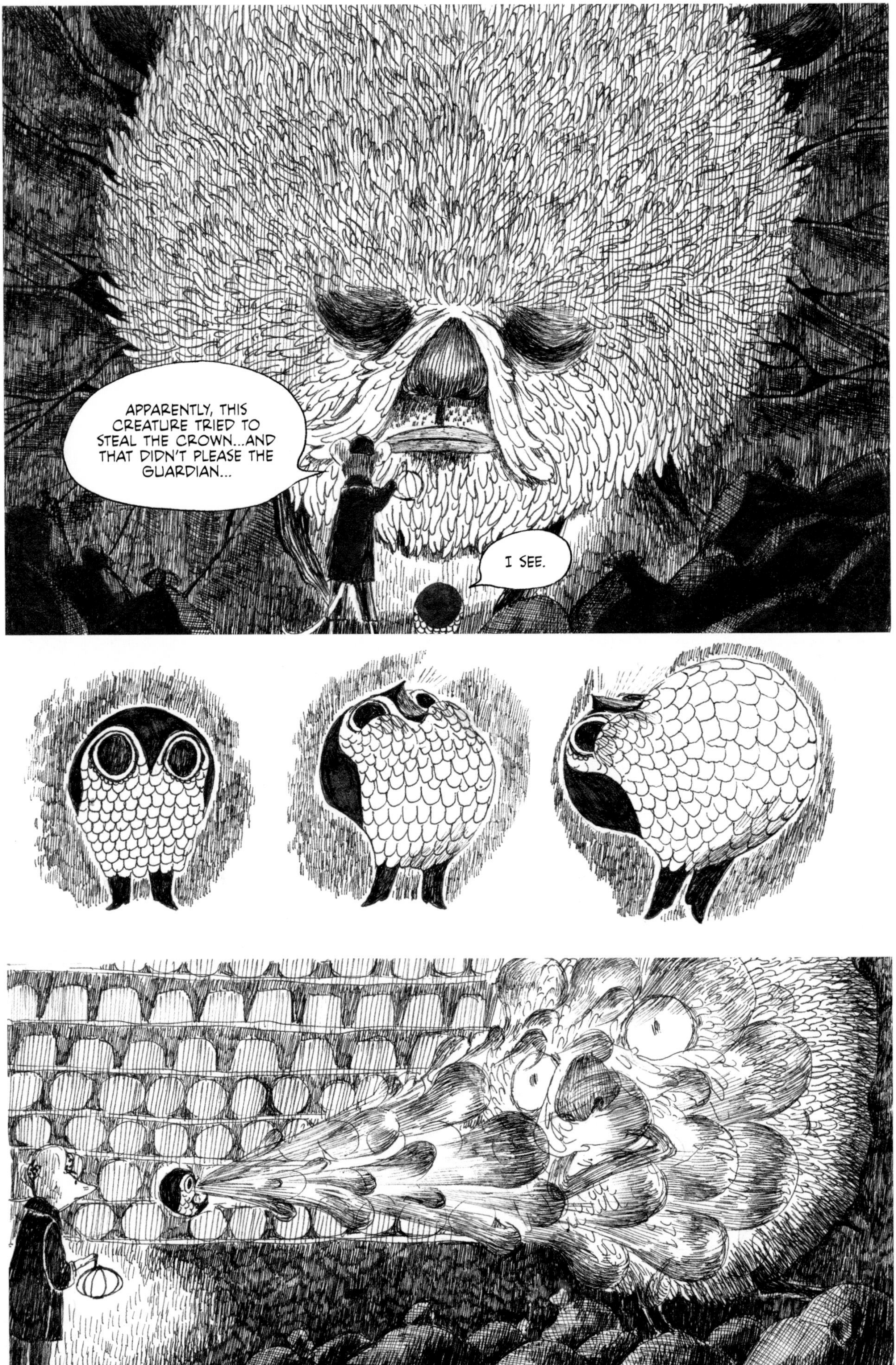
APPARENTLY, THIS CREATURE TRIED TO STEAL THE CROWN...AND THAT DIDN'T PLEASE THE GUARDIAN...
I SEE.

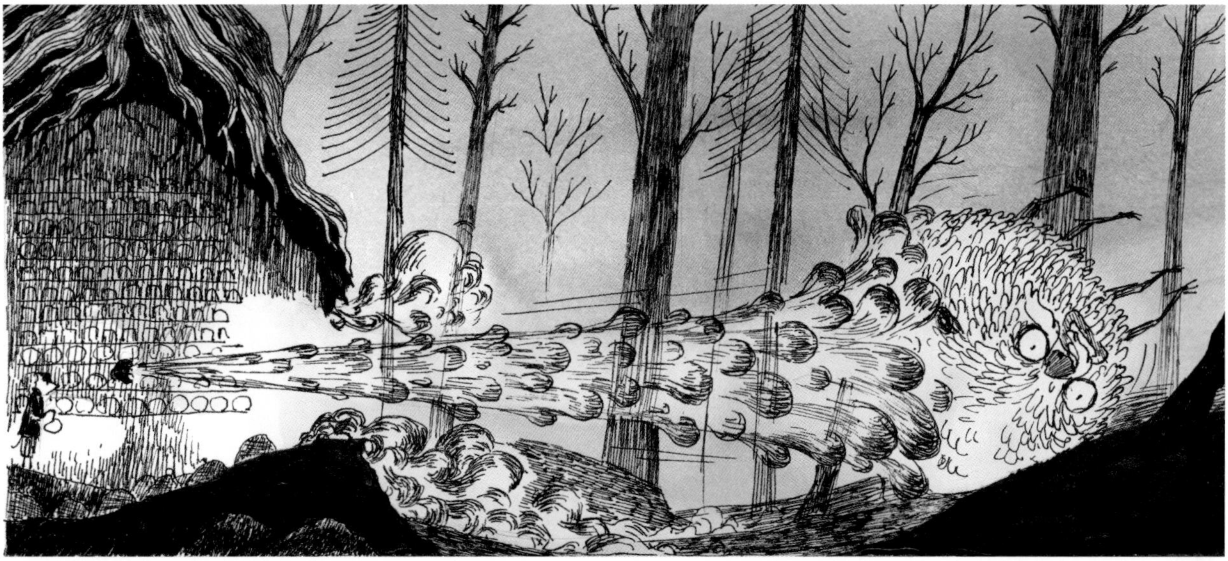

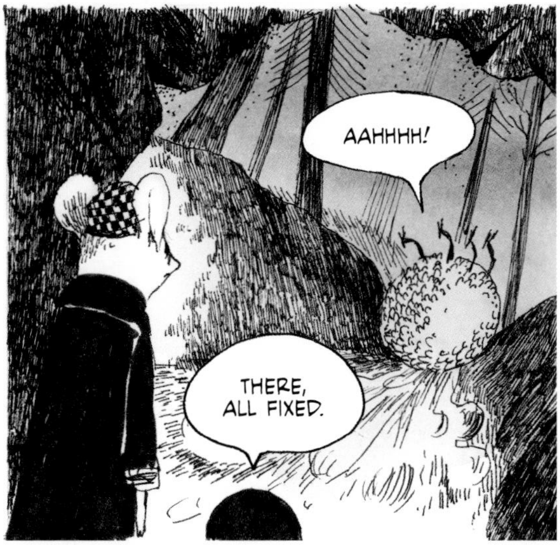
AAHHHH!
THERE, ALL FIXED.

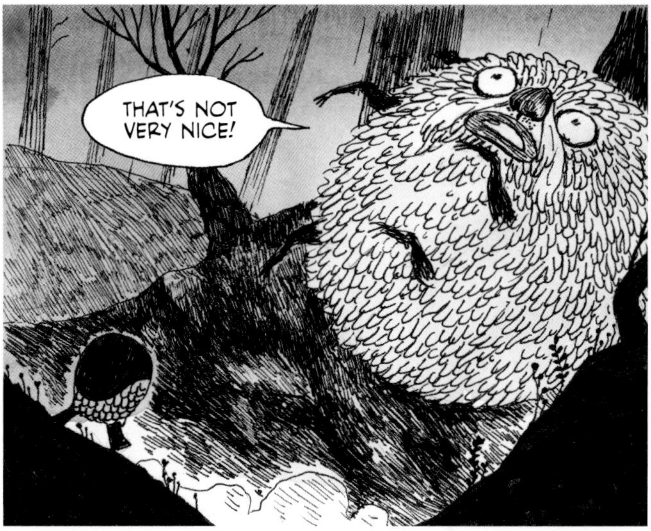
THAT'S NOT VERY NICE!

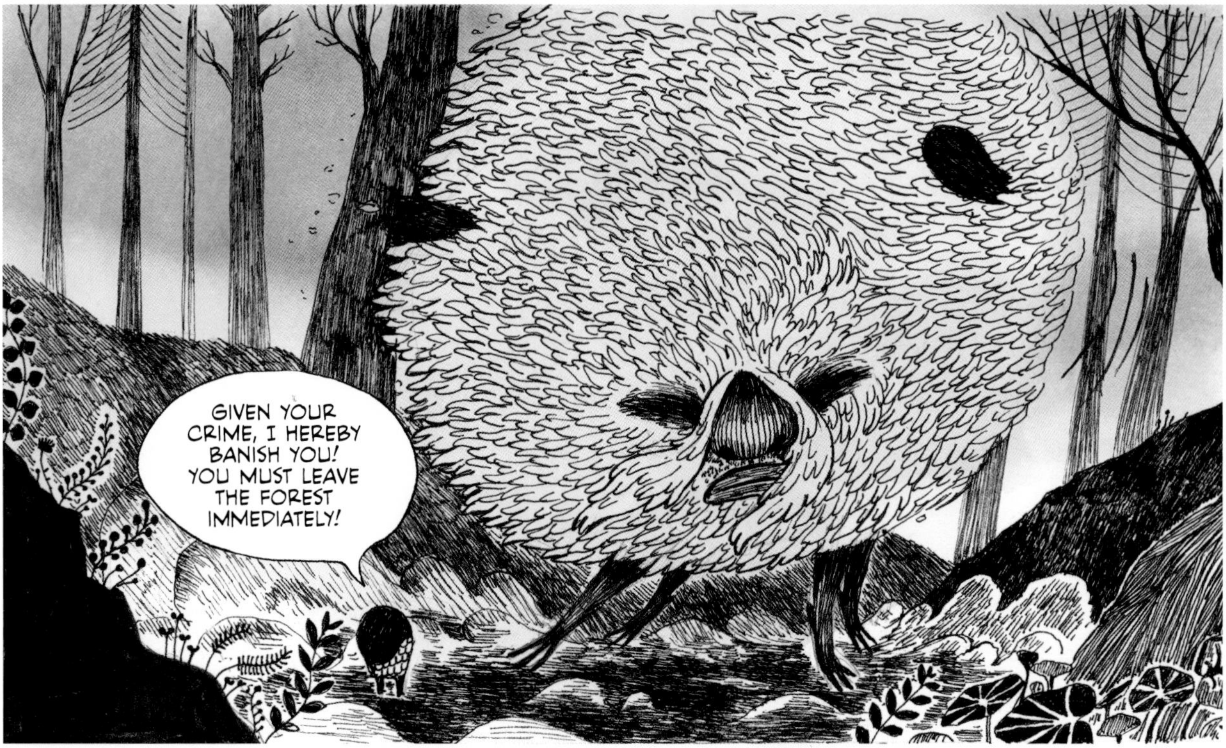
GIVEN YOUR CRIME, I HEREBY BANISH YOU! YOU MUST LEAVE THE FOREST IMMEDIATELY!

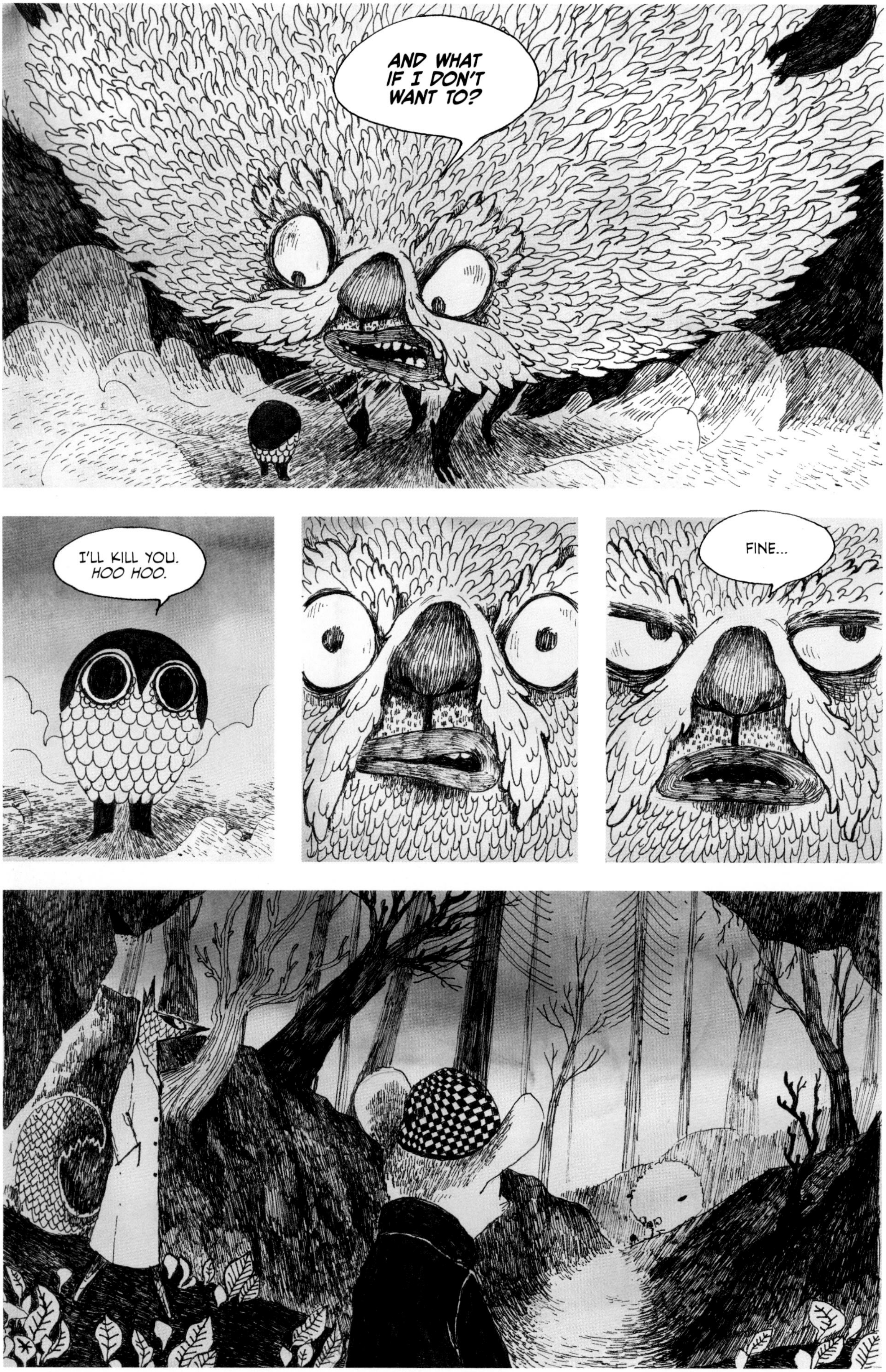
AND WHAT IF I DON'T WANT TO?
I'LL KILL YOU. HOO HOO.
FINE...

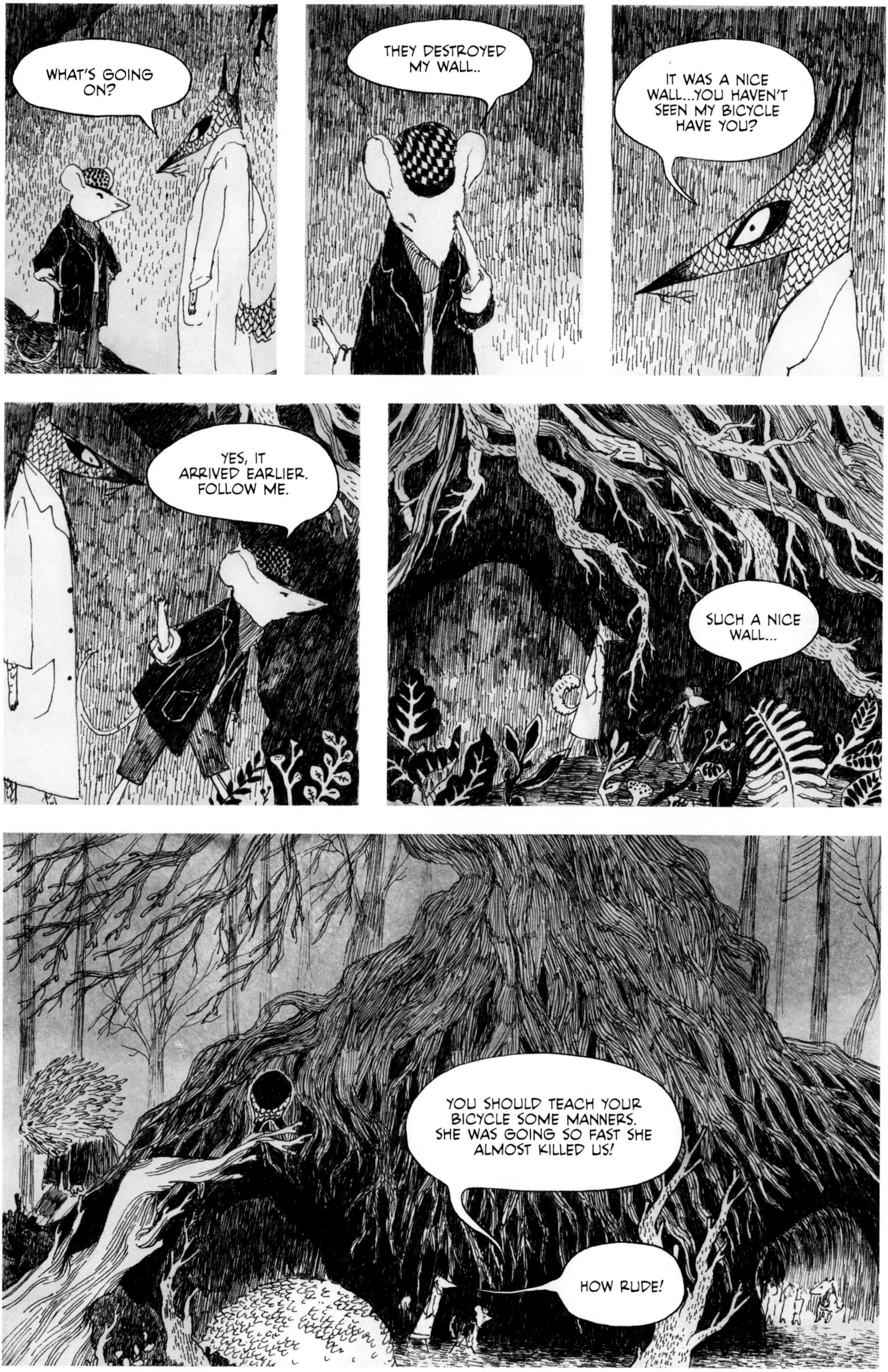
WHAT'S GOING ON?
THEY DESTROYED MY WALL..
IT WAS A NICE WALL...YOU HAVEN'T SEEN MY BICYCLE HAVE YOU?
YES, IT ARRIVED EARLIER. FOLLOW ME.
SUCH A NICE WALL...
YOU SHOULD TEACH YOUR BICYCLE SOME MANNERS. SHE WAS GOING SO FAST SHE ALMOST KILLED US!
HOW RUDE!

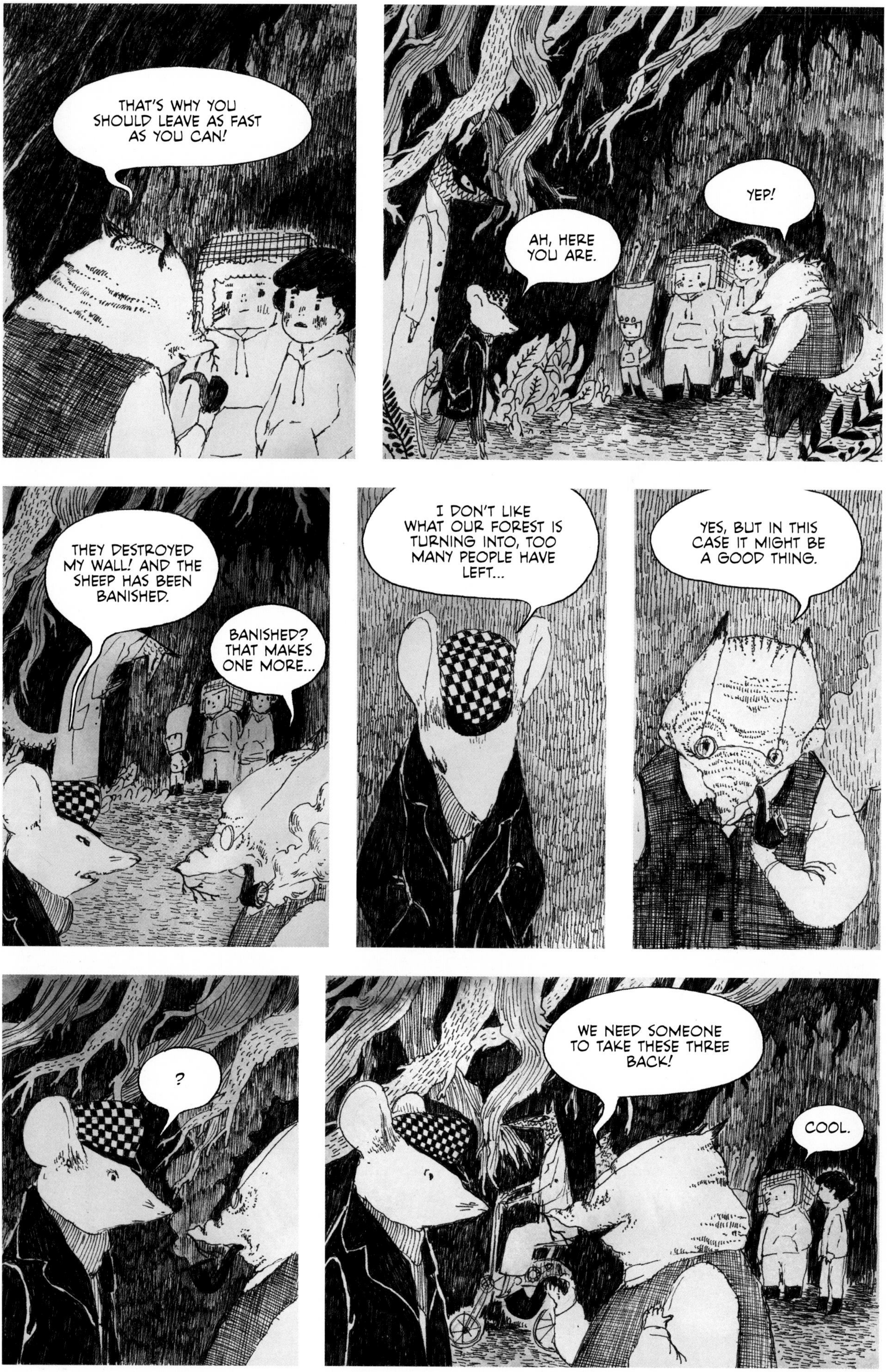
THAT'S WHY YOU SHOULD LEAVE AS FAST AS YOU CAN!
AH, HERE YOU ARE.
YEP!
THEY DESTROYED MY WALL! AND THE SHEEP HAS BEEN BANISHED.
BANISHED? THAT MAKES ONE MORE...
I DON'T LIKE WHAT OUR FOREST IS TURNING INTO, TOO MANY PEOPLE HAVE LEFT...
YES, BUT IN THIS CASE IT MIGHT BE A GOOD THING.
?
WE NEED SOMEONE TO TAKE THESE THREE BACK!
COOL.

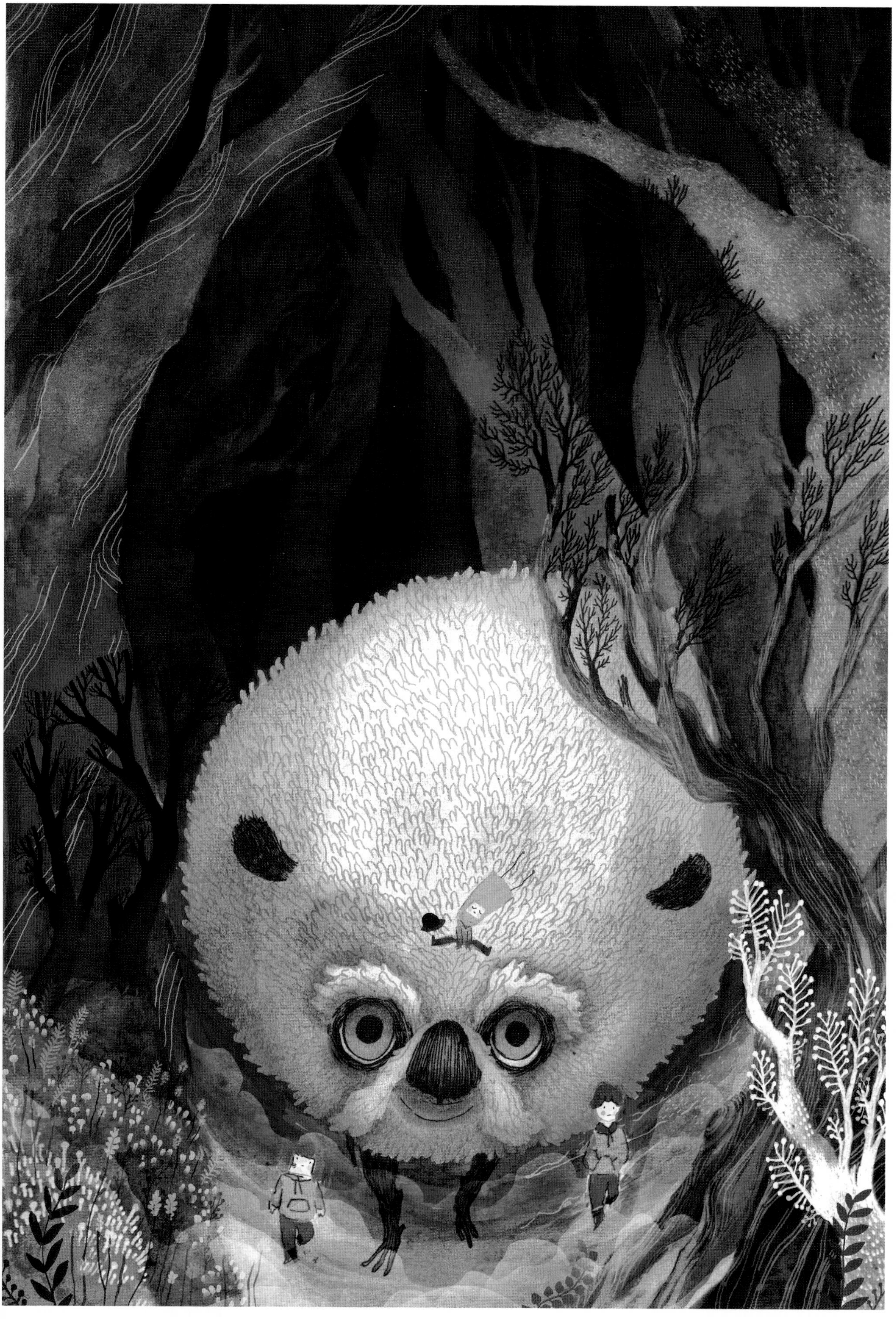

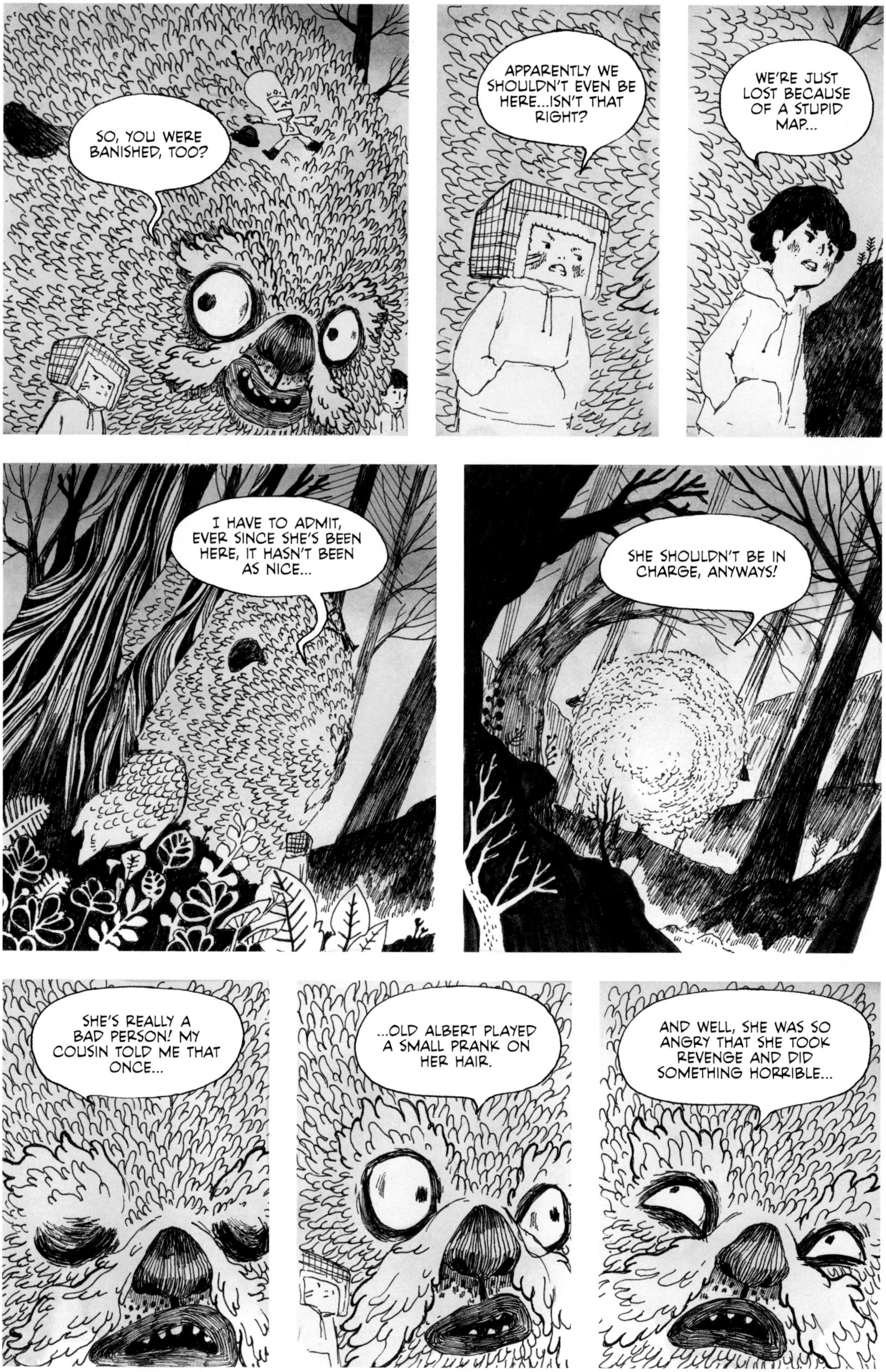
SO, YOU WERE BANISHED, TOO?
APPARENTLY WE SHOULDN'T EVEN BE HERE...ISN'T THAT RIGHT?
WE'RE JUST LOST BECAUSE OF A STUPID MAP...
I HAVE TO ADMIT, EVER SINCE SHE'S BEEN HERE, IT HASN'T BEEN AS NICE...
SHE SHOULDN'T BE IN CHARGE, ANYWAYS!
SHE'S REALLY A BAD PERSON! MY COUSIN TOLD ME THAT ONCE...
...OLD ALBERT PLAYED A SMALL PRANK ON HER HAIR.
AND WELL, SHE WAS SO ANGRY THAT SHE TOOK REVENGE AND DID SOMETHING HORRIBLE...

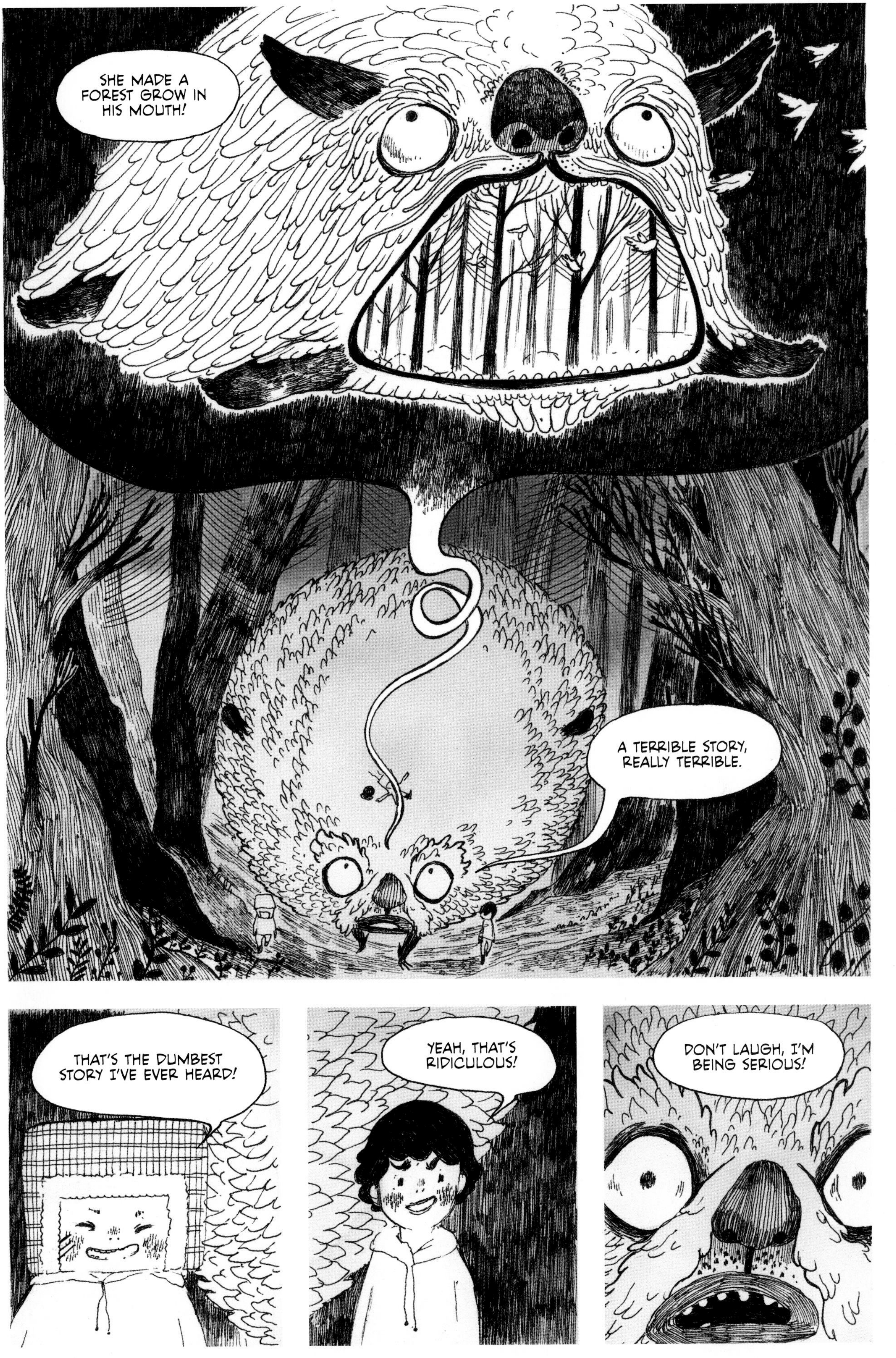
SHE MADE A FOREST GROW IN HIS MOUTH!
A TERRIBLE STORY, REALLY TERRIBLE.
THAT'S THE DUMBEST STORY I'VE EVER HEARD!
YEAH, THAT'S RIDICULOUS!
DON'T LAUGH, I'M BEING SERIOUS!

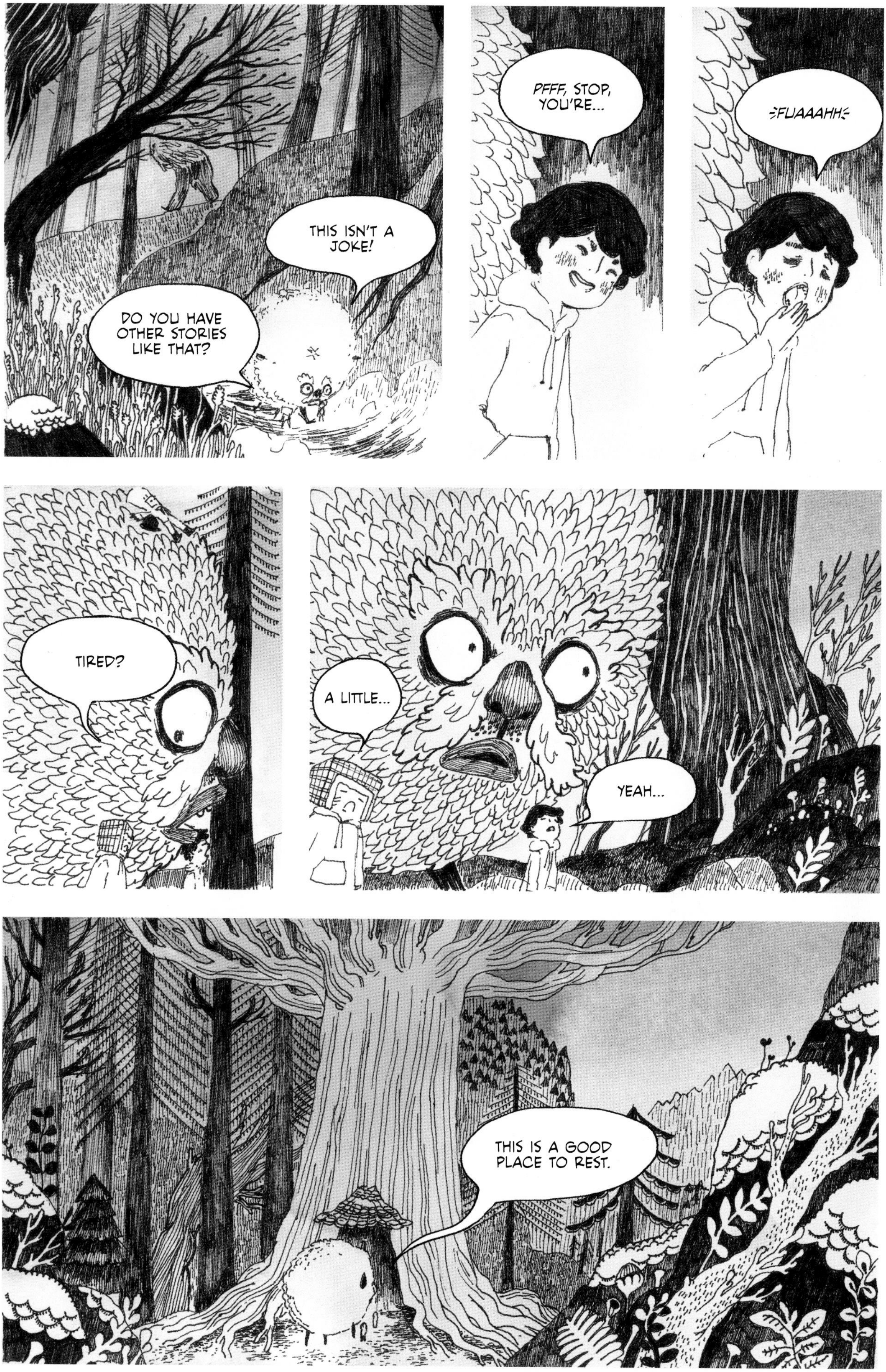
DO YOU HAVE OTHER STORIES LIKE THAT?
THIS ISN'T A JOKE!
PFFF, STOP, YOU'RE...
FUAAAHH
TIRED?
A LITTLE...
YEAH...
THIS IS A GOOD PLACE TO REST.

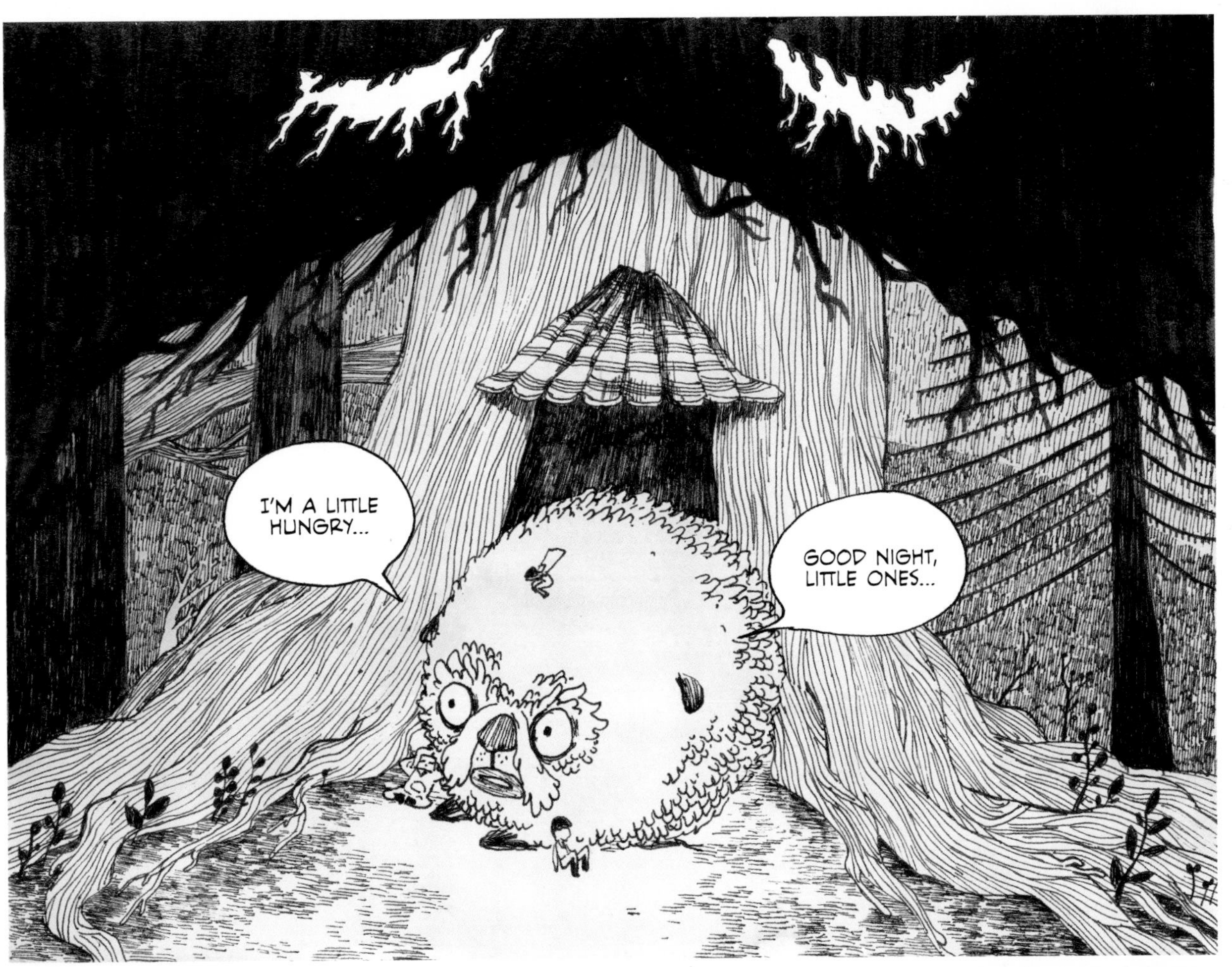
I'M A LITTLE HUNGRY...
GOOD NIGHT, LITTLE ONES...

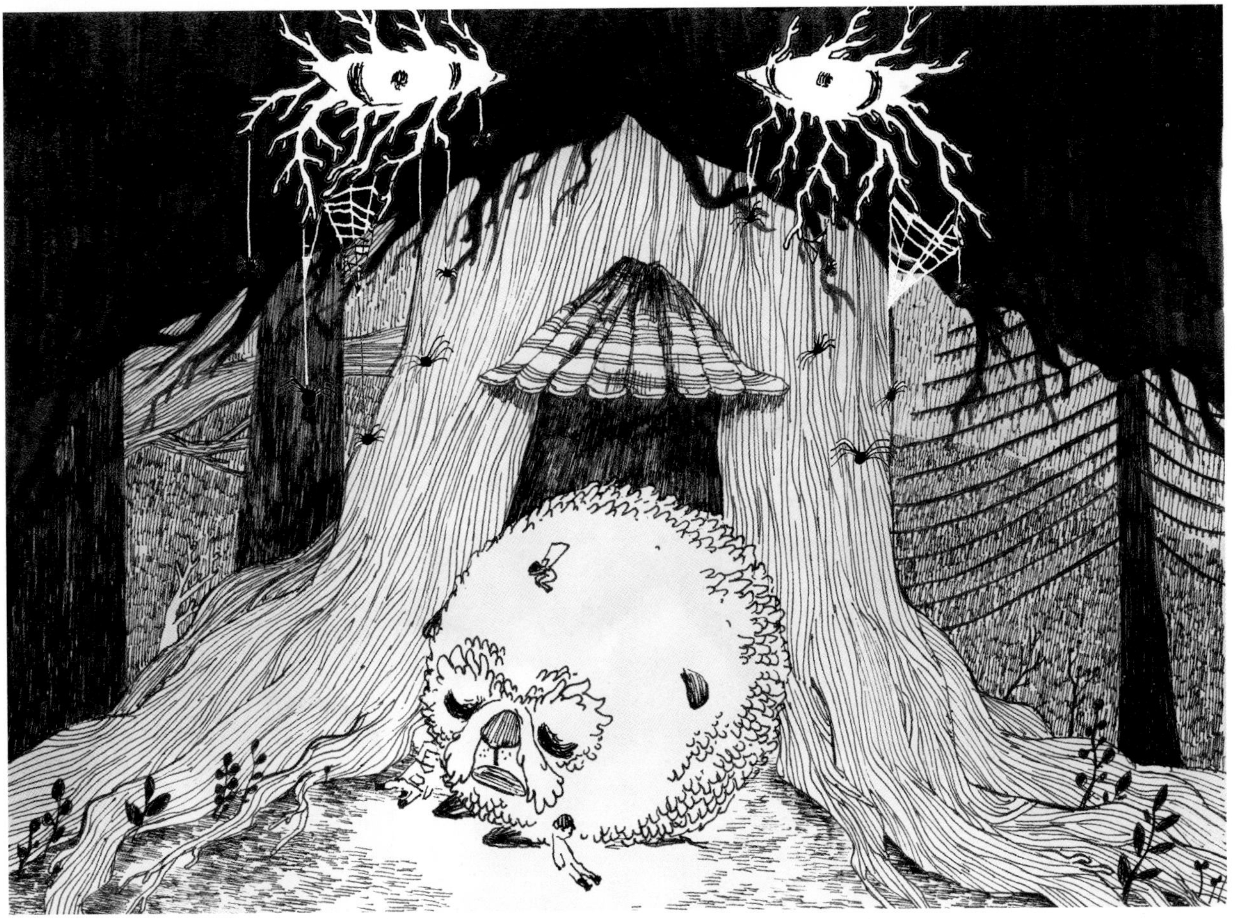

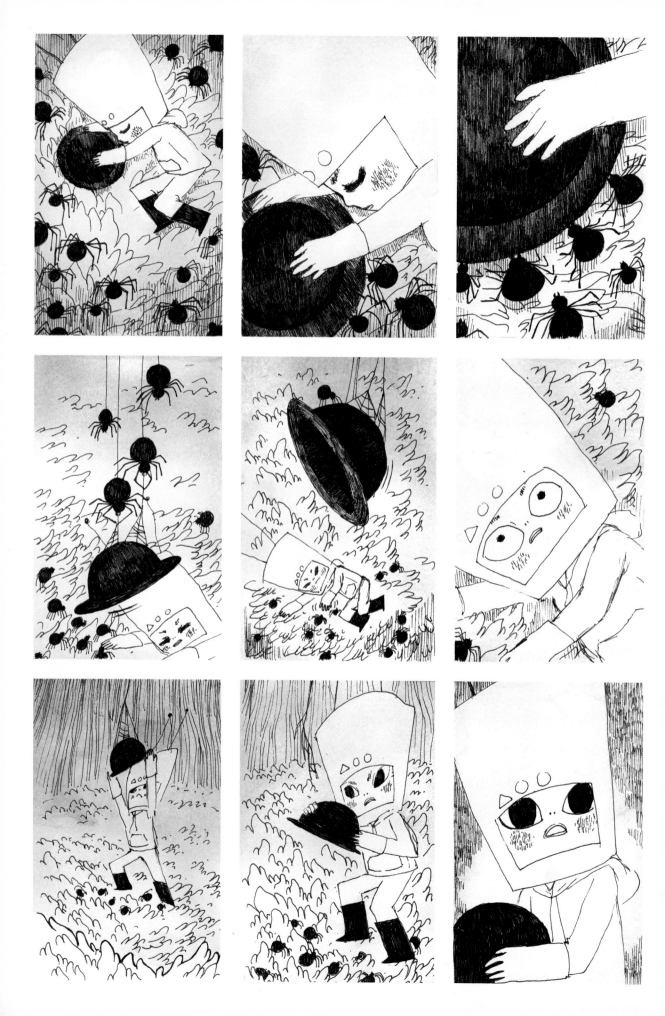

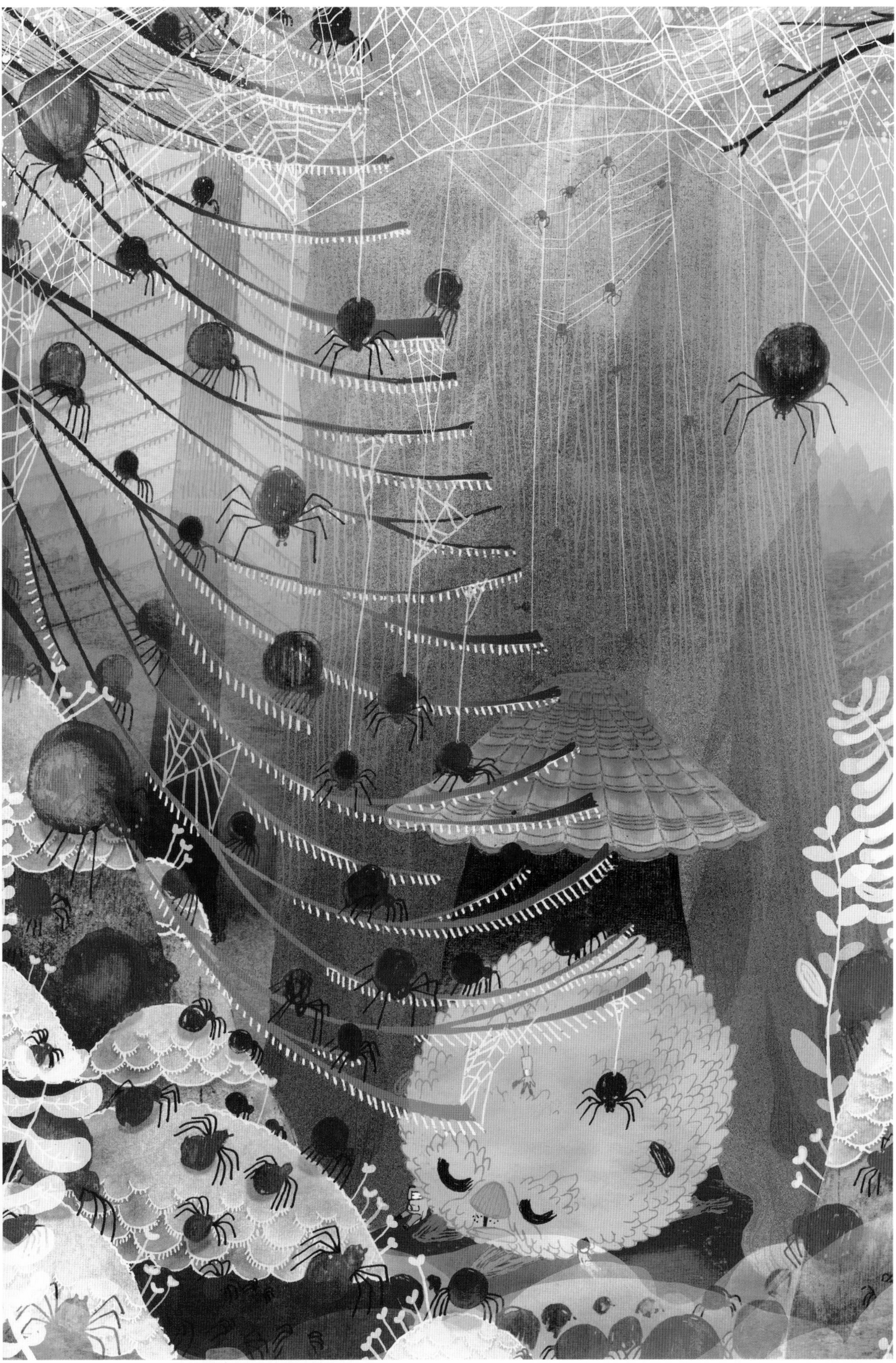

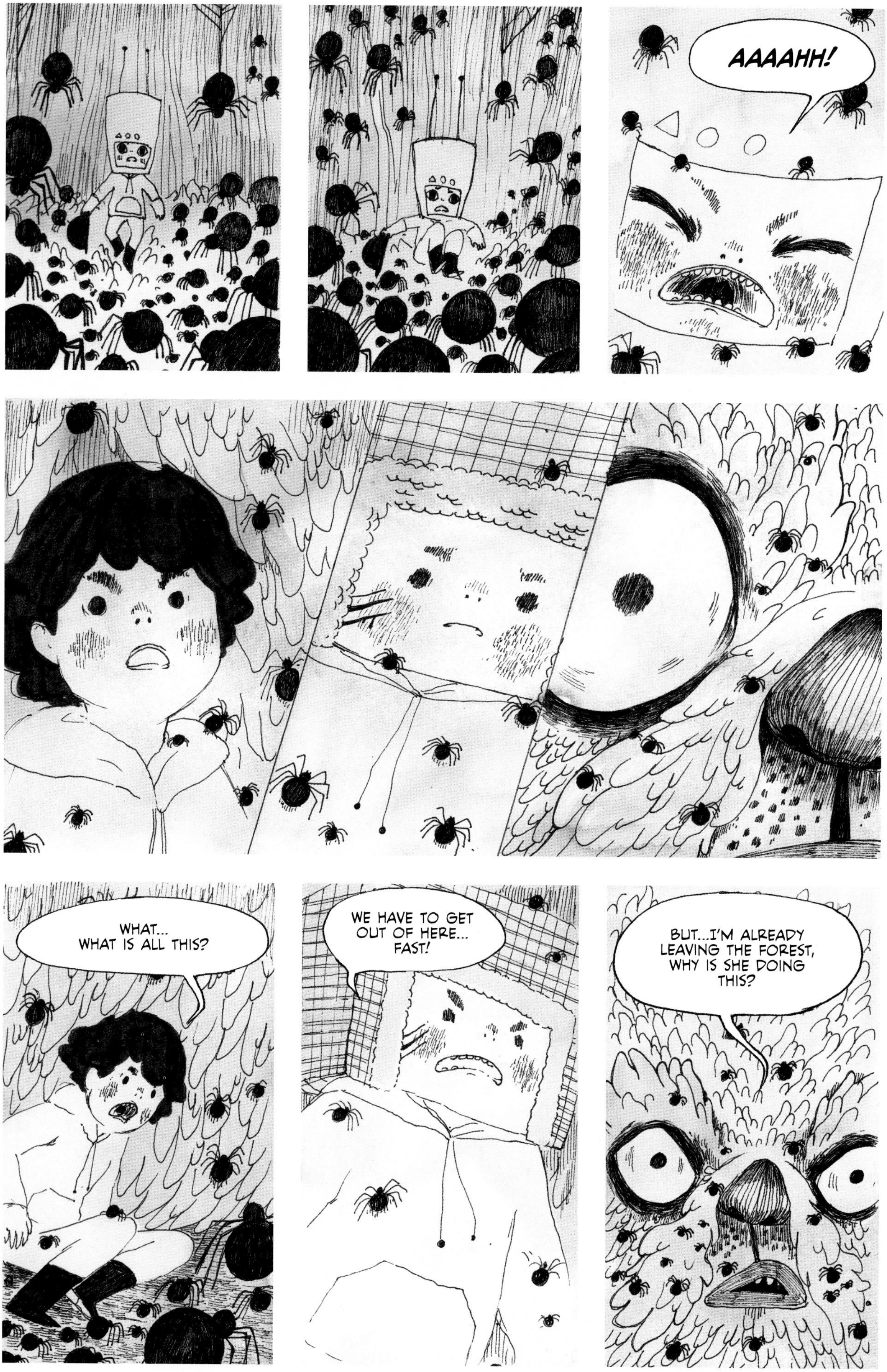
AAAAHH!
WHAT...
WHAT IS ALL THIS?
WE HAVE TO GET
OUT OF HERE...
FAST!
BUT...I'M ALREADY
LEAVING THE FOREST,
WHY IS SHE DOING
THIS?

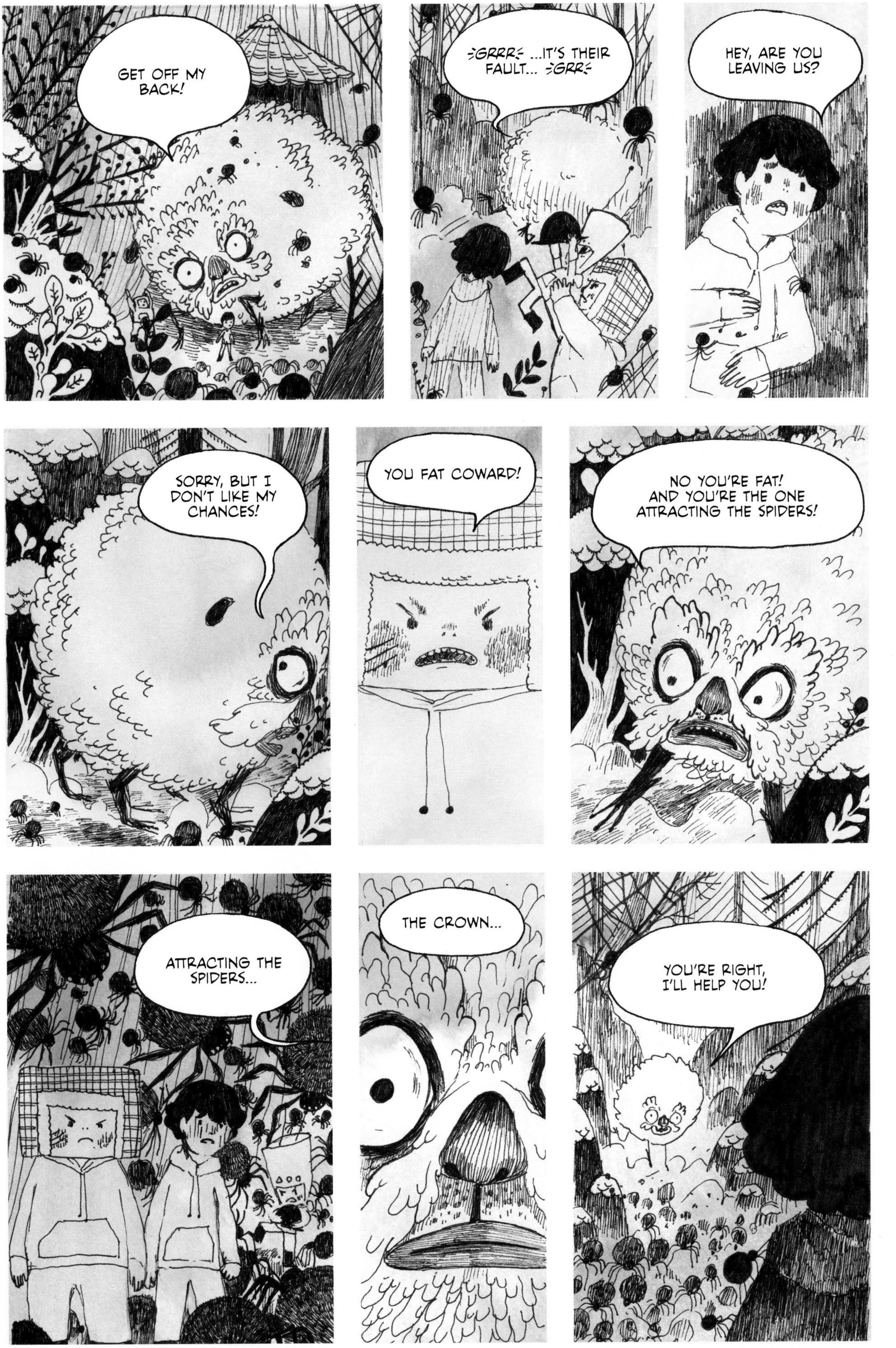
GET OFF MY BACK!
GRRR ...IT'S THEIR FAULT... GRR
HEY, ARE YOU LEAVING US?
SORRY, BUT I DON'T LIKE MY CHANCES!
YOU FAT COWARD!
NO YOU'RE FAT! AND YOU'RE THE ONE ATTRACTING THE SPIDERS!
ATTRACTING THE SPIDERS...
THE CROWN...
YOU'RE RIGHT, I'LL HELP YOU!

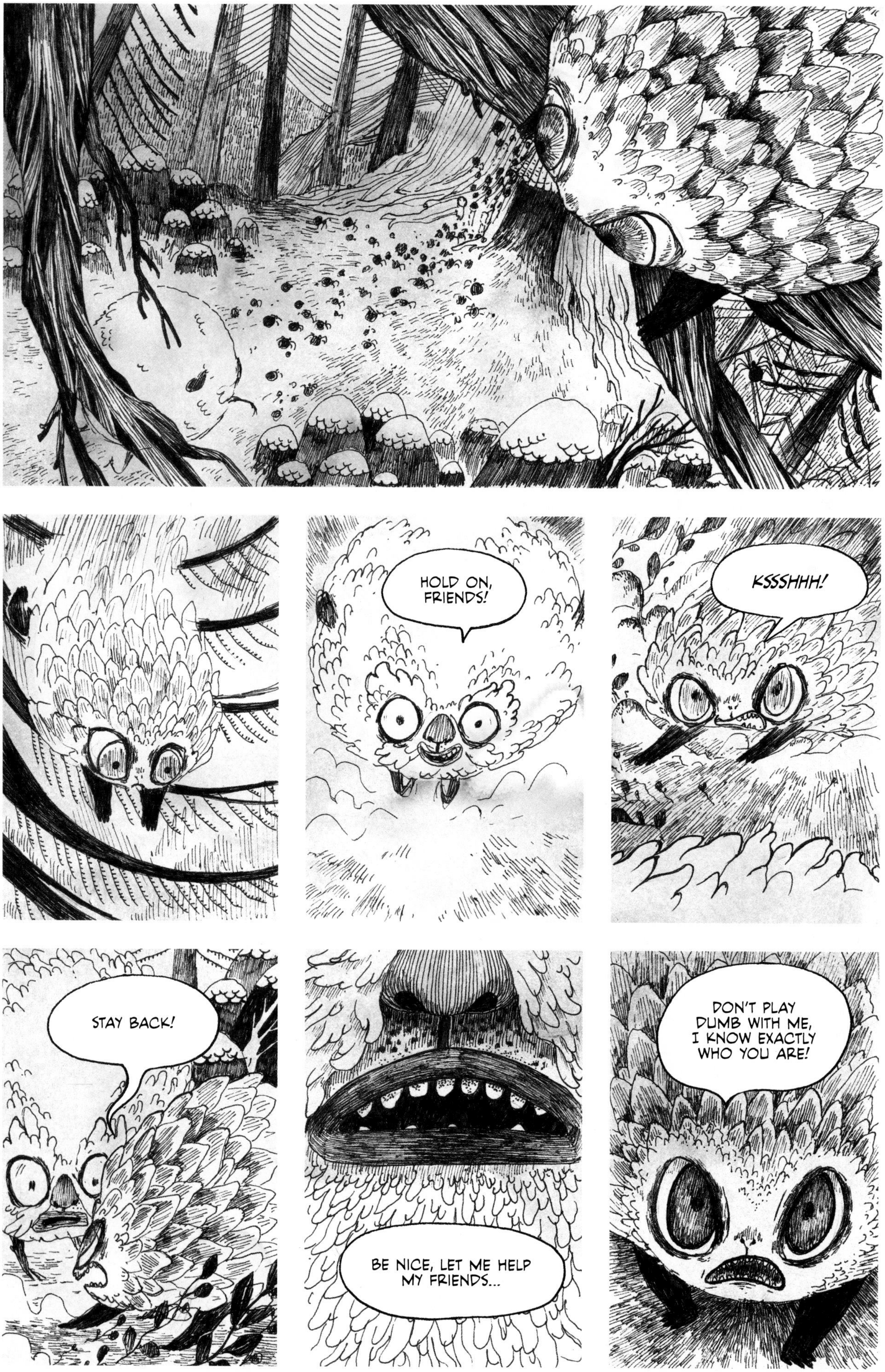
HOLD ON, FRIENDS!
KSSSHHH!
STAY BACK!
BE NICE, LET ME HELP MY FRIENDS...
DON'T PLAY DUMB WITH ME, I KNOW EXACTLY WHO YOU ARE!

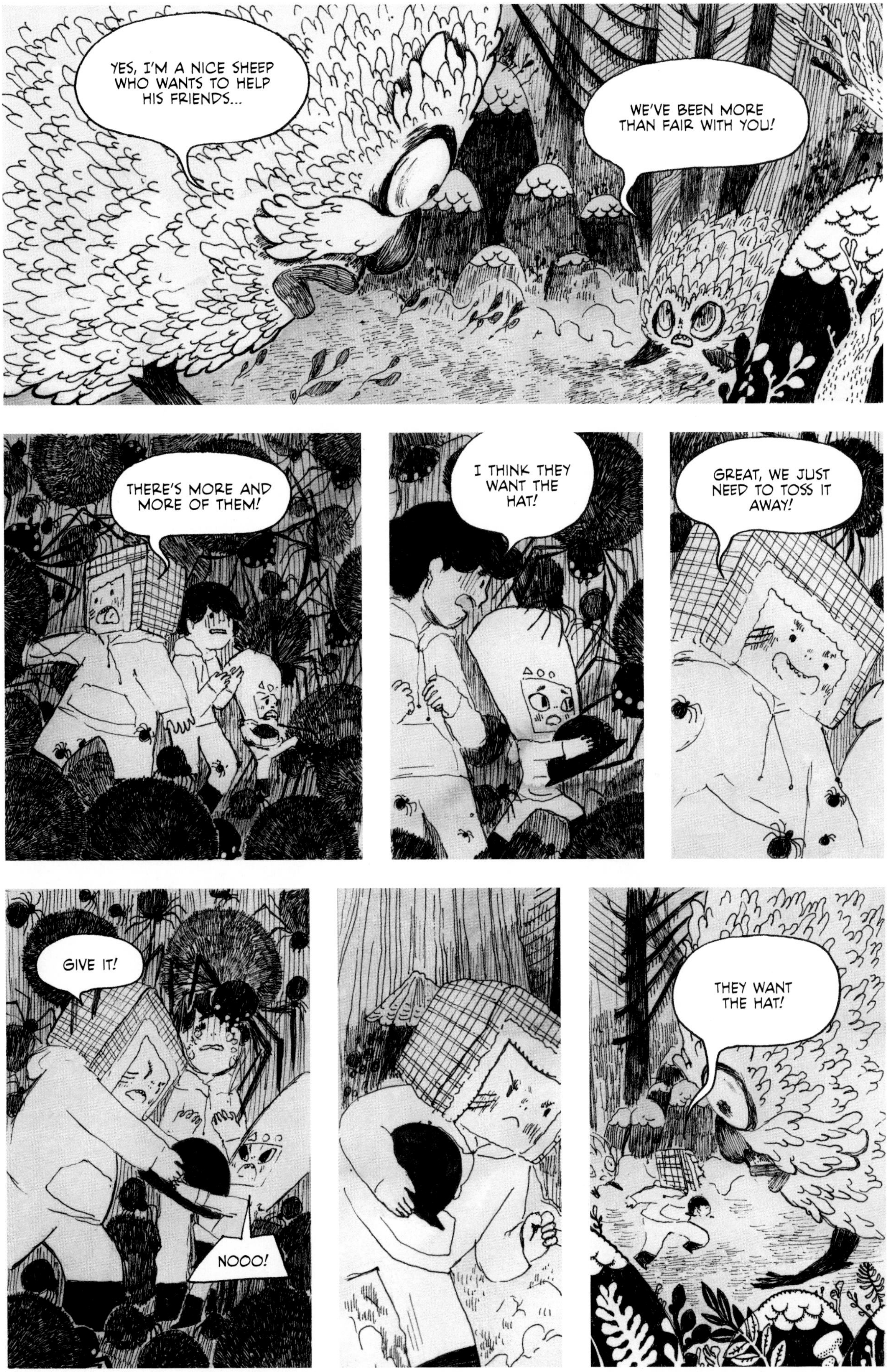
YES, I'M A NICE SHEEP WHO WANTS TO HELP HIS FRIENDS...
WE'VE BEEN MORE THAN FAIR WITH YOU!
THERE'S MORE AND MORE OF THEM!
I THINK THEY WANT THE HAT!
GREAT, WE JUST NEED TO TOSS IT AWAY!
GIVE IT!
NOOO!
THEY WANT THE HAT!

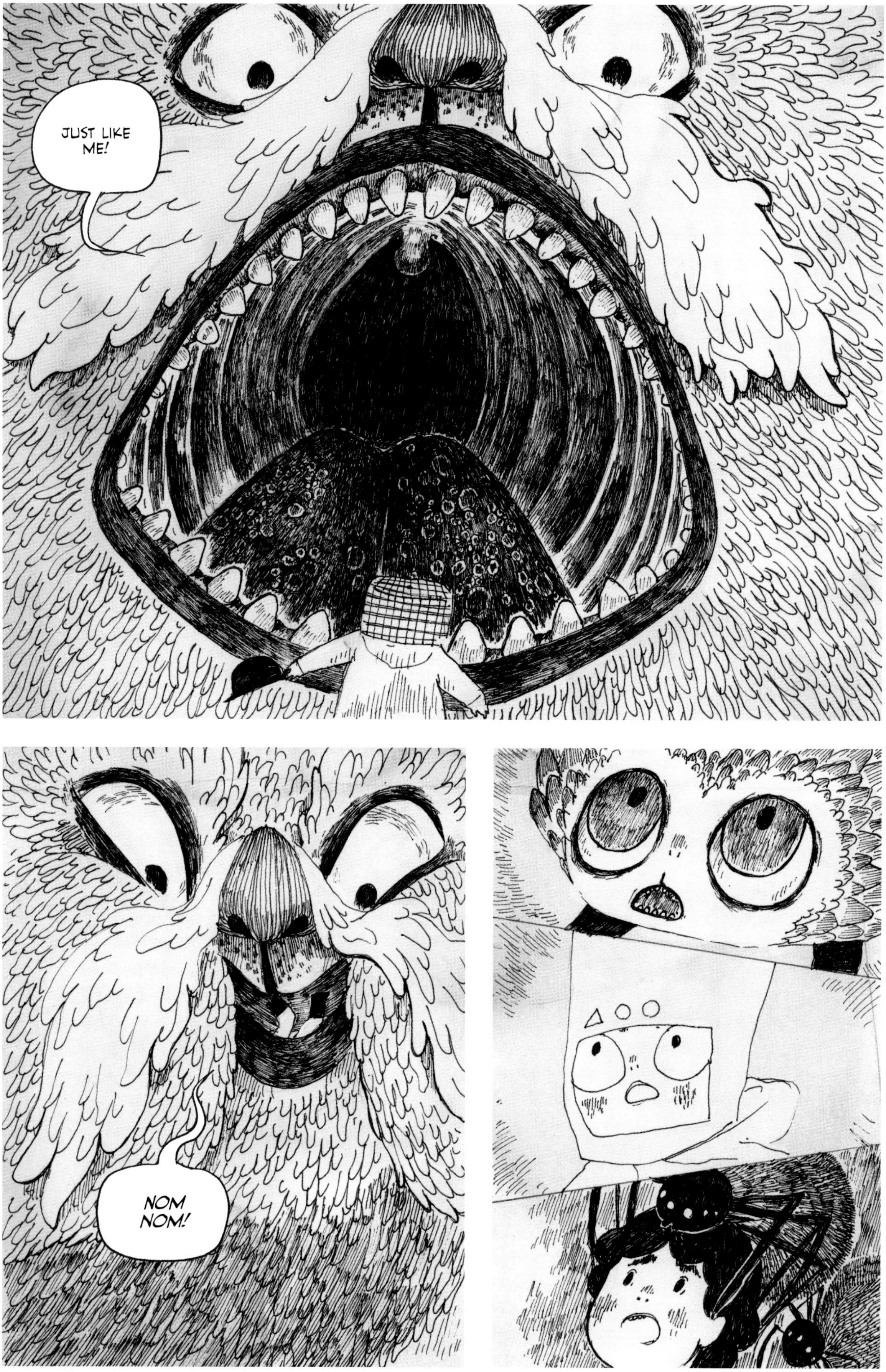
JUST LIKE ME!
NOM NOM!

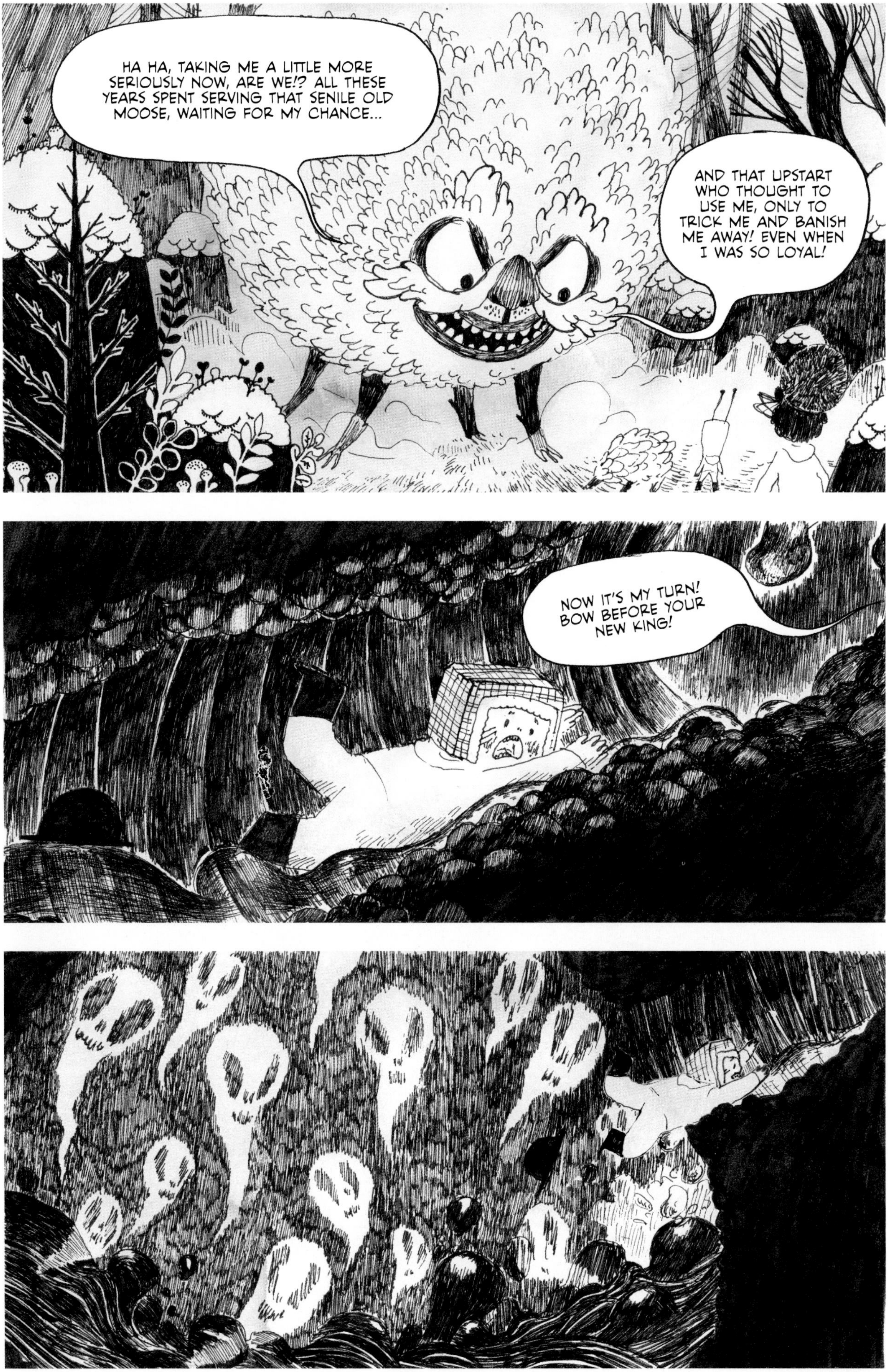
HA HA, TAKING ME A LITTLE MORE SERIOUSLY NOW, ARE WE!? ALL THESE YEARS SPENT SERVING THAT SENILE OLD MOOSE, WAITING FOR MY CHANCE...
AND THAT UPSTART WHO THOUGHT TO USE ME, ONLY TO TRICK ME AND BANISH ME AWAY! EVEN WHEN I WAS SO LOYAL!
NOW IT'S MY TURN! BOW BEFORE YOUR NEW KING!

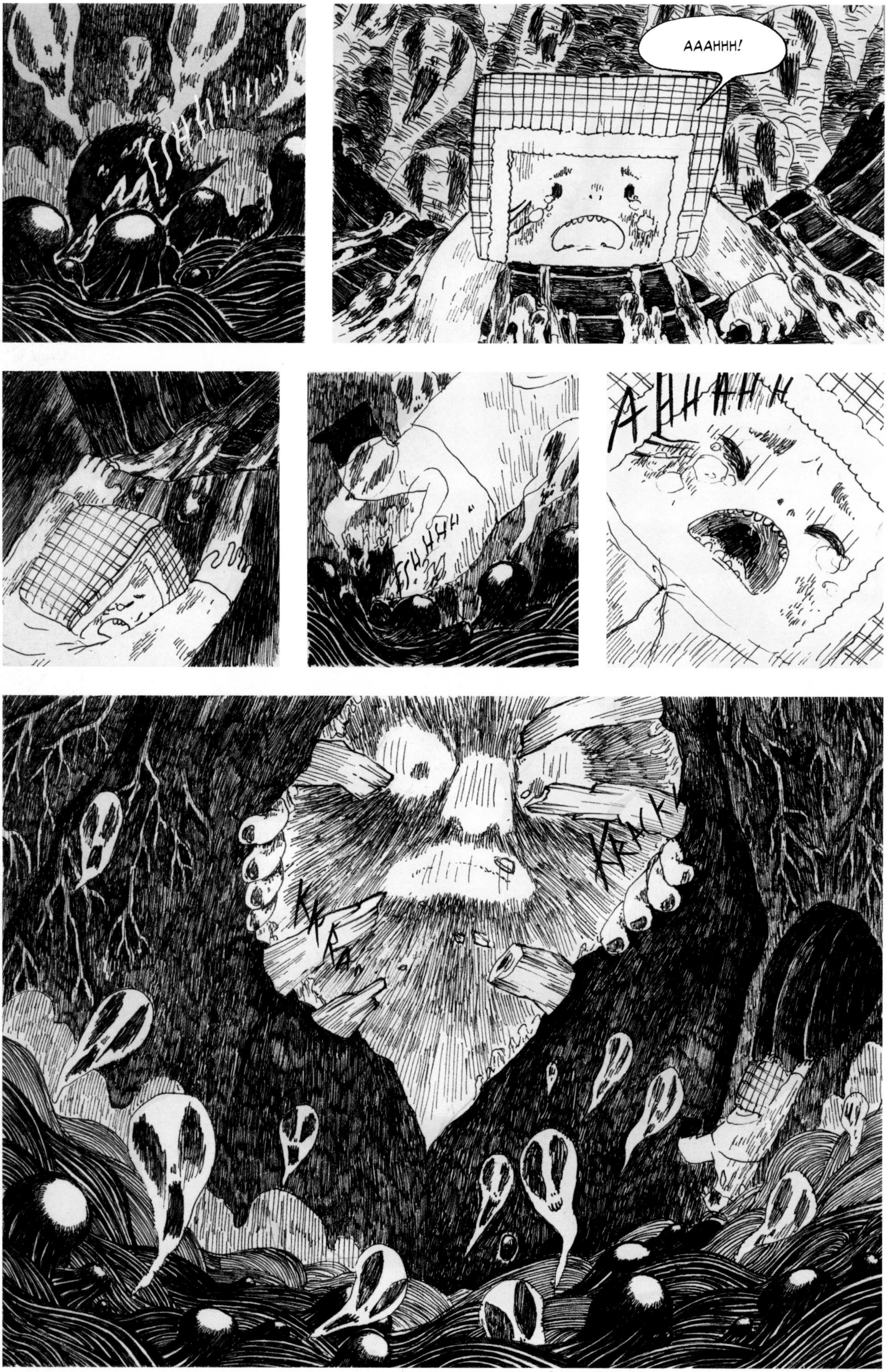
AAAHHH!
AHHHHHH

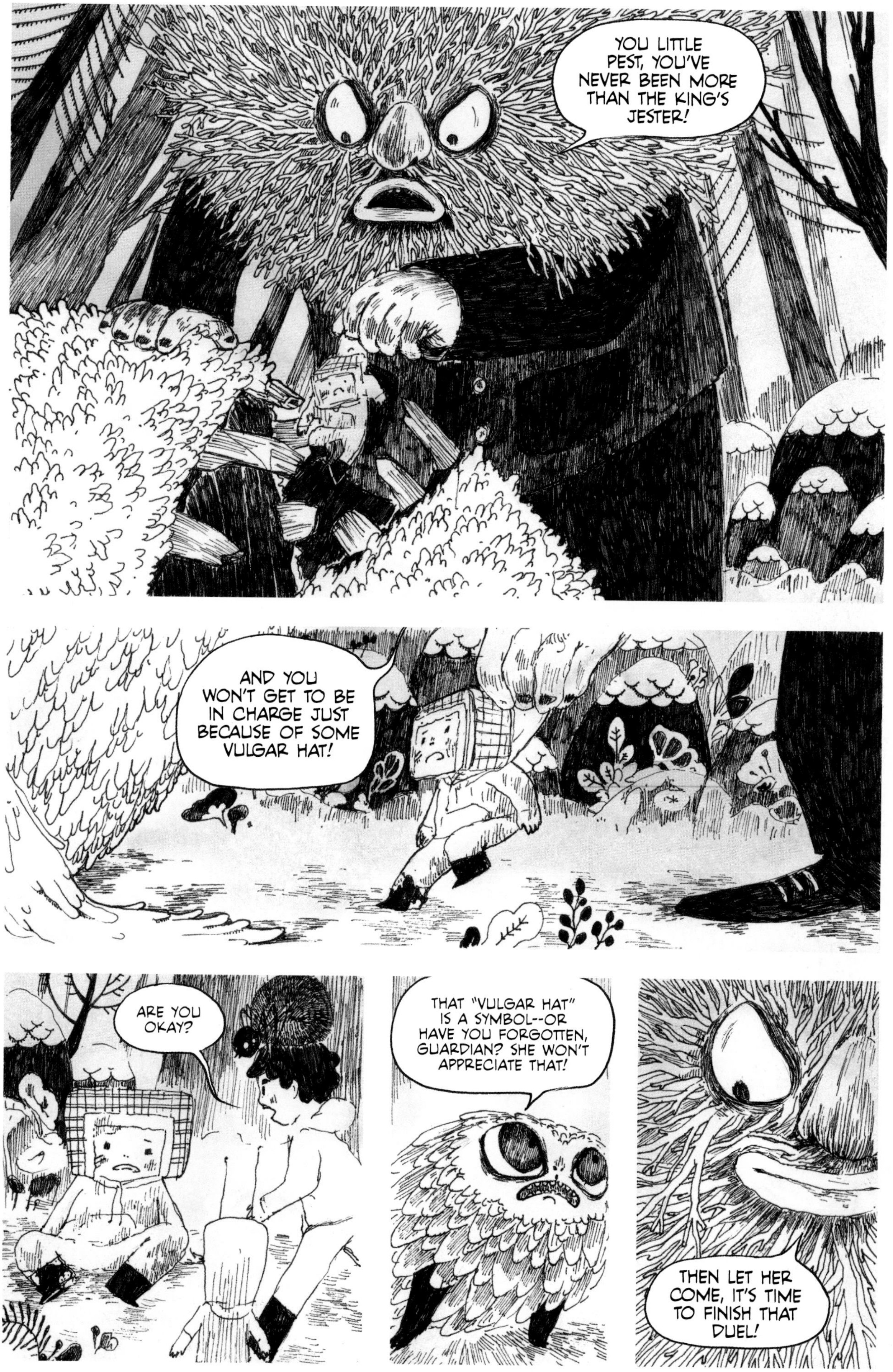
YOU LITTLE PEST, YOU'VE NEVER BEEN MORE THAN THE KING'S JESTER!
AND YOU WON'T GET TO BE IN CHARGE JUST BECAUSE OF SOME VULGAR HAT!
ARE YOU OKAY?
THAT "VULGAR HAT" IS A SYMBOL--OR HAVE YOU FORGOTTEN, GUARDIAN? SHE WON'T APPRECIATE THAT!
THEN LET HER COME, IT'S TIME TO FINISH THAT DUEL!

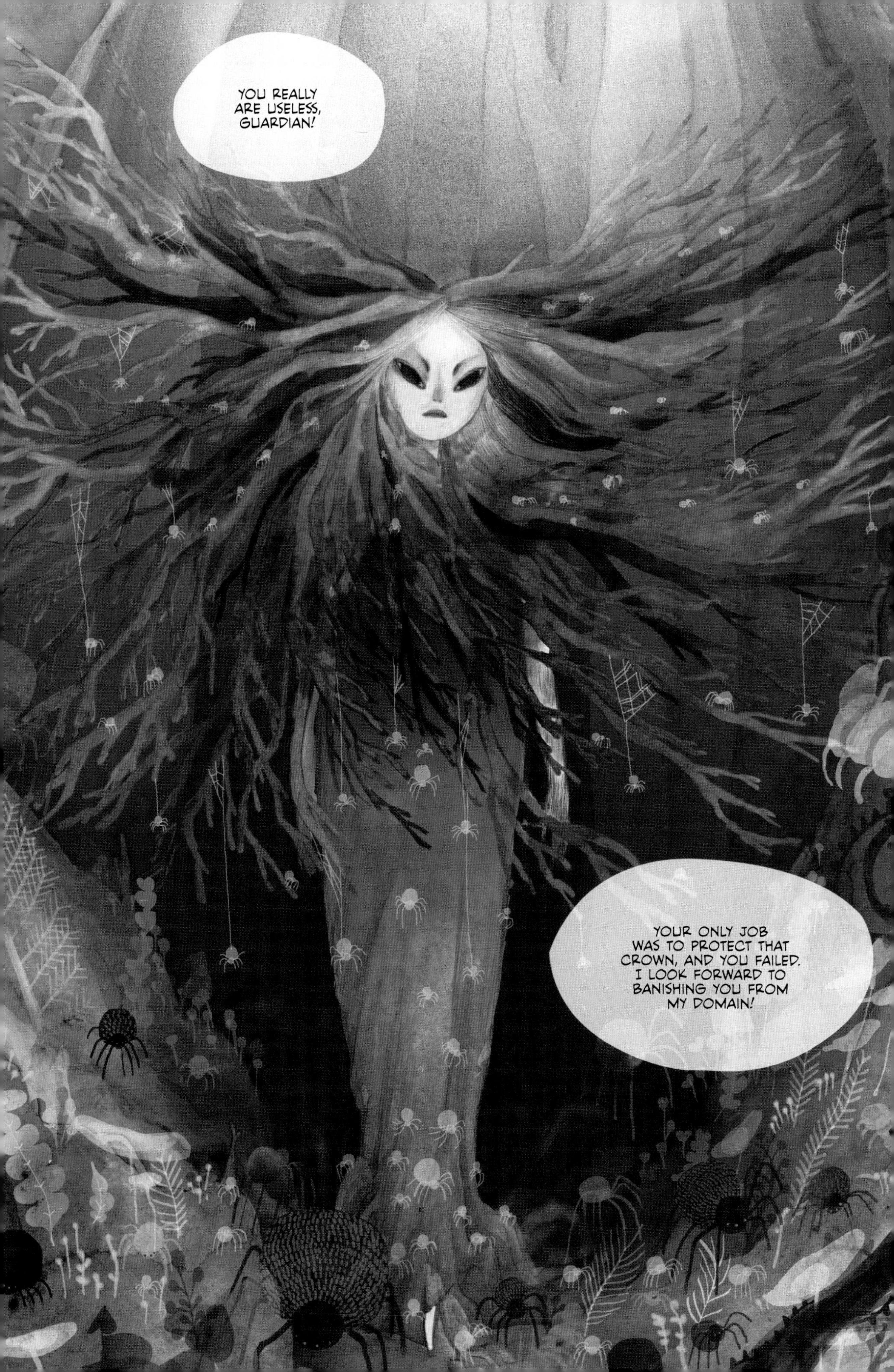
YOU REALLY ARE USELESS, GUARDIAN!
YOUR ONLY JOB WAS TO PROTECT THAT CROWN, AND YOU FAILED. I LOOK FORWARD TO BANISHING YOU FROM MY DOMAIN!

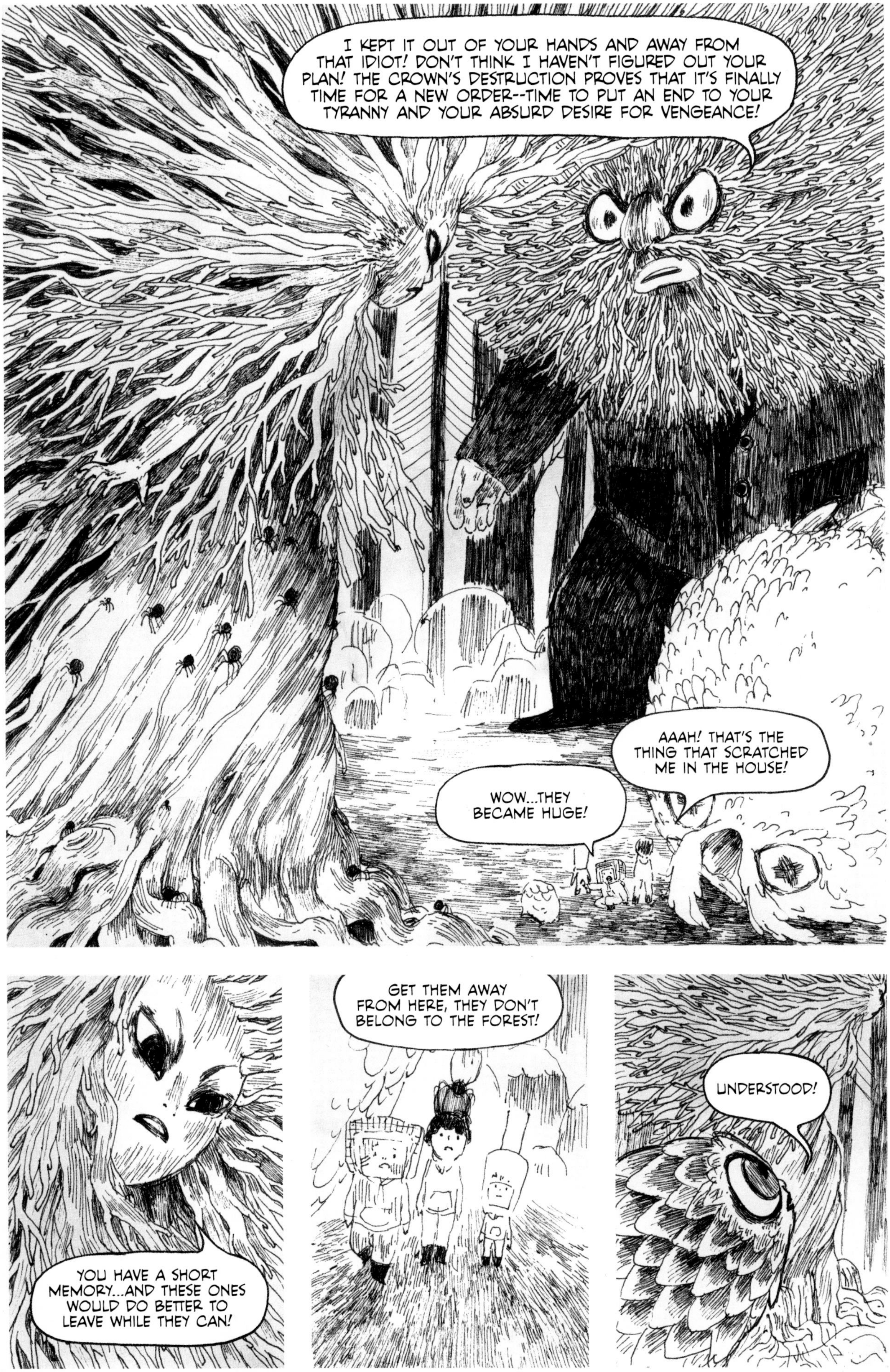
I KEPT IT OUT OF YOUR HANDS AND AWAY FROM THAT IDIOT! DON'T THINK I HAVEN'T FIGURED OUT YOUR PLAN! THE CROWN'S DESTRUCTION PROVES THAT IT'S FINALLY TIME FOR A NEW ORDER--TIME TO PUT AN END TO YOUR TYRANNY AND YOUR ABSURD DESIRE FOR VENGEANCE!
AAAH! THAT'S THE THING THAT SCRATCHED ME IN THE HOUSE!
WOW...THEY BECAME HUGE!
YOU HAVE A SHORT MEMORY...AND THESE ONES WOULD DO BETTER TO LEAVE WHILE THEY CAN!
GET THEM AWAY FROM HERE, THEY DON'T BELONG TO THE FOREST!
UNDERSTOOD!

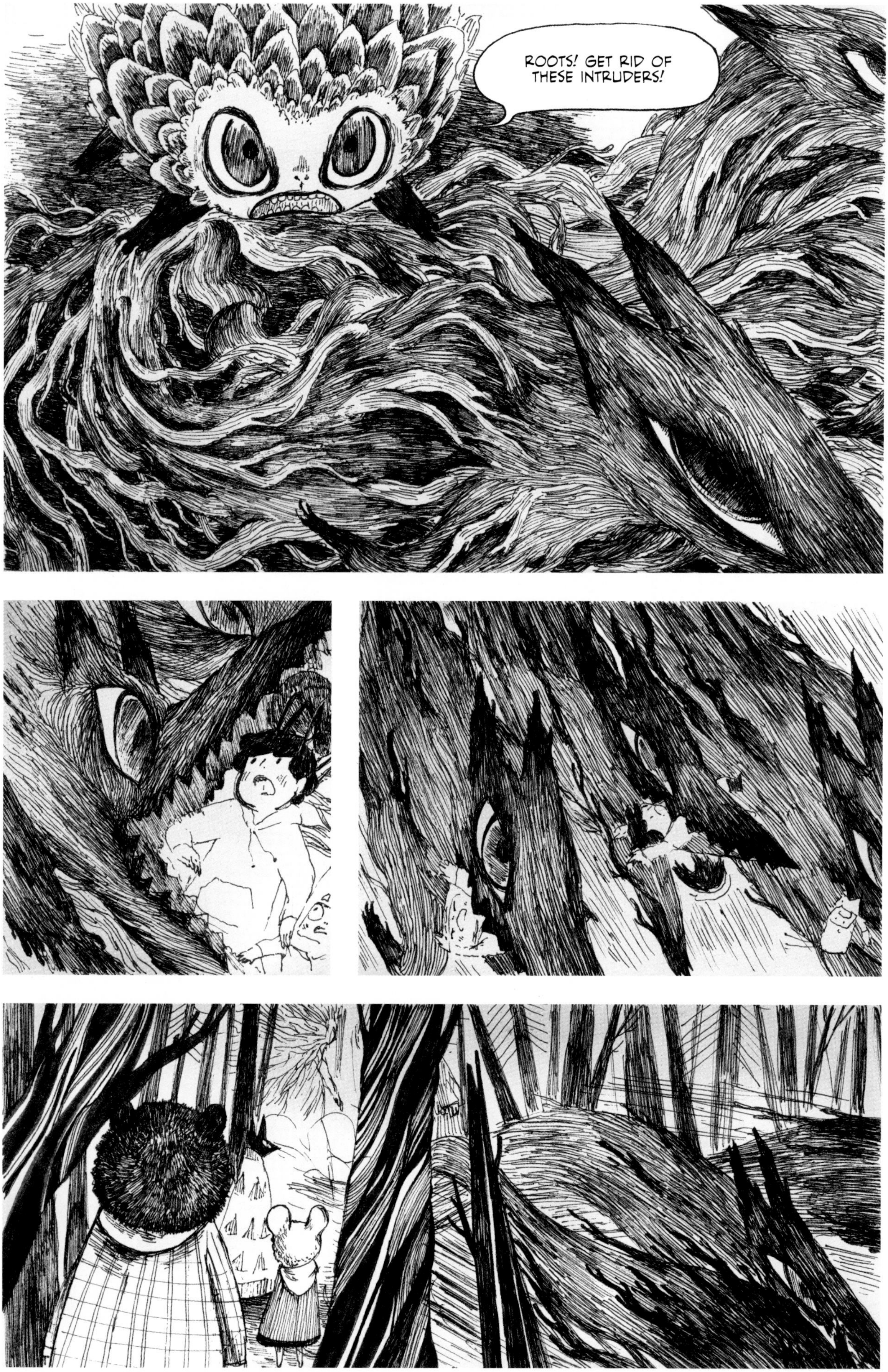
ROOTS! GET RID OF THESE INTRUDERS!

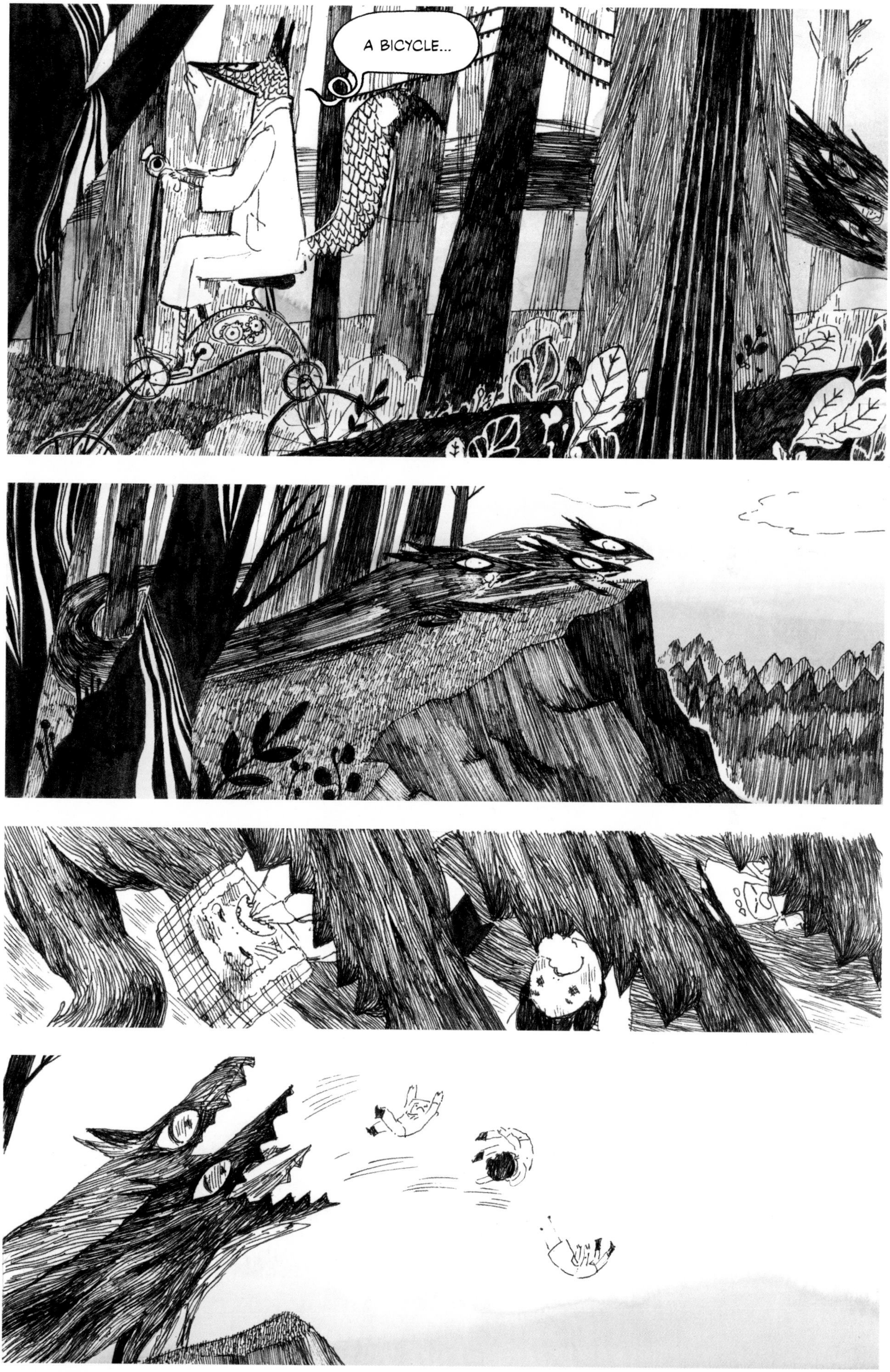
A BICYCLE...

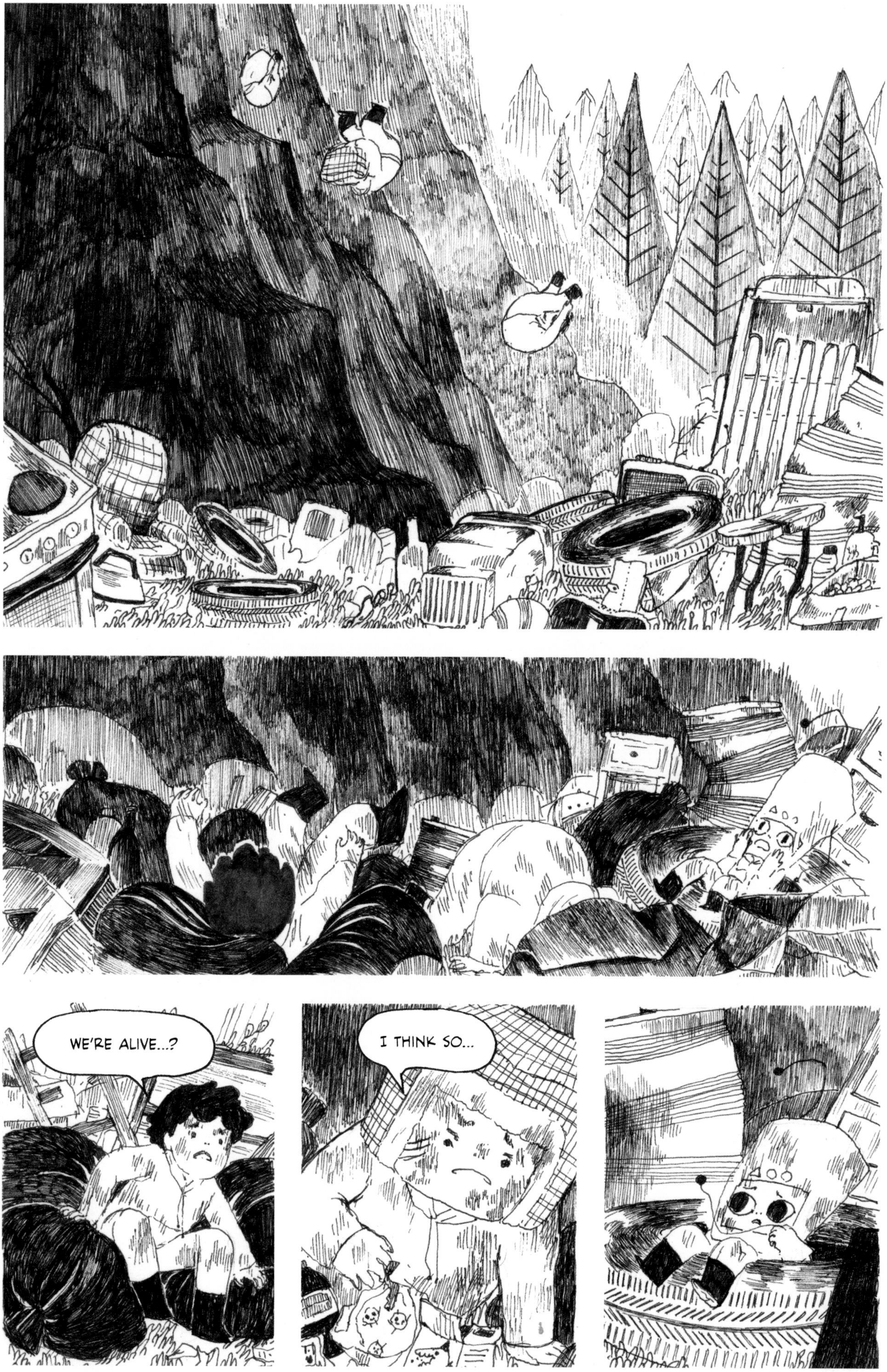
WE'RE ALIVE...?
I THINK SO...

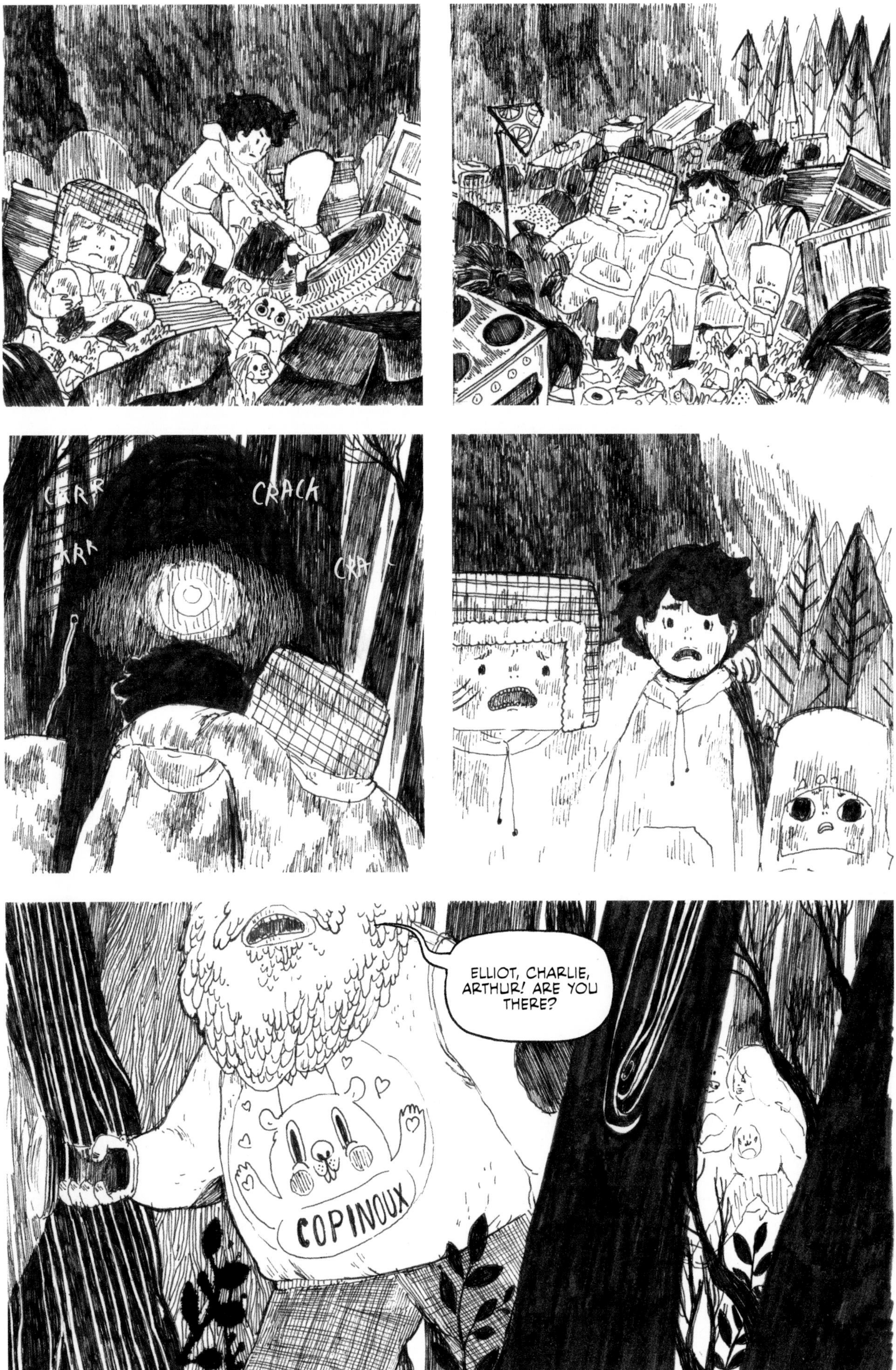
CRACK
ELLIOT, CHARLIE, ARTHUR! ARE YOU THERE?
COPINOUX

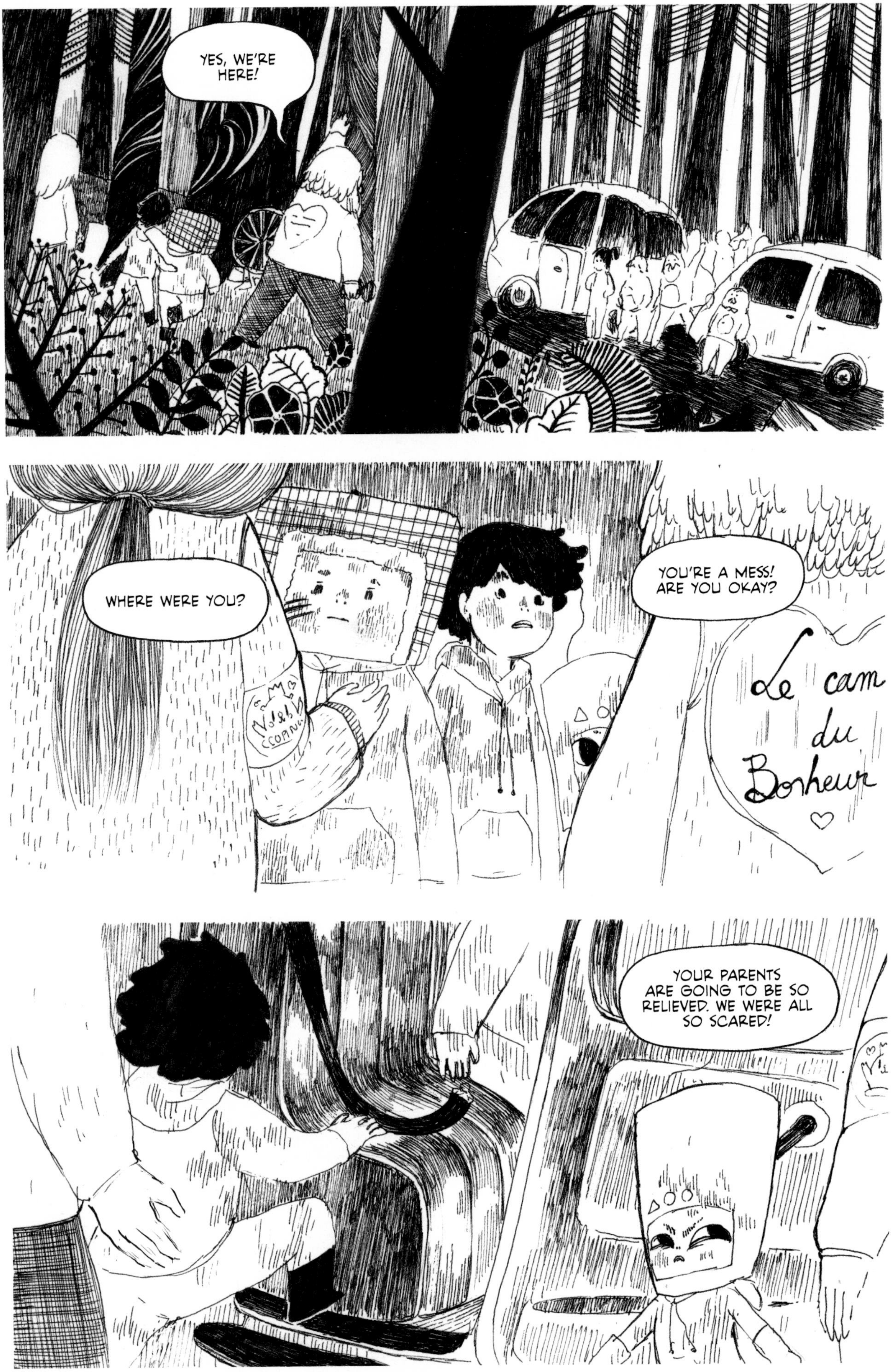
YES, WE'RE HERE!
WHERE WERE YOU?
YOU'RE A MESS! ARE YOU OKAY?
Le cam du Bonheur
YOUR PARENTS ARE GOING TO BE SO RELIEVED. WE WERE ALL SO SCARED!

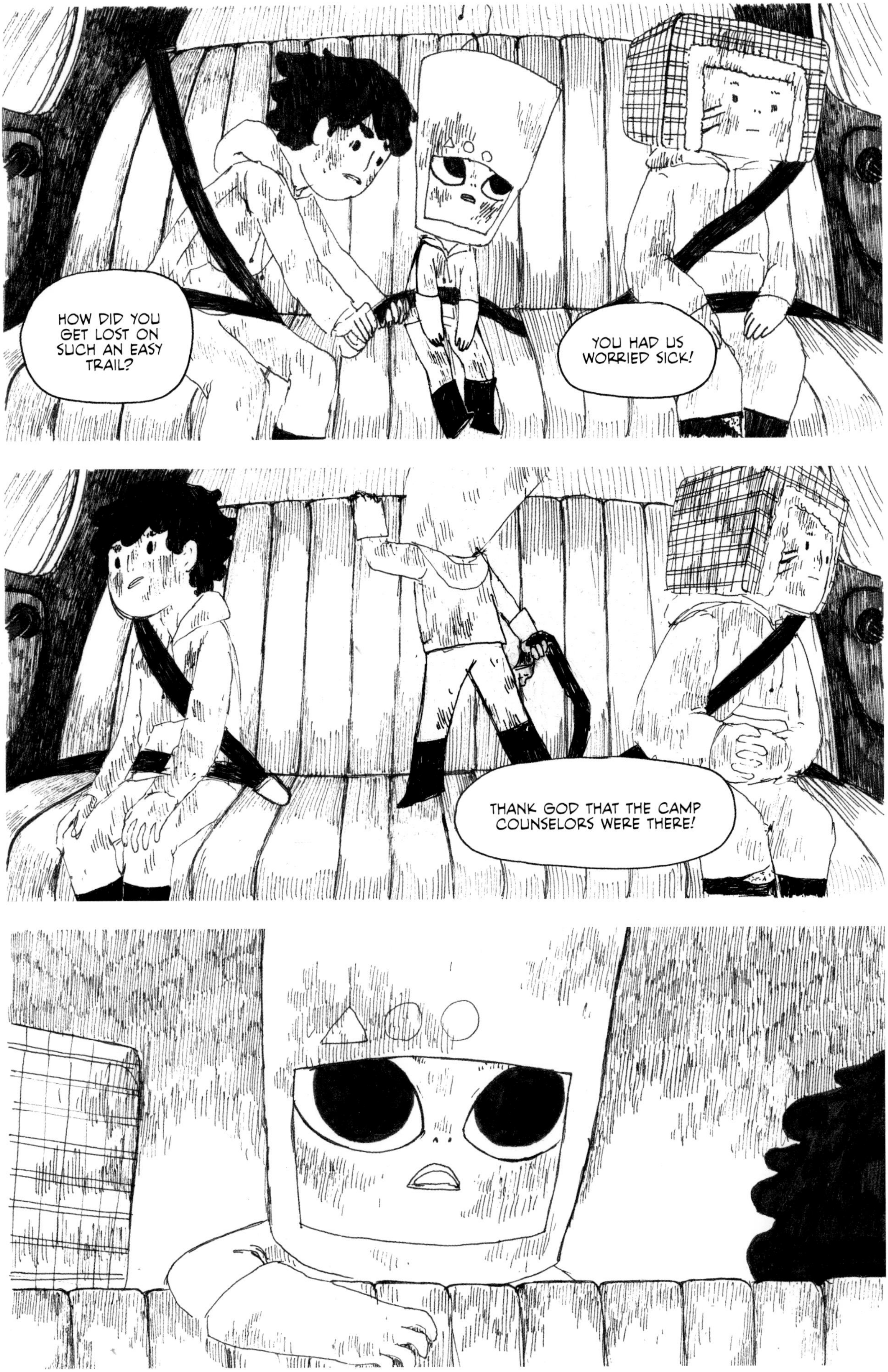
HOW DID YOU GET LOST ON SUCH AN EASY TRAIL?
YOU HAD US WORRIED SICK!
THANK GOD THAT THE CAMP COUNSELORS WERE THERE!

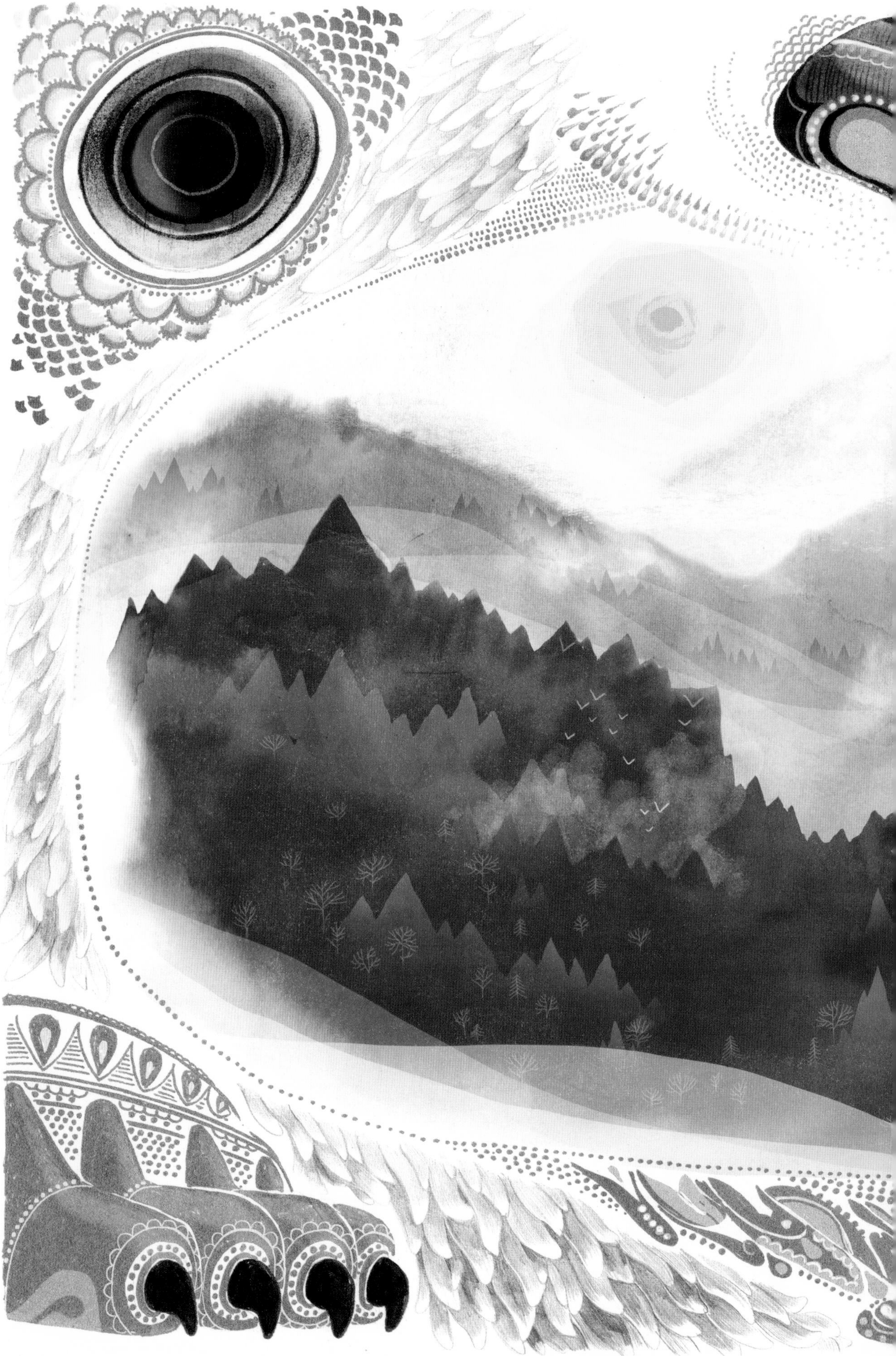

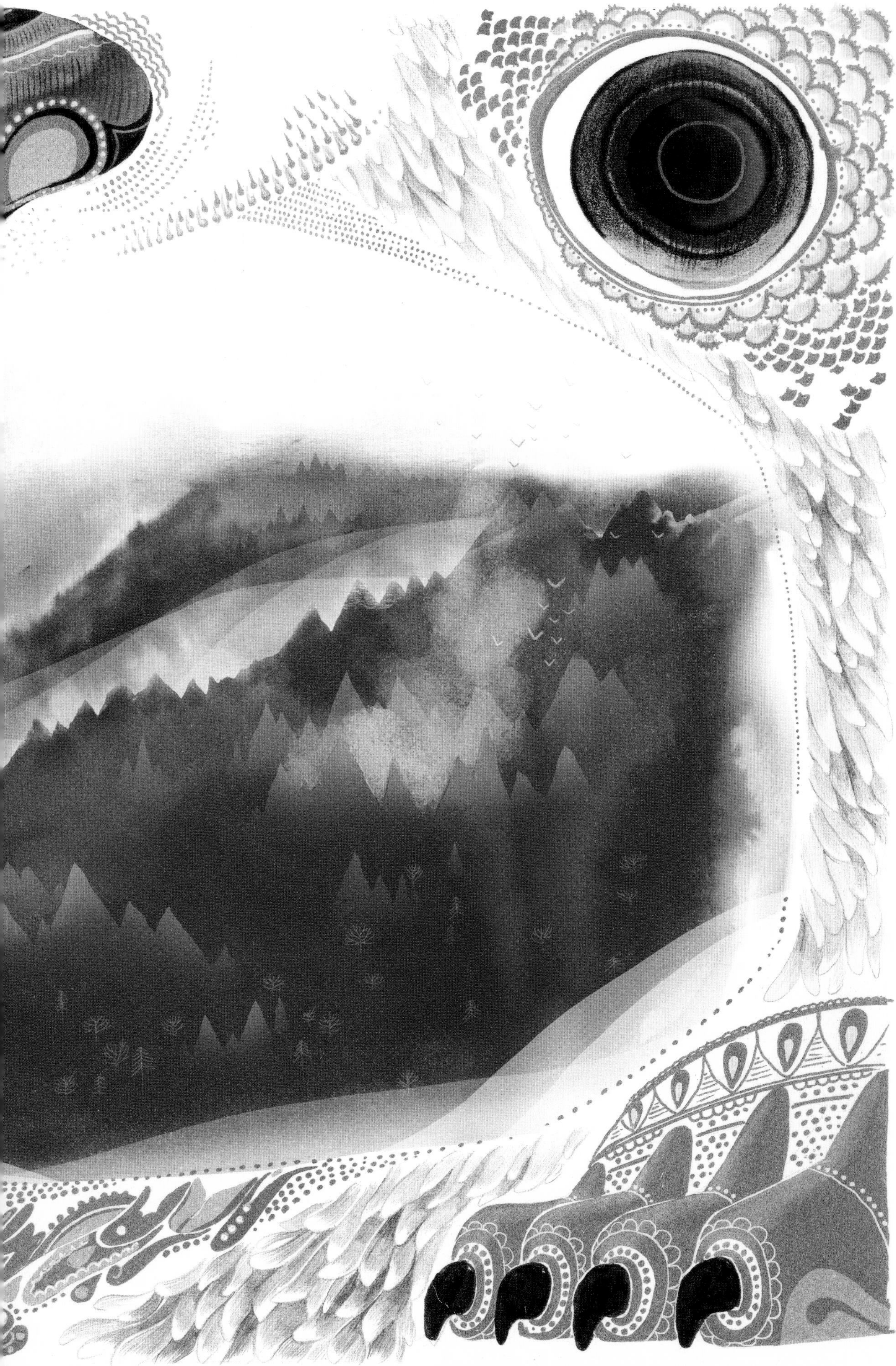

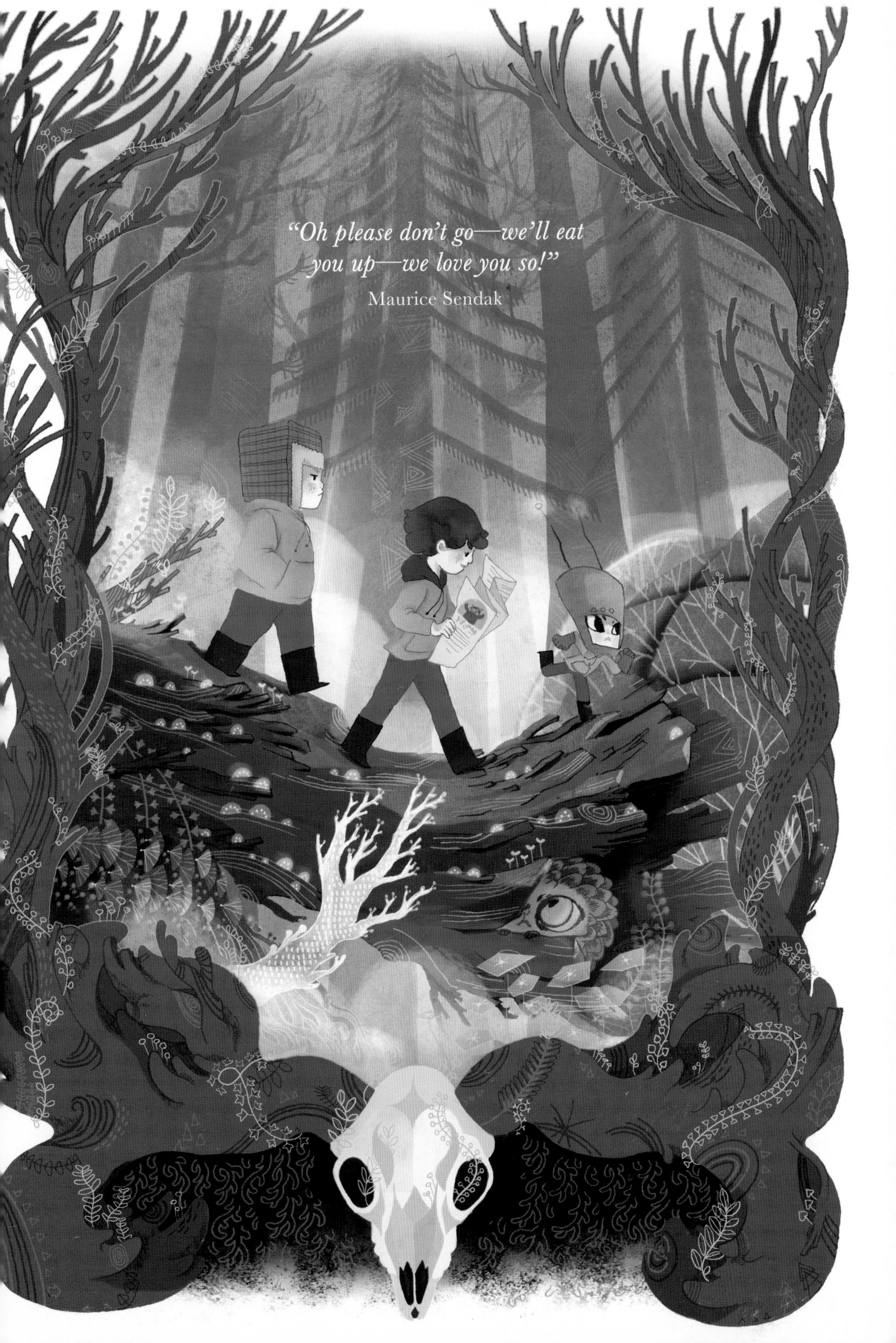

"Oh please don't go—we'll eat you up—we love you so!"

Maurice Sendak

First, I'd like to thank Jonathan, in particular, who started the project, followed it to the end, and cooked delicious crêpes for me all along the duration of this perilous adventure.

Thanks to my parents and Claire, who encouraged me to pursue this project.

Thanks to Rozenn and Jonas who helped me find a title that made everything click, and also for their delicious salted butter crêpes.

Thanks to Aurelie and Helene for their unfailing support and great jokes.

Thanks for Catherine and Suzanne for the war cry of Dinosaur Ninja Warrior 2.

Thanks to the friends, sometime lost, for all their inspiration.

And finally, thanks to Barbara and Clotilde for their enthusiasm, their help, and for their confidence in this project.

Amélie

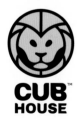

CUB™
HOUSE

ISBN: 978-1-941302-44-6
PCN: Library of Congress Control Number: 2017955338

The Lost Path, published 2017 by The Lion Forge, LLC. Originally published in French under the following title : Chemin Perdu, Fléchais © Editions Soleil – 2013

First published in the Métamorphose collection directed by Barbara Canepa and Clotilde.

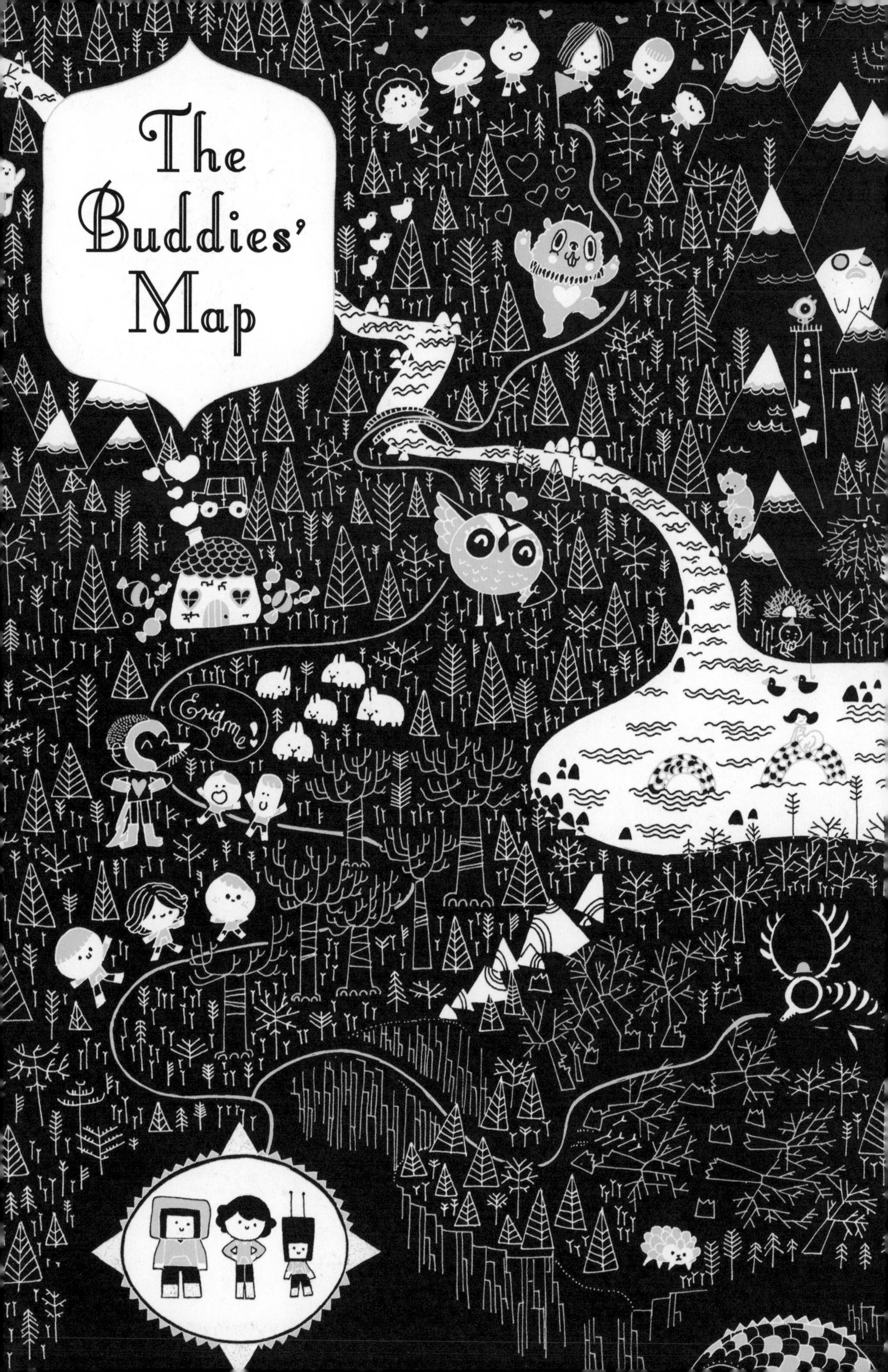
The Buddies' Map
Enigme!